Praise for the C

"I have been a Chet and Bernie fan from the start. Chet is a wonderful narrator—top dog, you could say—but he never descends to cuteness, and Bernie is as tough a PI as Spade or Marlowe, a man as quick with his .38 as he is with a Slim Jim for his sidekick. I'm already jonesing for the next one."

—Stephen King

"A tidy mystery, a good dollop of action, and a rumination on life after high school—who could ask for more? Chet, with his innate doggie wisdom, is sure to inspire loyal fans and seduce new readers." —*Publishers Weekly* on *Bark to the Future*

"Chet's narration provides humor and insight, and Bernie's search into his own past provides meditations on growing up and growing apart." —*Library Journal* on *Bark to the Future*

"Delightful . . . Dog lovers won't want to miss this one."
—*Publishers Weekly* on *Heart of Barkness*

"Would that we all were as infallible in our dogs' eyes as Bernie is in Chet's." —Susan Wilson, *New York Times* bestselling author of *The Dog I Loved*

"Cleverly plotted . . . Chet is a source of wisdom and innate doggie joie de vivre, making this a real pleasure for anyone who has ever looked into a dog's eyes and asked: Who's a good boy?"
—*Publishers Weekly*

A FAREWELL to ARFS

Spencer Quinn

 TOR PUBLISHING GROUP
New York

A FAREWELL TO ARFS

Copyright © 2024 by Pas de Deux

A Forge Book
Published by Tom Doherty Associates / Tor Publishing Group
120 Broadway
New York, NY 10271

www.torpublishinggroup.com.com

Forge® is a registered trademark of Macmillan Publishing Group, LLC.

The Library of Congress has cataloged the hardcover edition as follows:

Names: Quinn, Spencer, author.
Title: A farewell to arfs / Spencer Quinn.
Description: First edition. | New York : Forge, Tor Publishing Group,
    2024. | Series: A Chet & Bernie mystery ; 15
Identifiers: LCCN 2024012328 | ISBN 9781250331809 (hardcover) |
    ISBN 9781250331816 (ebook)
Subjects: LCGFT: Animal fiction. | Detective and mystery fiction. | Novels.
Classification: LCC PS3551.B64 F37 2024 | DDC 813/.6—
    dc23/eng/20240329
LC record available at https://lccn.loc.gov/2024012328

ISBN 978-1-250-33182-3 (trade paperback)

Our books may be purchased in bulk for promotional, educational, or
business use. Please contact your local bookseller or the Macmillan Corporate
and Premium Sales Department at 1-800-221-7945, extension 5442,
or by email at MacmillanSpecialMarkets@macmillan.com.

First Forge Paperback Edition: 2025

Printed in the United States of America

0 9 8 7 6 5 4 3 2 1

For Raphael

A FAREWELL TO ARFS

One

Who wouldn't love my job? You see new things every day! Here, for example, we had a perp clinging to a branch high up in a cottonwood tree. That wasn't the new part. Please don't get ahead of me—although that's unlikely to happen, your foot speed and mine being . . . very different, let's leave it at that with no hurt feelings.

Where were we? Perp in a cottonwood tree, nothing new? Right. Nothing new, not even the little detail of how this particular perp, namely Donnie the Docent Donnegan, was styling his shirt and tie with pajama bottoms. Seen that look once, seen it a . . . well, many times, just how many I couldn't tell you since I don't go past two. Not quite true. I have gotten past two the odd time, all the way to whatever comes next, but not today. No biggie. Two's enough. We're the proof, me and Bernie. Together we're the Little Detective Agency, the most successful detective agency in the whole Valley, except for the finances part. Bernie's last name is Little. I'm Chet, pure and simple.

We stood side by side, as we often do, and gazed up at Donnie. "Donnie?" Bernie said. "No wild ideas."

Donnie said something that sounded annoyed, the exact words hard to understand, most likely on account of the thick gold coin, called a doubloon unless I was missing something, that he was holding between his teeth. Donnie the Docent, an old pal, was an art lover with an MO that was all about museums. On this particular occasion our client was Katherine Cornwall who runs the Sonoran Museum of Art, also an old pal but not a perp, who we met way back on a complicated case of which I remembered nothing except that it ended well, perhaps only slightly marred by an incident in the gift shop involving something that hadn't turned out to be an actual chewy, strictly speaking. Katherine Cornwall was a woman of the gray-haired no-nonsense type. They don't miss much. You have to keep that in mind, which can turn out to be on the iffy side.

I should mention first that the gold coin between the teeth was also not the new part of this little scene, and second that this was the time of year when the cottonwoods are all fluffy white and give off a wonderful smell, a sort of combo of thick damp paper, sweet syrup, and fresh laundry. There's really nothing like rolling around in a pile a fresh laundry, possibly a subject for later. Also our cottonwood, standing on the bank of an arroyo, wasn't the only cottonwood in the picture. On the other side of the arroyo rose a second cottonwood, just as big and fresh laundryish or maybe even more so. In between, down in the arroyo, we had flowing water, blue and rising almost to the tops of the banks. That was the new part! Water! I'd seen water in some of our arroyos before but only in tiny puddles, drying up fast under the sun. I'm a good swimmer, in case you were wondering. There are many ways of swimming, but I'm partial to the dog paddle, probably goes without mentioning.

Meanwhile, high above, Donnie seemed to be inching his way toward the end of the branch, which hung over the arroyo. As did, by the way, a big branch on the far side cottonwood, the two branches almost touching. Below the far side cottonwood sat Donnie's ATV, engine running. How exactly we'd gotten to this point wasn't clear to me, even while it was happening, and was less clear now.

"Donnie?" Bernie said. "It's a fantasy."

Donnie said nothing, just kept inching along the branch, the gold coin glinting in the sunshine. His eyes were glinting, too, glinting with a look I'd often seen before, the look in the eyes of a perp in the grip of a sudden and fabulous idea. There's no stopping them after that.

"Donnie! Middle-aged, knock-kneed, potbellied? Is that the acrobat look?"

Donnie glanced down, shot Bernie a nasty glance. Then—and this is hard to describe—he coiled his body in a writhing way and launched himself into the air, his hands grasping at the branch of the other cottonwood. Wow! He came oh so close. I couldn't help but admire Donnie as he went pinwheeling down and down, landing in the arroyo with a big splash and vanishing beneath the surface. Also showing no sign of coming back up.

Bernie ran toward the water, but of course I was way ahead of him. I dove down, spotted Donnie at the bottom, flailing in slow motion, grabbed him by the pant leg and hauled him up out of there. Cottonwoody white fluffy things came whirligigging down and drifted away on the current. Case closed.

It turned out Donnie didn't know how to swim, so you could say we'd saved his life, but he forgot to say thanks. Maybe that had something to do with the fact that he'd gotten the gold coin stuck in his throat, although he'd soon swallowed it, but after X-rays at the hospital had established to Katherine Cornwall's satisfaction that it was still inside him but would appear in a day or two, she cut us our check—a woman of the no-nonsense type, as perhaps I didn't stress enough already.

"Very generous, Katherine." Bernie said. "It's way too much."

"I'll be the judge of that," Katherine said. I found myself in a very strange place, namely not on Bernie's side. "There's evidence that this particular doubloon was once in Coronado's personal possession."

Bernie's eyebrows—the best you'll ever see and there's no

missing them—have a language of their own. Now they rose in a way that said so much even if I couldn't tell you what, and he tucked the check in his pocket, unfortunately the chest pocket of his Hawaiian shirt. The Hawaiian shirt, with the tiny drink umbrella pattern, was not the problem, in fact was one of my favorites. The chest pocket was my problem. The check belonged in the front pocket of his pants, the front pocket with the zipper. I pressed my head against that pocket, sending a message. Bernie had great balance and didn't even stumble, hardly at all.

"He's so affectionate for such a formidable looking fellow," Katherine said.

"True," said Bernie, dusting himself off, "but this is more about chow time."

Chow time? It had nothing to do with chow time. But then, what do you know? It was about chow time! Chow time and nothing but! When had I last eaten? I was too hungry to even think about it. I eased Bernie toward the Beast. That's our ride, a Porsche in a long line of Porsches, all old and gone now, one or two actually up in smoke. The Beast—painted in black and white stripes in a rippling pattern, like a squad car showing off its muscles—was the oldest of all. We roared out of the museum parking lot, Bernie behind the wheel, me sitting tall in the shotgun seat, our usual set up, although once down in Mexico we'd ended up having to pull a switcheroo. This is a fun business, in case that's not clear by now.

Back at our place on Mesquite Road—best street in the Valley although far from the fanciest, which suits us just fine—we ate a whole lot in that quick and quiet businesslike way of two hombres after a long working day, and then went out back to the patio for drinks, beer for Bernie and water for me. He stretched out, his feet on a footstool, the check poking annoyingly from his chest pocket, like it was playing games with me. I was working on a plan for that check when Bernie said, "All those atmospheric river storms off the Pacific turned out to be good luck for Donnie." A complete puzzler. I waited for some sort of explanation but none came. Instead, without getting up, Bernie reached out and turned the tap at the base of the swan fountain. Then came a little sputter sputter, followed by a small bright stream flowing from the swan's mouth and splashing down into the dry pool with a lovely cooling sound. For me and my kind—the nation within the nation, as Bernie calls us—sounds can be cooling. Same for you? I won't even guess, the subject of human hearing turning out to be complicated but disappointing in the end. The fountain itself—and how nice to have it finally back on! Had Bernie forgotten to worry about the aquifer?—was all that Leda, Bernie's ex, left behind. Now she lived in High Chaparral Estates with her new husband Malcolm who had long toes and money to burn, although he wasn't the money burning type. Money burners in my experience—lighting up a smoke with a C-note, for example—never had much of it except for a sudden and nice little bundle, here and gone. But forget all that. I've left out the most important detail, namely Charlie, Bernie and Leda's kid, now living with Leda and Malcolm except for some weekends and every second Christmas and Thanksgiving, or maybe the other way around. At first, we'd left the mattress in his bedroom stripped bare, but now it's made up and Bernie even folds down one of the top corners so it's all set for getting into. I even sometimes get into it myself, who knows why.

On the other side of the patio fence that separates our place from Mr. and Mrs. Parsons next door, Iggy started barking. This is the time of year when old timers like the Parsonses keep their windows open, but there's no missing Iggy's bark, even if he's deep inside a trash truck, just to pick one instance out of many. A tiny guy but a mighty yip-yip-yipper. With an amazingly long and floppy tongue, by the way.

"Iggy," said Mr. Parsons, in his scratchy old voice. "Easy there. I can't hear."

Easy there does not work with Iggy. He dialed it up a notch.

"Billy?" Mr. Parsons said, also dialing it up, although only the scratchy part got louder. "Say again?"

Billy? We knew Billy, me and Bernie. He was the son of Mr. and Mrs. Parsons, a grown up son, unlike Charlie, and also unlike Charlie in other ways. An actual perp? I wasn't sure about that, but he'd been involved in the stolen saguaro case, one of our worst. Bernie had ended up in the hospital, the most terrible thing that had ever happened to me. I glanced over to make sure he was all right, and there he was, eyes closed, chest rising and falling in a slow rhythm, the best chest rising and falling rhythm I'd ever seen, and a bit more of the check peeking out from his pocket. My Bernie!

"Slow down a little, please, Billy," Mr. Parsons said. "I don't understand."

Was Mr. Parsons on the phone? When folks are on the phone I can often hear the voice of who they're talking to, but not this time, not with Iggy. But I could see Billy in my mind: shoulder-length fair hair, vague sort of eyes, that snakehead tattoo on his cheek. Plus, he had lots of ink on his arms as well. You see that arm ink on dudes that had done time although usually their arms are bulkier than Billy's. Northern State Correctional, if I remembered right, but not for the saguaro case. On the saguaro case we'd cut him a break and he'd split for Matamoros. Now you know all I know about Billy Parsons and possibly more.

"Refund?" Mr. Parsons said. That was followed by a long silence, if we're leaving Iggy out of it, and then Mr. Parsons said, "Payroll? But I—"

After that came another long silence. I could feel Mr. Parsons listening very hard, could even sort of see him holding the phone real tight. Mr. Parsons was a nice old guy.

"Two thousand?" he said at last. "Two thousand even? Well, Billy, I—I don't see why not. How do you want me to . . . yes, I've got a pencil. Hang on. Just need to . . . Okay. Shoot." Then more silence, again except for Iggy. Yip yip yip, yip yip yip. He doesn't even stop to breathe. You have to admire Iggy in some ways. "Yup," said Mr. Parsons. "Got it. Love you, son. Bye."

"You know what we should do first thing?" Bernie said the next morning at breakfast. "Zip on down to the bank and make a deposit." He waved the check in the air. Had a day ever gotten off to a better start? I was already at the door. Bernie laughed. "Got to shave first." We went into the bathroom. Bernie lathered up and shaved his beautiful face. I helped by pacing back and forth. You might say, beautiful face? Hadn't that nose been broken once or twice? Maybe, and Bernie had plans to get it fixed, but only after he was sure there won't be more dust ups in his life. Which I hope is never. No dust ups would mean no more chances to see that sweet, sweet uppercut of his. It lands on perp chins with just a click, like it's nothing at all, but then their eyes roll up. There's all kinds of beauty. That's one of my core beliefs.

We hurried out the door, me first, which is our system for going in and out of doors. It's actually my door system with everyone and even if they don't know at first they soon do. Humans are great at learning things, or certainly some things, a big subject I'd go into it now if it wasn't for the fact that over at the Parsonses' house a kind of a show got going.

All the world's a stage, Bernie says, just one more example of his brilliance. First out of the door was Iggy in full flight, tongue hanging out the side of his mouth. That part didn't last long, what with Iggy being on the leash. He came to a sudden stop in midair, his stubby legs still sprinting in a full speed blur. Then came the walker and finally Mr. Parsons, staggering a bit, trying to grip the leash and the walker with one hand and knot his tie with the other. Leash, tie, walker, Iggy, Mr. Parsons: for a moment they all seemed like parts to a single contraption, a contraption that was starting to tilt in a way that didn't look promising. But by that time we were there, Bernie steadying Mr. Parsons and me grabbing Iggy by the scruff of the neck. Iggy didn't like that. His eyes got wild and he tried to do who knows what to me with one of his tiny paws. You had to love Iggy and I do.

"You all right, Daniel?" Bernie said.

"Yes, thank you, Bernie. Well, no actually."

"How about we go inside and sit down?"

"No time for that," Mr. Parsons said. "I have to go to the bank."

"With Iggy?"

Mr. Parsons licked his lips, lips that were cracked and dry, and so was his tongue. "That wasn't the original plan."

"Then should we get the little fella back inside?"

"I'd appreciate that, Bernie."

"Chet?" Bernie made a little motion with his chin. It's not only his eyebrows that talk. The chin can jump in too, from time to time. There's no one like Bernie, in case you didn't know that already. I trotted into the house, dumped Iggy in the kitchen, and trotted back out. Bernie closed the door.

"Is Edna inside?" he said.

"Back in the hospital, I'm afraid." Mr. Parsons fished in his pockets. "Oh, dear."

"What's wrong?" Bernie said.

"I don't seem to have my car keys."

"What bank do you use?"

"Valley Trust, the Rio Seco branch."

"We'll drive you," Bernie said.

"Very nice of you, but—"

"Not a problem. We were actually headed there—it's our bank, too."

We got into the Beast. Normally the shotgun seat is mine, but in this case, I didn't mind letting Mr. Parsons have it while I squeezed onto the little shelf in back. Well, I did mind, but I did it anyway. I can do things I don't want to but not often, so please don't ask.

We rode in silence for a while, Mr. Parsons breathing in shallow little breaths, his twisted fingers busy with the tie, but having trouble. Finally, he gave up and lowered his hands to his lap.

"Where's our money?" he said.

Two

Bernie and Mr. Parsons started in on a complicated conversation that seemed to have something to do with Billy, but we happened to be on East Canyon Drive, two lanes each way, and in the lane next to us, going at the same speed, was a car with a cat in the back, a cat who seemed interested in gazing out at me. Maybe that's not quite right. The truth was the cat was looking through me. When a cat is looking through you—and I've had way too much experience with this—it's impossible to think of anything else. Your mind just goes *CAT CAT CAT* until finally it ends, you give yourself a good shake, starting at the head, rippling through to the tip of the tail and back again, and then your mind returns to its peaceful resting state, mostly blank. But here's the worst part. While your mind is going *CAT CAT CAT* the cat's mind is doing nothing of the sort. What the cat's mind is doing I couldn't tell you. All I know is it's not going *DOG DOG DOG*. That's what looking through someone must be all about, but I'm only guessing since I've never done it myself. The point of all this is that whatever Bernie and Mr. Parsons were talking about passed me by completely.

We turned off the highway, the cat's head slowly shifting to follow us, the cat's body remaining perfectly still in the most irritating way possible, but then we were in the Valley Trust parking lot and the cat had vanished in the heavy traffic over the Rio Seco bridge. Once I'd seen an accident on that very same bridge where a porta-potty truck had ended up swerving over the side and falling all the way to the bottom. Just a memory, no reason for bringing it up now, nothing to do with cats. But just imagine if . . . well, never mind.

Bernie switched off the engine and helped Mr. Parsons out of the car. I hopped out, gave myself the necessary shake, feeling better at once, and we entered the bank, after some confusion, with me first. I'd been here before. We'd had a problem or two with Ms. Mendez, the manager, something about overdrafts which had to be very strong drafts but today the air inside the bank was still. We were off to a good start.

Mr. Parsons stumped over to the nearest teller. We followed. "I'd like to see the manager, please." Mr. Parsons took a scrap of paper from his pocket and smoothed it out. "Miss Mendez," he said.

"Ms. Mendez," the teller said, "is in a meeting."

"Ah," said Mr. Parsons. "Ms., I see." He gazed at the scrap of paper, ran a finger over it. His lips quivered but no sound came out.

Bernie stepped forward. "We'll wait," he said.

The teller looked up at Bernie, a look that might not have been the friendliest appearing on her face.

"Meanwhile," Bernie went on, "Um." He handed over the check. All at once I felt the need to do some crazy running around, not much, only the merest sample. Bernie rested his hand on the back of my neck, not heavily, just there. The need for crazy running shrank down, not disappearing entirely since it's always there, but losing its immediate power.

The teller glanced at the check and said, "Certainly, Mr. Little. Right away. Are the two of you together?"

"Three," Bernie said. "But yes."

The teller looked my way, and in that look I saw at once she was a fan of me and my kind. "Three, of course. And I'll let Ms. Mendez know you're waiting."

We sat down in the waiting area. Getting from the walker to the chair seemed to take something out of Mr. Parsons. When he got his breath back he said, "Thank you, Bernie. You don't have to stay."

"But would it be helpful?"

Mr. Parsons closed his eyes and nodded a tiny nod.

"Then that's that," Bernie said.

"So nice to see you again, Mr. Little," said Ms. Mendez when we were seated in her office, the most pleasant thing she'd ever said to us. Ms. Mendez was a small, roundish woman of the no-nonsense type but much younger than Katherine Cornwall. "I read about you in the paper, you and Chet, of course. All about that aquifer case. Congratulations." She smiled. I'd never seen her smile before. It made her look less no-nonsensey. Not that she was suddenly on the side of big-time nonsense willy-nilly, but still a nice sight in my opinion. As for the aquifer case it had something to do with . . . with . . .

"Uh, thanks," said Bernie. "We're actually here with our neighbor, Mr. Parsons. He's a customer of yours and he's got a problem."

"Pleased to meet you, Mr. Parsons. Cecilia Mendez. How can I help?"

Mr. Parsons leaned forward. I could hear his heart beating, very fast and very light. When humans are nervous they sometimes tremble, and Mr. Parsons was trembling now, just slightly, but I didn't miss it. Me and my kind are close watchers of you and your kind. That's how this works. We're learning about you all the time—for example, now I knew that old men could get nervous, when here all along I'd thought it was only a young person's thing—but in a nice way.

"Our account," Mr. Parsons began, "Edna's and mine, is . . . I just don't under . . . gone."

"Your account is gone?" Ms. Mendez said.

"Empty. All the money. The funds. That's what I saw this

morning, when I checked on my computer. The computer account, for the bank. Oh, what's the word I'm looking for?"

"Online," Bernie said.

"Thank you, Bernie," said Mr. Parsons. "Online. Our online computer account is empty. When I checked last week it had over forty-five thousand dollars. And now zero dollars. It has to be a . . . a . . . a . . ."

"Glitch," Bernie said.

"Thank you, Bernie. A glitch. Doesn't it? Doesn't it have to be?"

"What's the account number?" Ms. Mendez said, turning to her screen.

"Four three six . . . no, seven . . . four three seven, uh . . ." Mr. Parsons patted his pockets. "I forgot my passbook."

"That's all right," Ms. Mendez said. "Daniel and Edna Parsons?"

"We've been married for sixty-five years," Mr. Parsons said.

Ms. Mendez gazed at the screen. "We're showing a withdrawal yesterday at four thirty-four p.m. in the amount of forty-seven thousand six hundred two dollars and thirty-one cents." She looked up. "Leaving a balance of zero. You say you're unaware of this transaction?"

"It's true?" Mr. Parsons said. "It happened?"

"The funds were transferred through something called Zapp."

"Where to?" Bernie said.

"We have no information on that," said Ms. Mendez.

"Zapp?" Mr. Parsons raised his hands, palms up. "I don't know any Zapps. I've never heard of these people."

Bernie and Ms. Mendez exchanged a look, the kind you sometimes see, especially when smart humans are around, a quick but silent conversation. Bernie is always the smartest human in the room so my takeaway was that Ms. Mendez was not too shabby in the brains department.

"Mind if I ask Daniel a question?" Bernie said.

"Please," said Ms. Mendez.

He turned to Mr. Parsons. "Have you ever made an online transaction from or into your account?"

"No, never." Daniel, already kind of flushed, flushed some more. "Now that I think, damn it, I guess you could say, well, it's not true. There was one transaction, a withdrawal I suppose you could call it."

"When was that?" Bernie said.

Mr. Parsons shook his head. "I just don't understand what's going on," he said. "It was yesterday."

"Yesterday?" said Ms. Mendez, her voice rising in surprise.

Bernie's voice went the other way, lower and calmer, like . . . like things were hunky dory. That wouldn't have been my guess, but I'm with Bernie, end of story.

"Tell us about it."

"The transaction? But didn't I already tell you on the ride over?"

Bernie smiled. "Again, if you don't mind," he said. "I wasn't clear on a couple of points."

"A withdrawal, yes, a withdrawal for certain," said Mr. Parsons. He leaned forward, his hands now on Ms. Mendez's desk. "Don't you see it there? It should be on the screen."

Ms. Mendez blinked. "Sir? Are you referring to the forty-seven thousand·plus?"

"Oh, no. No no no. It was only two thousand. Two thousand even. Don't you see it? It should . . ." He sat back, leaving damp palm prints on Ms. Mendez's desk. I resisted a sudden urge to lick them away. What comes over me sometimes?

"There's no record of a two thousand dollar withdrawal here," Ms. Mendez said.

"Maybe . . . maybe it was recorded as . . . as what did you call it? Not transaction. Transfer!" His voice rose to a shout. He took a deep breath and softly went on. "Maybe it's there as a transfer. Ma'am."

Ms. Mendez shook her head. "The only entry is the one we've

noted—forty-seven thousand six hundred two dollars and thirty-one cents."

"So a true one isn't there but a false one is?" said Mr. Parsons. "Doesn't that prove it?"

"Prove what, sir?" said Ms. Mendez.

"Why, that it's all a glitch. One of those computer snafus you read about. You know, an error." He snapped his fingers but they failed to make any sound at all. "A coding error!"

Bernie and Ms. Mendez exchanged another look. Her phone, lying on the desk, made a beep beep beep. She poked it with her finger, poked it nice and hard, a fine idea in my opinion, and it went silent.

"Can you tell us a little more about the two thousand dollar transaction, Daniel?" Bernie said.

"The real one?" Mr. Parsons said.

Bernie nodded yes. He's an expert nodder, with many nods for this and that, including some that meant yes in different ways. I'd seen this particular nod once before, last Christmas when Charlie said, "Is Santa real, Dad?" Same nod but there was one big difference because then Bernie had said, "Go open your presents," and now he said nothing.

"Okay, then," Mr. Parsons said. "Let me just get my ducks lined up."

Would it be true to say that I was totally on top of things up to this point? No. But no way was I expecting ducks. Where were they? I didn't have to look around for ducks. They have a very distinctive smell—a sort of combo of down pillows and an oven getting opened on Thanksgiving morning—and there wasn't a trace of it here in Ms. Mendez's office. That was the moment I realized we were dealing with a tough case, if this was in fact a case, and who was paying, by the way?

"Now that I think about it, I'd actually just gotten off the phone," Mr. Parsons said. He glanced at Bernie and at Ms. Mendez, maybe to see if they were following along. As for me, my mind was still more or less on the ducks. "I'd been talking to Edna. Edna's my wife, Miss, um, Ms. Mendez."

"Right," said Ms. Mendez. "A joint account."

"Edna's in the hospital, dealing with health issues, as they say." He looked down. "What they mean is she's sick. But—" Now he looked up and raised a finger, not quite pointing it at Ms. Mendez. "But she doesn't complain and we're dealing with it. I visit every day and I'd already had my yesterday visit when she called to tell me the result of some new test. It wasn't good, but I didn't get the details, on account of Iggy, I'm afraid, although I can't blame the poor little fellow. He's our dog—did I mention that?—and I think he can actually hear her voice on the other end of the phone, and he misses her dreadfully. He's family."

Mr. Parsons paused, maybe waiting for Ms. Mendez to say something. When she did not, he went on, "Well, maybe he can't hear her, but he can sense her presence. Of that I'm sure."

What was that all about? Iggy—strange in so many ways— was still a member of the nation within. Of course he could hear Mrs. Parsons on the other end. My teeth suddenly wanted to gnaw on something, say, one of the legs of Bernie's chair. But it was a metal chair. What was the point?

Mr. Parsons sighed. "Maybe it doesn't matter. The main . . . oh, what's the word? Not thing but . . . well, thing will have to do. The main thing is that Iggy was already upset when the phone rang right away, the moment I put it down, you see, and when he's upset he gives way to barking quite a lot." He turned to Bernie. "I hope his barking doesn't disturb you, Bernie."

"We never hear it," Bernie said.

Excuse me? Bernie's metal chair turned out to have rubber wheels. I tried one of those.

"Oh, that's a relief," said Mr. Parsons. He got a faraway look in his eyes and went silent.

"Sir?" said Ms. Mendez.

Mr. Parsons came slowly back to us. "Yes?"

"The second call?"

"Yes, of course. The whole point. It was our son Billy on the phone although I could hardly—well, I've already explained. We don't hear from him often but it's always a pleasure. He's turned his life around—I must have told you that, Bernie."

"Last year," Bernie said, "but I don't think you went into detail."

"ProCon," said Mr. Parsons. "Capital P, capital C. It's one of those NGOs. Billy got a job there—a good legitimate job—and now he's risen to director. We couldn't be more proud of him."

Meanwhile, Ms. Mendez was tapping at her keyboard and watching her screen. "ProCon, based in Gila City?"

"That's right," said Mr. Parsons.

Ms. Mendez's eyes—quick, dark, bright—went back and forth, back and forth. "They work with former inmates?"

Mr. Parsons nodded. "Pro ex-convicts is the idea. Helping them get back on their feet and such. Billy himself is a former inmate. That's no secret. Although, as Edna puts it, it's Billy's secret sauce."

"How so?" said Ms. Mendez.

"Why, it gives him instant credibility with the clients. And that's not all. Edna was talking about it just the other day." He went silent again.

"What did she say?" said Ms. Mendez.

"It's on the tip of my tongue."

Then we just sat for what seemed a bit too long. At last Bernie said, "Was it something about leading by example?"

"Bingo! You're a mind reader, Bernie. That's what Edna said. The fact that Billy has been through what they've been through and come out the other side makes him a shining light. That's what she called Billy—a shining light. You must understand, Bernie—knowing that world and all." He clapped his hand over his mouth. "Oh, dear. Miss, uh, Ms. I don't mean to say Bernie's an ex c . . . former inmate. It's just that he's a private investigator, so . . ."

"Understood," said Ms. Mendez. "What was Billy's call about?"

Mr. Parsons looked surprised. "Didn't I say? The real what-chamacallit, entry on your ledger. The two thousand dollar transaction."

"Billy asked for two thousand dollars?" Ms. Mendez said.

"Just until Monday. Then he'd be paying us back. There was a supply chain problem at the bank they use and he needed it to make payroll."

"A supply chain problem at a bank?" Ms. Mendez said.

"Maybe not supply chain exactly," said Mr. Parsons. "But something of that nature."

"And you agreed to lend him the money?" Ms. Mendez said.

"Of course! It wasn't a king's ransom, and only for a few days. Plus they're a legitimate company, an NGO for heaven's sake!"

"How were you supposed to send the money?" Ms. Mendez said.

Mr. Parsons thought. "Well, it was complicated, like just about everything nowadays. Edna says technology was good enough in 1956. We should have stopped then."

Ms. Mendez smiled, one of those smiles that was just a turning up of the corners of the lips, no eye involvement. Those would be pretty scary if I was the type who gets scared. "Do you remember the details?"

"I can try," said Mr. Parsons. "But what difference does it make? I don't mean to be rude but the money never got sent."

Ms. Mendez sat back. "Forty-seven thousand six hundred two dollars and thirty-one cents," she said. "It all got sent."

All the flushness drained out of Mr. Parsons' face at once. He toppled over. Bernie caught him before he hit the floor, caught him the way he catches everything, simply folding him in.

Three

"My apologies," Mr. Parsons said, now back up sitting in his chair and sipping a glass of water. "I didn't mean to cause so much trouble. Inexcusable, and—"

"No apologies necessary," Ms. Mendez said, who'd been busy on the phone and now reached for it again. "How about I call the ambulance?"

"What for?"

"To take you to the hospital. Get you checked out."

Mr. Parsons turned to Bernie. "Do I have to?"

"It's up to you."

Mr. Parsons thought about that. "Then, no. Thank you, Bernie. Do you know that decades went by—decades and decades— when we never went to the hospital, Edna and I? Blessed with good health, simply blessed." He took another sip of water, then set the glass carefully on Ms. Mendez's desk. The water trembled until the glass was out of his hand. I moved a little closer to the side of his chair, meaning we now had me on one side and Bernie on the other. A fine setup, in my opinion. Maybe Mr. Parsons thought so, too, because he sat up straight, one of those human moves when they're pulling themselves together. "What's next?" he said.

"In terms of . . . ?" said Ms. Mendez.

Mr. Parsons' wrinkly forehead wrinkled some more. "In terms of getting our . . . in terms of recovering the money."

"I've already notified the Financial Crimes Unit," Ms. Mendez said. "Anything else you can think of, Mr. Little?"

"Calling Billy," Bernie said.

Mr. Parsons blinked. "To let him know the two thousand dollars didn't go through?"

Ms. Mendez opened her mouth to say something but Bernie spoke first. "Sure," he said. "And are you okay with putting the call on speaker?"

"I don't know how to do that," Mr. Parsons said. "And of course I'd be telling Billy we were on the speaker from the beginning."

"Understood," Bernie said.

Mr. Parsons took out his phone. "And also who is in the room."

"That too."

"Hello, Billy? It's me, Dad."

"Hey, Dad! Nice to hear your voice."

Ah, yes, Billy. Hearing his voice coming from Mr. Parsons' phone, now lying on Ms. Mendez's desk—a nice voice, light and pleasant, not like Bernie's which also can be light and is certainly pleasant, but always has a mighty rumble way down deep, letting you know what's what—the whole stolen saguaro case came back clearly in mind. Well, not clear from start to finish, or what it was all about, but at least the last time we laid eyes on Billy, on the back of a motorcycle driven by a woman named Dee. Did he have a cashbox in his hand? Whose cashbox was it? But we'd let them vamoose, so there couldn't have been anything fishy going on. Impossible anyway, since this was all happening way out in the desert where fish are hard to come by. There you have it, the whole enchilada, enchiladas actually a fascinating subject which maybe we can get to later.

"Ah, yes, um, and the same to you, son," Mr. Parsons said. "But on the other hand we spoke just—"

"Dad? It sounds like you've got me on speaker."

One more thing about the pleasantness of Billy's voice I maybe should have mentioned already. There was a tiny tiny breeze in it, like feathers were fluttering somewhere way down deep. But not easy to hear. You might have missed that feathery part. No offense.

"Why, yes, that's true. I didn't realize you could hear the diff—"

"Is Mom with you? Are you at the hospital?

"No, nothing like that," Mr. Parsons said. "This is actually about yesterday." He paused, maybe waiting for Billy to speak. When Billy did not, Mr. Parsons went on. "I'm talking about our call."

"Whose call?"

"Our call, Billy. Yesterday afternoon. About the two thousand dollars. I'm at the bank now with the manager, Miss . . . Ms., uh . . ."

"Mendez," said Ms. Mendez. "Cecilia Mendez."

"Ms. Mendez," Mr. Parsons said. "And Bernie very kindly drove me here. Bernie Little, our neighbor."

"I know Bernie, Dad," said Billy. "But I don't understand what you're talking about."

"The phone call, Billy. The two thousand dollars to help with payroll." Mr. Parsons licked his lips. "Your NGO and the . . . the shortfall, whatever it was."

Then came a long silence.

"Dad?" Billy said at last. "There was no phone call yesterday, not between you and me. The last time we spoke was when I called you and Mom at the hospital on Easter Sunday."

"But," said Mr. Parsons. "But, but, but . . ." A thin drooly trickle shone at one corner of his mouth.

"Billy?" Bernie said. "This is Bernie."

"Hi, Bernie. I'm a little confused here."

"Same," said Bernie, and as he spoke did something very quick and kind of amazing. He leaned forward, took a tissue from a little tissue box on Ms. Mendez's desk, wiped away Mr. Parsons' drool and stuffed the tissue in his own pocket. But so fast and smooth you could have missed it easily, like it never happened. "Where are you right now?" Bernie said.

"My office," Billy said. "In Gila City."

"Can you come up here and help us sort this out?" Bernie said. "We're at Valley Trust, the Rio Seco branch."

"See you in ninety minutes," Billy said.

"Oh, thank you," said Mr. Parsons. "I know we talked because, well, a son's voice is something that—"

Mr. Parsons' phone started up with a droning sound, rather hard on my ears. Ms. Mendez leaned forward, gave it a poke, and it shut up. I was beginning to like Ms. Mendez.

"How about Chet and I take Daniel out to breakfast in the meantime?" Bernie said.

Breakfast! Bernie's brilliance: it can pop up at any moment, just another wonderful thing about him. I was already on my way to the door but before I got there it opened and a man entered, a roly-poly type man in a suit that made him seem roly-polyer, if that makes any sense. He was bald with a mustache, a look you often see although it makes no sense to me, hard to explain why. A cop, of course. Shoe polish, gunpowder, doughnuts: the smells are impossible to miss, at least for me.

The roly-poly cop glanced around. "Bernie? Whoa! This is a surprise." He hurried into the room, his stride a kind of quick-stepping waddle, and shook Bernie's hand. "Lookin' good, Bernie! Haven't changed a bit! And this must be the famous Chet!"

The air in Ms. Mendez's office, which had been still, perhaps even on the stale side, began to stir and even freshen up. That was on account of my tail—a realization I came to almost at once—ramping up to high gear. It can change the weather, although only in small spaces.

Meanwhile Mr. Parsons and Ms. Mendez were looking puzzled.

"Daniel Parsons and Cecilia Mendez," Bernie said, "say hi to a former colleague of mine back when we were both at Valley PD, Trummy Pizzicato."

Everyone said hi.

"The thing is, Bernie, I'm actually back on the force," Trummy said.

"How is that possible?" Bernie said. "After what . . . well, just after."

Trummy shook his head, his jowls lagging slightly behind. Bernie sometime talks about how Billie Holiday, one of our favorites, lags behind the notes, although how that fits in here I don't know. Except . . . except maybe there was something musical about Trummy's chubby face. Wow. There's all kinds of beauty in life, as I may have mentioned too much already and will try not to do again.

"Bygones," Trummy said. "Plus, the old guard is out and, the new guard doesn't know . . . well, in short, I'm not only back, but feast your baby blues on the deputy chief of the fraud squad." A baby blue feast? I was lost and somewhat alarmed. Before I could even start to find my way, he turned to Ms. Mendez. "You called?"

"I did."

"Fraud squad?" said Mr. Parsons, but so quietly no one heard but me.

Trummy took out a notebook, pulled up a chair, licked his thumb, flipped through the pages. A dusty orange flake popped free and drifted down to the floor, where I snapped it up. Cheeto— the smell and the taste powerful and unmistakable. "Take it from the top," Trummy said.

A long and complicated conversation got going, with Ms. Mendez and Trummy doing most of the talking, then Bernie, and Mr. Parsons hardly at all. I could smell how anxious he was, could hear his heart beating so fast and light, could see how heavy his eyelids were getting, could feel how hard he was trying to keep them from closing. But mostly my mind—now under some sort of Cheeto command—was on breakfast. Hadn't that been the very next thing on the schedule? *BREAKFAST! BREAKFAST! BREAKFAST!* My mind kept that up for some time, but at last my own eyelids got heavy. Far away, like a distant storm, there was rumbling about Zapp and numbers far past two. No eyelids on earth can fight off that kind of thing. I lay down close to Mr. Parsons.

A door opened. At the sound my eyes did the same thing, security being a big part of my job. A man entered, perhaps slightly familiar, but I couldn't place him, not by sight alone, plus he hadn't spoken yet and his smell was hard to get at, somewhat lost in little ripples of after shave, toothpaste, deodorant.

"Ah, Billy," said Mr. Parsons. He'd been slumped in his chair, but now he straightened and rose to his feet, not easily and with a cracking sound or two, but he did it. Billy—so changed from the last time I'd seen him, changes I'll try to remember to describe when I get a chance—came over and hugged his dad, and Mr. Parsons hugged him back, his eyes growing watery. "So good of you to come, son," he said, and then stepped back. "Now please tell these nice folks about our call yesterday."

Billy gave Mr. Parsons a worried look. "We didn't speak yesterday, Dad," he said. That was when I noticed that although I had remembered the sound of his voice—hard to forget what with that interesting feathery part—it had changed a bit, now deeper than before, and more relaxed, if that makes any sense. "Are you thinking about our call on Easter Sunday? That was the last time we talked."

Mr. Parsons' voice rose, high and trembling. "No, I am not."

Billy turned to Bernie. "Hi, Bernie," he said. "Could someone tell me what's going on?"

Bernie nodded. "This is Ms. Mendez, bank manager, and Sergeant—"

"Lieutenant," said Trummy.

"Um," said Bernie. "Lieutenant Pizzicato from the Valley PD fraud squad. Maybe one of them will fill you in."

Billy sat slowly down.

"It's pretty straightforward from our end," said Ms. Mendez. "Yesterday at four thirty-four p.m., Mr. Parsons withdrew forty-seven thousand six hundred two dollars and thirty-one cents from his Valley Trust account."

"But I did not!" said Mr. Parsons. "I sent two thousand dollars to Billy, and only till Monday."

Billy shook his head very slightly, his gaze, not a happy one, on Mr. Parsons.

"How did you do that, sir?" said Trummy.

Bernie's eyebrows, with that language all their own, made a very slight movement. That's how they show surprise, hardly moving at all.

"Online," Mr. Parsons said. "Is that what you mean? I didn't drive down here to the bank or anything like that."

"You're comfortable doing things online?" Trummy said.

"I wouldn't say comfortable," said Mr. Parsons.

Trummy licked his thumb again, turned another page in his notebook. "So what were the steps? Walk me through it."

"The steps? Well, I just gave Billy the password. Then he handled the steps, whatever they were. Isn't that right, Billy?"

Billy shook his head in that same sad way. Maybe this is where to get to what I promised before, the part about how changed Billy looked. The last time I'd seen him, almost at the end of the terrible stolen saguaro case, he'd looked so young, almost still a kid, a long-haired kid with vague sort of eyes, which you often see in kids, and a small snakehead tattoo on his face, which you hardly ever see. Now his hair was short and neatly trimmed, his eyes were in the here and now, and the snakehead tattoo was gone. Hadn't he been sporting a lot of arm ink as well? If so, there was no way to tell at the moment: Billy wore a jacket and tie and sky-blue button down shirt.

Trummy turned to Billy. "Anything to say on this?"

Billy reached over and touched Mr. Parsons' shoulder. "Sorry, Dad."

"So it didn't happen?" said Trummy.

Billy shook his head.

Mr. Parsons tried to rise but couldn't quite do it.

"What we get in these cases, over and over, is impersonators," Trummy said.

"Impersonators?" And now, with a tremendous effort, Mr. Parsons rose to his feet. For a moment I thought he was about to shake his fist, but he didn't, although the fingers of one of his hands shook, like they were thinking of folding themselves into one. "I know the voice of my own flesh and blood."

"Hate to say it, sir," said Trummy, "but I've heard that one plenty of times. That's how this works. They can do all sorts of things, like distorting the connection, or they catch a break and someone's got a leaf blower going on the receiving end, or a dog is barking. It doesn't take a whole lot, because—" And now he turned to Bernie. "Because they're counting on the will to help. That's the . . . what's the word I'm looking for?"

"Heart," said Bernie.

Trummy nodded. "Right. That's the heart of it. Did you hear about that old lady in Florida? A grandson impersonator in her case. It was on the news. I'll be damned if she didn't hop on a plane to Romania to get her money back. But a very different case—the FBI knew the scammers were in this one particular town, for one thing. Here we got nothing like that, no leads at all."

There was a silence. Then Mr. Parsons said, "I'm not blaming Iggy."

Everyone turned to him.

"You must have some questions, Daniel," Bernie said. There was a long silence. Then Mr. Parsons said, "Edna and I—are we getting our money back?"

He looked up at Ms. Mendez. Ms. Mendez looked down. Bernie looked at Trummy. Billy looked at Bernie and so did I, always my preference in any case.

"It depends," Trummy said. "If Zapp turns out to be real, there's a chance. If not . . ."

"Real?" Mr. Parsons said. "I'm lost."

I was totally with him on that.

Four

Billy took Mr. Parsons out to the parking lot and Trummy followed. Bernie and I lingered behind, me because he was doing it and Bernie for reasons of his own. I'm no expert on reasons, but Bernie is. For example, once he said, "The heart has its reasons that reason knows not of." Unbelievable! Although I don't have a clue what it means, from start to finish. This happened a while back at a bar when Bernie told Lou Stine something very important that I hope to remember real soon.

But here's what I remember about that bar, Lou Stine, and the heart having its reasons. Lou's an old buddy and now a captain on the Valley PD, that promotion finally happening on account of us somehow. And maybe I'll remember that, too! What a day that would be! Captain Stine's a hard-faced man and not to be messed with. On the other hand, as humans like to put it—and more than once I've heard Bernie say that if people had more hands they'd have more opinions—when he and his wife had a kid they named him after Bernie, maybe the middle name, perhaps a bit of a complication. Chet is all the name I need.

Forget all that. What I'm getting at is Bernie and Captain Stine at Akbar's Ack-Ack Bar and Grille, a tough place but all the tough guys and gals were giving us plenty of room. Akbar's a real big guy who was in the desert—not our desert but a far off one, back in Bernie's army days before we got together, him and me—the night Bernie hurt his leg so bad, although you wouldn't know it now, not unless he was wearing shorts, which he never does, or it's late in the day on a long hike so you might catch him limping just the slightest. Whenever we run into any of the guys who were there that far off night we pay for nothing, which is why we hardly ever go to Akbar's, Bernie wanting to pay at least sometimes. But on this particular occasion, we'd gone on account of Captain Stine wanting to check out the place. So we were down at the end of the bar, drinking from the top shelf—which was where Akbar kept the best bourbon and also my water bowl—when Bernie said that important thing, which was . . . which was . . . Got it! What a lucky break! All this luck: why me? Well, that last thought was somewhat uncomfortable, and I forgot it at once.

"Got a bit of news," was what Bernie said. "I asked Weatherly to marry me."

Oh my goodness! I didn't realize that once I got started down this road I'd have to fill you in on Weatherly! And meanwhile we've got Billy, Mr. Parsons, and Trummy out in the bank parking lot. This will have to be quick. Weatherly's a sergeant at Valley PD, with a big future as Captain Stine himself has said. We met on account of Trixie, a member of the nation within that some folks would call Weatherly's dog, a way of seeing things that's a bit of a puzzler to me. The point is we'd rescued Trixie from a cave or abandoned mine, me and Bernie. So far, a normal day at the Little Detective Agency. Then it turned out Trixie had been kidnapped, which was how Weatherly came into our life. Weatherly loved us for finding Trixie. No problem there, I suppose. The problem is that Trixie and I—this is from what I've heard, not really seeing it myself—look alike. Why would anyone think such a thing? Just because our coats are the same—glossy black except for one white ear? Didn't my being so much—or at least somewhat—bigger count for anything? And here's a bothersome fact: aside from the she-ness of her scent and he-ness of mine, they were rather similar. But who knew that other than Trixie and me and every single member of the nation within? Certainly not Bernie or Weatherly. So how had they arrived at the strange idea that Trixie and I must have been puppies together? Strange and unacceptable.

Meanwhile Captain Stine had put down his glass and was turning to Bernie.

"And she said yes?"

"You sound disappointed."

"It's not that. I kind of thought this was coming. I'm happy for both of you."

They clinked glasses, raised them to their lips, and then paused. "But?" Bernie said.

"Well, you've been married before."

"So?"

"So why formalize things now? You're older."

"Marriage is for the very young?"

"Let's just say the young."

"I'm not even forty."

"Call that young if you want. But you're way too smart to believe you can start over in this life. A slight course change is the best you can do."

Bernie thought that over and then nodded. But what was going on? Were they buddies or not? I was on the point of doing who knows what when Bernie said the brilliant thing that got me started on all this.

"The heart has its reasons that reason knows not of."

"You son of a bitch," Captain Stine said. "I'll drink to that."

Down at the end of the bar Akbar had been dusting bottles, his back turned to us. But now he wheeled around and hurried over our way. A man of that size—and Akbar was enormous—on the move and, in fact, moving pretty fast, is an alarming sight. I got ready for anything.

"Me, too!" he said. Akbar had one of those powerful voices even when, like now, he wasn't shouting. My paws could feel that voice through the floorboards. He grabbed a glass, banged it down on the bar, and filled it to the brim with that top shelf bourbon. "That's the best damn thing I ever heard and it happened right here in my own bar." He clinked each of their glasses, some bourbon spilling, a few drops landing on my shoulder. I licked them off. I'd tasted bourbon once or twice in my career and wasn't a fan but now found that bourbon mixed with a touch of something Chetish was a different story. You can learn things in this life. All you have to do is be there! Anyone can do it.

"Down with reason and all that bullshit," Akbar said, his good eye glittering like it had a life of its own, which I suppose eyes do, if I ever stopped to think of it, which probably won't happen. I should point out that the space where Akbar's other eye was was covered with a patch, all that having something to do with that same far away night when Bernie's leg got hurt.

They drank. Akbar smacked his lips; a terrific human move you don't see nearly enough. Actually, it's the sound and not the sight that appeals, but let's leave that for now.

"Ever think of being a preacher, Bernie?" he said.

"Ha ha ha," said Captain Stine.

Akbar turned slowly to him. "You're some kind of cop?"

"That's right."

"Thought so. Let me tell you something. The heart has its reasons? That's preacher material right there. You think just anyone can make up gems like that?"

Captain Stine stopped laughing. They both shot Bernie a glance, quick but admiring.

"Um," said Bernie.

So that's the story of the heart and its reasons, more or less, but put your money on less. Now back to Ms. Mendez's office where Bernie and I seemed to be lingering even though I was pretty sure the action had moved out to the parking lot.

"Something on your mind, Mr. Little?" Ms. Mendez said.

Bernie gazed at her, maybe making up his mind about something. "From a few things Daniel has said to me in the past, I got the impression that he and Edna lived off social security and a few small pensions. They own their house free and clear but as for savings it was all here in the account that's now empty."

"I'm sorry to hear that, but there's nothing—"

Bernie held up his hand. "I know that. But what I'd like you to do is tell him the bank has a special fund you can dip into sometimes and so you've dipped into it to the tune of ten grand. Make it twenty."

Ms. Mendez sat back. "Didn't I just say—or try to—that what you're suggesting is impossible?"

"Right," Bernie said. "I shouldn't have interrupted. Take the twenty K from my account."

"Excuse me?"

"Won't the check I deposited cover it?"

I didn't know what this was all about, but I sensed it was going south. South is where things go when they're headed in the wrong direction. From the look on her face, I was guessing Ms. Mendez's take was the same as mine.

"It's my duty to counsel prudence," she said.

"Yes or no?" Bernie said.

"I'll have a document drawn up."

"'Preciate that."

Ms. Mendez reached for a pad of paper. Were her eyes slightly damp? Probably not, what with her being a woman of the no-nonsense type. Their eyes stay nice and dry in my experience, even in the rain.

Out in the parking lot, Billy and Mr. Parsons were driving off in a red pickup, not new, what with the paint all faded, but very clean. Trummy was standing by his squad car watching them go. He pointed with his chin.

"The last generation that's going to be suckers for this crap," he said.

"Yeah?" said Bernie.

"Think of their formative years, Bernie. No computers, no internet, no passwords. The only screen was a blurry box with rabbit ears on top. Now they're helpless, like some stone age tribe when the invaders arrive with muskets and cannons."

Bernie gave him a close look.

"What?" Trummy said. "What's that about?"

"You were good in there, that's all."

"What are you saying?"

"Nothing," Bernie said.

"Come on, Bernie. This is all about how I was a complete screw up before."

"Let's not do this," Bernie said.

"I don't mind," said Trummy. "In fact, I'd like to. I was a complete screw up, and worse. So now that I'm doing all right, the guys like you aren't quite buying it."

"Guys like me?" said Bernie.

"The hard guys. The guys who don't believe in fresh starts."

Bernie's eyes got an inward look, deep and almost like he'd felt a sudden pain. Whoa! I put my paw on his foot, all I could think of to do at that moment.

"You were good in there, Trummy," he said again. "Anything we can do to help just ask."

"Got this," Trummy said. "But I'll loop you in."

"Thanks," Bernie said.

"Don't mention it," said Trummy. "That old guy likes you."

☼　☼　☼

When we got home, the red pickup was parked in the Parsons' driveway. Mr. Parsons was still in the passenger seat, head resting on the head rest, eyes closed, and Billy was outside sweeping off the front steps to the house.

"Dad nodded off," he called over in one of those loud whispers humans use from time to time. Where do they come up with this stuff? They sure do like to entertain, one of the best things about them. "I'm letting him snooze."

We walked over. The instant I stepped in their yard Iggy started up inside the house, no surprise there. Mr. Parsons' eyes opened slowly. He saw Bernie and frowned. "I know the voice of my own son."

Bernie began to say something, but Mr. Parsons cut him off. "Iggy barking or not! Makes no difference."

Billy leaned the broom against the side of the house and walked up to us. "I know, Dad. But let's not worry about it now. How about we go inside and grab something to eat?"

"I'm not hungry."

"Then just rest."

"Rest? What about your mother?"

"I'm sure she's resting, too."

"But Billy! What am I going to tell her?"

Billy opened the pickup door and helped Mr. Parsons out. "Let's think about that later," he said.

"Later?" said Mr. Parsons. "My later is . . ." He took a deep breath, although not a Bernie-type deep breath, his chest not moving all that much. ". . . sliced thin."

Billy didn't say anything, just supported Mr. Parsons on the way to the front door and then inside. The door closed. Iggy's yip-yip-yipping amped down to a whine and then he went silent.

Meanwhile, Bernie was walking slowly around the red pickup, giving it a real close look. Because it was so clean and he was hoping to pick up a few pointers? That was as far as I could take it on my own.

"I wonder," Bernie began, but before he could go on Billy came out of the house, perhaps with a bit of a bounce in his step. "How's he doing?" Bernie said.

"Better," said Billy. "You'll never guess why. The bank manager—Ms. Mendez?—just called him." Billy held up his hand. "And no, they haven't found the money. But it turns out they have some kind of grant program that partially covers cases like this, and they've put twenty grand into Dad's account. He fell asleep on the couch thirty seconds after she hung up. I could almost see the tension flowing out of him."

"Good to hear," Bernie said, "but the case—the criminal case—is still open."

"Of course," said Billy, sounding a little less lively. "Sure."

"Which leads me to a question," Bernie said. "Did Trummy— Lieutenant Pizzicato—ask to see your phone?"

Billy's head went back. "My phone?"

Bernie nodded.

"No," Billy said. "Why would he have?"

"You can figure that out," Bernie said.

Billy's eyes shifted to the side, just for an instant, but in that instant I thought I saw the old Billy, from back in the days of the stolen saguaro case.

"It must have slipped Trummy's mind." Bernie held out his hand. "So now I'm asking unofficially."

Five

Billy stepped back. A real hot look flashed in his eyes, the kind of look you see right before fisticuffs. I didn't bother moving in front of Bernie. When it comes to fisticuffs, he's in danger from nobody, and certainly not from the likes of Billy. But no fisticuffs happened out here on the walkway to the Parsons' house. The hot look vanished fast, and in its place rose something much cooler, even cold.

"Even back on my most messed up day I'd never do anything close to what you're suggesting—not to anybody let alone my own parents," Billy said.

Bernie just stood there, saying nothing. Billy tossed him the phone, not in a playful way but not hard or anything like that, which made the fact that . . . that Bernie dropped it—yes! That really happened—even more surprising. Bernie catches everything. You name it—balls of all kinds, and not just balls but scissors, for example, burning candles, even a live diamondback on one occasion—in that same easy way, his hand just folding whatever it was inside. But not Billy's cell phone, which thunked off the palm of his hand and tumbled to the ground. I grabbed it up at once, like the whole thing hadn't happened, and held it out for him in easy reach.

Bernie took it and gazed at the screen, tapping it from time to time. Billy was watching in a way I didn't like one little bit, like he was looking down his nose at Bernie. Billy's little turned-up nose compared to the magnificence of Bernie's? What was he thinking?

Bernie looked up, walked over to Billy and handed back the phone. Billy stuck it in his pocket.

"I could have used someone else's phone," Billy said. "Or a burner."

"True," Bernie said.

"You planning to check out those possibilities?"

Bernie shook his head.

"I'm not sure I believe you," Billy said. "Do you trust anyone?" What a crazy question! There I was, as trusted as they come, and within easy leaping distance of this dude. Especially him! We'd cut him a break on the saguaro case. The details escaped me but one thing for sure: this was turning into a confusing day.

Meanwhile, Billy seemed to be waiting for an answer and Bernie wasn't saying anything.

"I mean it," Billy said. "I'm curious."

Bernie thought about that and was still thinking when his own phone buzzed. He glanced at the screen, said, "I have to take this," and stepped away. "Hi, Leda," he said.

Leda being his ex, and mother of Charlie, as I hope you don't mind me reminding you. I heard her on the other end. "Sorry to bother you, Bernie," she said. Her voice had an underlying—I don't want to say harshness—but lately, especially when she was talking to Bernie, it did not. "I could use a favor." Then she got started on a long story about being stuck at LAX, whatever that was, or maybe it was Malcolm stuck at LAX and she was stuck someplace else. Billy was still watching Bernie in a way I didn't like. I watched Billy right back. He noticed me watching, a sight that maybe startled him a bit. He turned and went into the house.

"No problem," Bernie said, tapping his phone and putting it away. He looked at me, his face lighting up as though the sun had come out from behind the clouds, even though the sky today was cloudless. He took a quick glance at the Parsons' door and then said, "Let's go get Charlie."

I sprang all the way from where I was on the Parsons' lawn into the shotgun seat of the Beast parked in our driveway. Perhaps there'd been an initial bound or two, but of that I have no memory.

We drove up to Charlie's school just as the kids were getting out. I myself know a little bit about school, having spent some time at K-9 school which was lots of fun right up to the very last day when all that remained was the leaping test—and leaping, as you just saw, is something I'm not too shabby at, in fact could be called my very best thing—and . . . and I can barely think of it, even now! I flunked the leaping test! Yes, me, Chet the Jet! How had that happened? There are still nights when I wake up and try to figure it out, but all that comes back to me is the involvement of a cat, and possibly some blood. But—and this but is the kind of but Bernie calls a big one—that day of the leaping test was also the day I met him. Bernie! So there you have it, all I know about everything.

Back to the kids getting out of school. They came out fast which is how kids come out of school, kids going in being a very different story. Kids are lighter on their feet than adults but their balance tends to be iffy, so this whole stream of them looked like it could come tumbling apart at any moment but it did not, instead split into little streamlets heading toward the buses or to the long line of waiting cars by the playing fields, which was where we were. And there was Charlie! What a kid! Who else would think to carry a backpack like him? Every single kid out there had bought into the backpack on the back approach, but not our boy, meaning mine and Bernie's, although I suppose I should include Leda. Our boy was the only one who knew that a backpack didn't have to be on your back! It didn't even need to be carried at all. Not if you could kick it, kind of like an odd lumpy ball. And then one of his sneakers flew off! How amazing is that?

"Good God in heaven," Bernie said quietly, which must have meant he was a proud dad.

Meanwhile Esmé, Charlie's best friend and the smartest kid in the class, was picking up the sneaker and handing it to him. She seemed much taller than he was, but most of that was her topknot, bigger every time I saw her. Now an odd little scene started up. First Charlie dropped the sneaker. Then Esmé, reminding me for a moment of Ms. Mendez, funny how the mind works, spoke to him in what appeared to be no uncertain terms, although on account of them still being quite distant and also all the kid type hubbub going on, I couldn't hear a word, except possibly for *baby*. Then she knelt down and—what was this? Grabbed Charlie by his bare foot, the sock somehow missing in action, jammed the sneaker on it and zip zip just like that laced it up? Wow! I'd never seen such fast and smooth lacing up, certainly not by Charlie but also not by anybody. Finally, she picked up his backpack, and slung it over her shoulder.

"Boy oh boy," Bernie said, maybe even prouder.

They came toward us.

"Hey, Dad! Hi, Chet!"

"Hi, Mr. Little."

"Hi, Esmé. You know you can call me Bernie."

"I do. Thanks, Mr. Little."

"Guess what, Dad! Soon toasters are going to be smarter than us."

"Oh?" said Bernie.

"That's what Esmé says. It's all about AIEEE!" Charlie's voice rose to a shout on the AIEEE part.

"A.I.," Esmé said.

"Ah," said Bernie.

"My dad works on A.I.," Esmé said.

Bernie smiled. He has a special smile that's just for kids. "I thought your dad was a jazz trumpeter."

"Both," said Esmé. "Why not?"

"No reason," Bernie said.

"For sure. They both come down to numbers."

"I hadn't gotten that far."

She gave Bernie a long look and then nodded. Something was going on in her mind but don't ask me what. "The toaster's hype, by the way."

"What's hype?" Charlie said.

"Hyperbole," said Esmé. At that point there was a beep beep from a car on down the line and Esmé waved bye bye and ran off.

Grammy's Kick Ass Country Cookin' is where Charlie likes to go for an after school snack. Grammy's has tables out back with old wooden barrels to sit on.

There are also barrel cactuses growing here and there. That—the wooden barrels and the barrel cactuses—always makes me think and I always get no place, but today I didn't bother because Weatherly was sitting at one of the tables, waiting for us. I hurried over to greet her. Weatherly's not real big but she's strong for her size and greeted me right back no problem, not getting knocked over or anything like that. Greeting Weatherly can't be done without picking up Trixie's smell, but Weatherly also has a very nice smell of her own, a smell that reminds me of those soft mountain breezes that come as the sun sets. This time I also sniffed ink, specifically the kind used for fingerprinting perps.

Weatherly tilted up her face and Bernie gave her a kiss. Then she turned to Charlie and patted the barrel next to her. He climbed up and sat.

"Hey, buddy." She gave him a smile. Weatherly's teeth are

the best human teeth I've seen. Not big or sharp, of course, goes without mentioning, but white, shining, even. "How was your day?" she said.

"Toasters are gonna be smarter than us," Charlie said.

"Oh?"

"Charlie and Esmé have been discussing A.I.," Bernie said.

"Ah," Weatherly said.

"Dad? What are the toasters gonna say?"

"Don't butter me up," said Bernie.

Weatherly made a good grief sort of face, but Charlie started laughing. He fell off the barrel and rolled around on the deck, laughing and laughing. When rolling around on the deck gets going, I'm in, as I'm sure you've guessed. That was around the time the waitress came to take our order. She smiled one of those killer smiles you hardly ever see.

Charlie had PB&J, and Bernie and Weatherly had tacos, pork for Bernie, beef for Weatherly, and I made do with a chewy, on account of . . . well, I'm not sure. But no worries because here's the thing about tacos: they're a kind of roll up with holes at the ends. Holes at the ends! What a brilliant human invention! Where do they get these ideas? Holes at the ends mean there's no way that's what's inside stays inside. In short, I recommend Grammy's tacos, especially the beef.

"There's something we should go over," Weatherly said, and with a slight wince pulled a bunch of papers from her pocket.

"Hey," Bernie said, "you all right?"

"Fine," said Weatherly, smoothing out the pages on the table and sorting through them. "We've got that meeting with the caterer coming up and I just wanted to nail down a thing or two. You wrote down the Muertos, for example." She looked up. "How many Muertos were you thinking?"

Ah. This was about the wedding. The tone of her voice—loving, but—and the way Bernie said, "uh," were the tells. Tells are one of those things we law enforcement types are always on the look-out for. In the nation within, the tail is very useful when checking for tells. Tell tails, right? Surely, you've heard that one. Humans lack tails, of course, one of those tragedies life comes up with sometimes, although most humans just soldier bravely on, so let's hear it for them. But the point is, humans have all sorts of other tells you have to learn if you want to be successful in our business, tells like loving, but . . . and many different kinds of uhs. You can find yourself wondering if in fact they're nothing but a collection of tells. My advice? Don't go there.

Back to the Muertos, a motorcycle club or possibly gang. They throw the best Christmas party in the whole Valley, and we always go. Everybody checks their guns at the door of the Muertos hangout—and not just guns but knives, brass knuckles, chains, axes, nunchuks, crossbows, and some nasty one-of-a-kinds that have no name—but some of the bikes themselves are allowed in, because otherwise how could indoor racing be part of the evening?

"How many Muertos were you thinking?" Weatherly said. "I checked their file downtown—three hundred and forty-two known members, not counting seventy-six currently in lockup."

"Oh, no, certainly not all of them," Bernie said. "How about just the board?"

"The board is mostly in rehab or witness protection."

"Then why not just Junior and his wife?" Junior being the chief Muerto.

"And leave out his mom?"

"Can't do that," Bernie said, perhaps recalling an incident involving Junior's wife, his mom, and the nunchuks I mentioned earlier.

"Junior, wife, mom," Weatherly said, writing on one of the

pages. She folded them up and stuffed them back in her pocket, wincing again.

"Hey!" Bernie said. "You all right?"

"Fine."

Charlie has a way of piping up just when you think he's completely zoned out, one more reason that he's the greatest kid around. "Didja get into a fight with a bad guy?" he said, or something like that, not so easy to tell with his cheeks bulging with PB&J.

Weatherly smiled. "Not what you'd call a fight."

"What happened?" Bernie said.

"Nothing."

"It sounds like something."

"But it wasn't."

Her phone beeped. She glanced at the screen and rose. "See you later, boys." She kissed Bernie, mussed Charlie's hair, gave me a quick pat, and walked away. Bernie watched her closely. Was she limping slightly? That was my take. Bernie started to say something but at that moment his own phone beeped.

"Bernie? Trummy here. Quick update. According to our tech gal, that app—Zapp, or whatever the hell it was—turns out to be what she calls a ghost code, here and gone. It moved the old man's money to something called Greta Analytics, ghost number two. But there's a catch. In between it—meaning the forty some grand—touched down in a checking account at the Gila City National Bank."

Bernie's hand tightened on the phone.

"You see where this is going?" Trummy said.

Bernie didn't answer.

"The account's in the name of Billy Parsons," Trummy said.

Bernie took a long slow breath. "Are you going to pick him up?"

I heard Trummy taking a long slow breath on the other end. "I like that old man," he said at last. "So what's justice here?"

"You're telling me you're not bringing him in?" Bernie said.

"Oh, I'm bringing him in all right. But softly."

"Meaning you'll give him a chance to return the money?"

Trummy nodded. "And turn himself in."

"He might need some persuading," Bernie said.

"I wondered," Trummy said.

"How about I handle that?" Bernie said.

"Works for me," said Trummy.

Bernie had a sudden idea. I could feel the change in him. "Trummy?"

"Yeah?"

"Uh, maybe you could do me a favor. It's not a quid pro quo so say no if it's no."

"I'm all ears" said Trummy.

Humans: sometimes clueless. You had to love them.

"Weatherly collared someone today," Bernie said. "I'd like to know who."

There was a long, long pause. I felt a question coming, maybe a whole bunch of questions, but finally Trummy just said, "I'll get back to you."

Six

"The old Gila City highway," Bernie said the next morning. "It'll take a little longer than the interstate, but—the open road, big guy!"

Ah, yes, our kind of day: the open road, two lane blacktop with hardly anyone around, and feeling tip top. The Beast was in a real good mood, rumbling beneath us, and I sat tall in the shotgun seat, protecting us from . . . well, you name it. Roof up, the wind in Bernie's hair and my fur, the hills as green as they ever get, with flowers in all sorts of colors popping up here and there. Since Bernie says I'm not good when it comes to colors, I'll leave picturing them to you. As for the smells in the air, where to even start? With that saguaro standing tall by a big red rock, giving off that characteristic aroma of—

"Should we let Billy know we're coming or make it a surprise?" Bernie said taking his phone out of the cupholder.

I wasn't sure where this was going but surprises can be fun. Take, for example the Torquemada runaway case—Torquemada being the runaway, but also a giant tortoise, so the case was over almost before it began—where I'd surprised the big fella by flipping him over on his back. Fun for sure, although the expression in Torquemada's upside-down eyes had perhaps been a bit on the murderous side. Were we planning on flipping Billy over on his back? Why would we do that? Still, it sounded promising. The heart has its reasons that—whoa! For one wonderful and very brief moment I understood all.

"I don't want to believe that we're all of us either wolves

or sheep," Bernie said, cutting off whatever I'd been thinking about, cutting it off stone cold. All of us either wolves or sheep? I gave him a close look, saw nothing but my normal Bernie, a lovely sight. There was a faint sheepish smell in the air—not unusual in these parts—but not the least wolfish hint. I'd come across a wolf or two in my time—their smells reminding me of me in a way, with something coyoteish mixed in and something else, hard to name, that made me think of blood—but only at a distance, what with how they wanted nothing to do with ol' Chet. But none of that was important. What was Bernie saying? We were somehow all sheep or wolves? Sheep and wolves? Had I ever been so confused?

"And," Bernie went on, "I don't want to think of Daniel and Edna as sheep."

I was totally with him on that. I knew both their scents very well, and neither had the slightest hint of sheep. So the answer was clear. We weren't going to think of the Parsonses as sheep. I never had, but from now on I'd be on guard to make sure I never would.

Whew. I was getting that nice bullet-dodging feeling—a feeling we know well, me and Bernie, from real bullets—when he said, "Also I don't want to think of us as wolves." He took his hand off the phone, leaving it in the cupholder.

Bernie's always the smartest human in the room, but anyone can have an off day. Which was why now, for the very first time, I was waiting for him to . . . to catch up to me in the thinking department? I didn't even want to go there.

"But what are we going to call ourselves?" he said.

That one had an easy answer: The Little Detective Agency. Bernie would be landing on it any moment now and then his head would clear and we'd be back to normal.

"Is there a creature that protects sheep from wolves? Like

bears, for example? Although not bears per se. A top of the food chain type, like tigers or eagles."

Now we were bears? Or tigers—whom I knew from Animal Planet and are actually giant cats, the kind of thing that pops up in the very worst dreams—or eagles? Eagles? Aren't eagles birds? Correct me if I'm wrong. But as for protecting sheep, didn't we in the nation within already handle that? Sometimes Bernie doesn't get enough sleep. That had to be it.

"Or am I oversimplifying?" Bernie said. "Are we all made up partly of sheep and partly of wolves? Or under the right circumstances can any of us be a sheep or a wolf?"

He glanced over at me. I had no idea what to do. How about biting the steering wheel, something I'd never done or even considered? I was going back and forth on that when the phone buzzed. Whatever this was had to be better than what we had going. I've been lucky all my life.

"Bernie? Trummy here."

"On the road to Gila City." Bernie said.

"Early bird catches the worm," said Trummy. He left out the part about how the bird then scarfs it up. Fish also go for worms. Not my kind of thing and I've never even considered it. Except for once. Or possibly twice. "Got the deets you wanted," Trummy went on.

"Deets?"

"Details, Bernie. Gotta keep up. Otherwise you get left behind." Trummy paused, maybe waiting for Bernie to say something. When he didn't, Trummy said, "Anyways it was a collar. Bit of resistance. Weatherly handled it, took the guy in, booked him. Finito."

"Who was riding with her?"

"Nobody. Staffing issues plus it was a crime in progress situation."

"What kind of resistance?" Bernie said.

"Huh?"

"What went down?"

"The usual. Some sort of scramble."

"Got the deets on that?" Bernie said.

"Just that it was over pretty quick. Oh, and the perp had . . . what was it? A wrench?"

Bernie got very quiet. "He hit her with a wrench?"

"Don't know that for a fact. But there is this additional charge of resisting and assault on an officer. The initial charge is attempted arson. She caught him red-handed, all set to torch one of those warehouses where the feedlots used to be. Long rap sheet. That's what he does professionally—arson for hire."

"What's his name?" Bernie said.

There was a long pause. Then Trummy said, "Werner Irons. You know him?"

"No. Where have they got him? Downtown or in the South Pedroia lockup?"

"Neither one. He made bail."

Bernie eased off the gas. The rumble of the Beast got quiet. Bernie said nothing.

"Bernie? You there?"

"How much was bail?"

"A grand, maybe?"

"For arson, assault, resisting?"

"You know how it is," Trummy said. "What are you plan—"

"Thanks, Trummy." Bernie clicked off, slowed down a little more, pulled a U-ee, and floored it.

Bernie hardly ever gets angry. Is that why when he does get angry he starts looking way more dangerous than the dudes who are pretty much angry twenty-four seven, which is a complicated number meaning I'm not sure what? The angriest I've ever seen him was the night of the broom closet case, not that we didn't solve it. The problem was we got there too late. The little girl's name was Gail Blandino. At dawn the next morning, when we'd done what we'd never done before or since, namely taken care of justice in our own way, Bernie said, "Never think of this again." Oh, how I wish. But there you go. I'm thinking about it again right now! When all I was trying to get to was how Bernie looked angry now—as we drove back to the Valley, interrupting a fun ride to wherever it was we'd been headed—although not as angry as on the night of the broom closet case. Here's a strange thing about his face when he's angry. It hardly changes at all! You have to really know him, and who knows him better than me? His face—such a beautiful face!—loses none of its beauty when he's angry. It just looks a little bit thinner, like he hasn't been eating enough. Thinner and harder. That's it.

Back in the Valley we took the Cactus Town exit. Cactus Town was the oldest part of the whole shebang, if I understood right, and also the shadiest, where the trees were big, and the houses were small. We stopped in front of a little bungalow with a desert-type yard like ours and a front porch. An old woman— not as old as Mrs. Parsons but older than Katherine Cornwall— sat in a rocker, smoking one of those thin cigars, possibly called a cheroot, and not rocking. The smoke rose up in little puffs, nice and straight.

"She hasn't changed," Bernie said.

I took his word for it, pretty sure I'd never seen this woman, but even if I had and she'd changed big time, I'd still have taken his word. The woman didn't look at us but she started rocking. Now the little puffs rose in a wavy way.

"Etta Kohn," Bernie said. "Of Etta's Crime Beat in the Tribune, the old Tribune before they sold out. No one knows more about crime in the Valley than Etta."

Of course he'd meant to add "except for us." Some things—maybe most!—are just understood between me and him. We walked up to the porch.

"Well, well," Etta said, "I won't say look what the cat dragged in, since there's no cat in the land of the free who'd mess with the likes of this one. And obviously I don't mean you, Bernie." She tapped a cylinder of ash off her cheroot. "This must be the famous Chet, turnaround specialist."

"What does that mean?"

"He's turned your career around, if the rumors are true."

"Funny," said Bernie, although he didn't seem to be even close to laughing. But meanwhile, cats were suddenly in the picture, which was usually how they made their entrance. Cats dragging things in was something you heard surprisingly often, but never like this. Somehow Etta knew from the get-go that cats don't mess with the Chetster. She and I were off to a great start.

Etta puffed out a nice round smoke ball and added, "Except for the finances part." Wow! Why was I just now meeting her for the first time? She held out her hand, a woman's hand and much smaller than Bernie's, but square and strong-looking. They shook. "Take a seat," she said.

We sat, or rather, Bernie did. I went sniffing around the porch, doing a quick recon. We had a snake or two somewhere down under the porch floor, nothing unusual about that, not in these parts.

"You haven't changed," Bernie said.

"Bullshit," said Etta. "Capital bull, capital shit."

"You don't like retirement?"

Etta shrugged. "The word itself sucks. And I loathed how it went down. I'm a capitalist but I can't stand this late capitalism stage. Early capitalism was also putrid."

"You like middle capitalism?" Bernie said.

"Exactly." Etta glanced around. "Is it whiskey o'clock yet?"

"Not for me."

Etta gave him a close look. "You've changed, too."

"Oh?"

She nodded. "I was just thinking about you the other day."

"Why?"

"Does there have to be a reason?" she said. "We've known each other a long time."

Bernie smiled. "I remember when we met."

"You do?" Etta sounded surprised. Why? Bernie has a pretty good memory. The only thing he tends to forget is that he quit smoking.

"Sure," he said. "I was still on the force and you were doing a story on vets in the Valley PD."

Etta smoked her cheroot, breathing out smoky streams from her nose. "Actually," she said, gazing through the smoke, "that wasn't the first time."

"What am I forgetting?" Bernie said.

Etta looked up. "Nothing. There's no way you'd remember. I was my younger self and you were maybe eight years old."

Bernie sat up straight.

"Do you recall the batting cages that used to be off the old airport road?" Etta said.

"I hit there with my dad. Every Saturday morning in spring."

"Exactly," said Etta. "That's where it was."

"You met me at the batting cages?"

"What I just said."

"You used to hit at the cages?"

"Did I say that?"

"Were you working on a story?" Bernie said. "A dads and baseball kind of thing?"

"Hell no. I don't read crap like that, let alone write it. It was an outing."

"An outing with my dad?"

Etta gazed into the distance. "Harry, you, and me," she said. "I was along for the ride."

"You knew my dad?"

"Bingo," Etta said. "How old were you when he died?"

"Eight."

"When's your birthday?"

"September."

"Then you must have been seven, since it was spring."

Harry was the name of Bernie's dad? Was I following this right? How can anyone keep up with all the incoming stuff? All I knew—from hearing a bit of talk one night from Bernie's bedroom, he and Weatherly inside and me dozing out in the hall—was that Bernie had lost his dad a long time ago, way before he and I had gotten together, which was too bad since I'm pretty much an expert on tracking down the lost and bringing them back. I knew Bernie's mom, of course—she calls him Bernard!—still going strong in Florida. Too strong? What a strange thought, and not even nice! I wiped it out at once, in fact, before I'd even finished thinking it. What an ability!

At that moment, finding myself at the far end of the porch and just about out of the range of snake scent, I caught a break. This particular break happened to be the end of a burned sausage, just lying there, with hardly any ants on it at all. Yes, amigos, a break of the best kind. I snapped that little treasure right up. Does anyone else have a life like mine? I hope so.

Meanwhile Etta was smiling at Bernie. There are all kinds of human smiles but one of the best is the one they call the warm smile, which was what Etta was flashing now. "You had such a smooth swing, Bernie, so easy and natural. That's why I was thinking about you the other day—a player on TV had a swing that reminded me of it." She shook her head. "He was in awe."

"Who?" said Bernie. "What?"

"Are you having a slow day, Bernie? I'm talking about Harry. Your dad. He was in awe of that swing."

"He said that?"

"Not in so many words," Etta said. "But I could tell."

"You could tell," Bernie said, which sounded to me like what Etta had just said, but slower, quieter—and also stranger in a way I couldn't help hearing but also couldn't understand.

Etta made one of those open handed gestures. At times I think their hands do what the tail does in my world. In this case it meant yeah, I could tell, so what? Or something like that.

"How well," Bernie began, then stopped and started again, also a human thing although I didn't remember ever seeing it from Bernie before. "I never realized you'd known him."

"Right," said Etta.

"Why didn't you let on?"

"I'm letting on now."

Bernie thought about that for a few moments and said, "How did it come about—you knowing him?"

"I was working in a real estate office at the time," Etta said, "writing the ad copy, just starting out. Harry walked in. He wanted to sell off the last lot he had on Mesquite Road, across the street from where you live now, if you still do."

Bernie nodded. "So you wrote his ad copy?"

"Yup."

Bernie folded his arms across his chest, a human gesture you see now and then but this was the first time I'd seen it from Bernie. "And did you know my mother?"

"Never had the pleasure," Etta said. She stubbed out what was left of the cheroot in an ashtray. "But my apologies. You're not here to dig up all this, are you?"

I was hoping Bernie would say yes, digging being my second best thing—after leaping, of course—but after what seemed like a lot of backing and forthing in his head, he said, "No." Kind of quietly, maybe not forcefully, but a no just the same. Then he glanced over at me in a way that made me think he wanted help. What kind of help? There was no gunplay going down on this shady porch and there wouldn't be, since we weren't carrying and neither was Etta. My nose is on top of that at all times. I went over to Bernie and sat on his foot, a foot that was tense and then was not.

"Do you still keep that index?" he said.

"AZ Desperados A to Z?" said Etta. "I do, but now it's just a hobby."

"We're looking for someone."

"You must have contacts at Valley PD," Etta said. "Rick Torres? Lou Stine?"

Bernie gazed at her and said nothing.

"Bernie, Bernie, Bernie," she said. "Still walking on the wild side."

"I wouldn't say that."

"Of course not—that's part of the syndrome." Etta rose. "Name?"

"Werner Irons," Bernie told her.

She went into the house. Bernie's eyes got sort of blank, like he'd gone someplace else for a while. I heard sounds from deep inside the house: Etta moving around, an opening drawer, a whirring printer. She came back and handed Bernie a sheet of paper.

"Don't be a stranger," she said.

Seven

We rode down Etta's block, turned a corner and parked by a hydrant. How considerate of Bernie, but at the moment I had no need for a hydrant. Not that I couldn't produce a little something since I always retain a splash or two for marking purposes. So what were we doing? Did Bernie need to go? That was as far as I could take it on my own.

Bernie smoothed Etta's sheet of paper over the steering wheel and began reading. Ah, I got it. Not that he wasn't capable of reading and driving at the same time. He most certainly was! Who could forget the last time, when that eighteen-wheeler seemed to surprise him and . . . kind of oddly it seemed that I had forgotten what happened after that! The mind plays all sorts of tricks on you, mostly good in my case.

Bernie tapped the sheet. "Arson. Burglary. Possession of stolen goods. Violating a restraining order. Assault. Assault and battery. Hijacking. Arson. Human trafficking. Arson. Assault with a deadly weapon. Attempted arson. Resisting arrest. Assault on a police officer." He looked up. "Those are the highlights. A lot of arson, big guy—his profession." The way he said that sounded like he was being funny—and there's no one funnier than my Bernie—but there was no fun in the look in his eyes. Somehow that gave me the idea that marking the hydrant was the right play after all, but before I could make the first move we were already rolling.

After not long at all—and this is just one of those things that make the Valley so interesting, as Bernie has told me on more than one occasion, although I haven't heard him say it to anyone else, some things being "for your ears only" as he's also told me on more than one occasion—we were in South Pedroia, a very different kind of place from Cactus Town, but still part of the Valley, which goes on forever in all directions. South Pedroia isn't where you go for shady trees or neat little houses with shady porches. It's where you go for the old, abandoned railyard, brick warehouses with blackened bricks, stucco apartment buildings that haven't been freshened up in some time, and—no forgetting this one—a whole block of nothing but self-storage units.

A very bothersome fact is that one of those self-storages is ours. You'll never guess what's inside so I'll tell you: Hawaiian pants, stacked from floor to ceiling, balled up on shelves, hanging from wall hooks. Hawaiian pants are just like Hawaiian shirts, except for being pants. Plus—and this is pretty much the reason our finances are what they are, if we leave out the tin futures play, perhaps for a later time—there's another difference. A lot of guys, Bernie included, love Hawaiian shirts but it turns out that none, not even one lone dude, loves Hawaiian pants. How does that make any sense? I still remember the moment Bernie snapped his fingers and said, "Hawaiian pants! Chet! We're rich!" After that, things happened fast and soon a whole boatload of Hawaiian pants arrived, made special in some far off place. Then things began to happen slow—actually not at all, meaning we didn't sell one single pair, and selling them was part of the plan from the get-go, as I later learned. Sometimes we go to our self-storage and just hang out, Bernie having a smoke and sitting on a stack of Hawaiian pants and me lying on a bed of them. Usually, he falls into a deep silence, but on our last visit he said, "Rich is when you have lots. Poor is when you have little. But when you owe, what's the word for that? Gotta be a word for less than poor." He thought for a bit and said, "But I can't think of one, so maybe we're doing all right." Then his face brightened, and he began to laugh. We got out of there in a hurry, Bernie laughing all the way.

I glanced over at him. Was he in a laughing mood? Was that what this visit to South Pedroia was about, finding a good place to hang out and laugh for a while? Bernie didn't look like he was in a laughing mood, not close, so I wasn't surprised when we drove right past the self-storage block without turning or even slowing down and headed down a street lined with boarded-up buildings. We came to a single unboarded-up building at the end of the block, a one story building with a dusty window and in that window a sign of what I believe is called the neon type. When something goes wrong with neon signs they flicker and make a buzzing sound that hurts my ears. I'd been picking up that buzzing sound long before the building came in sight, and from the smell I already knew what was inside: a bar, of course, the smell of bars from the fanciest to the crummiest being impossible to miss, and that's without counting the boozish part. Every possible scent humans can leave is left in bars—in their floors, chairs, walls, ceilings, and don't even get me started on the bathrooms. Has there ever been a bar where at least one toilet didn't get blocked each and every day? Not this one, baby, that was for sure—a plumbing disaster if I'd ever smelled one. I knew it before we'd even stepped inside.

It was still a plumbing disaster hidden behind the scenes, as I could see the instant we entered. A visible plumbing disaster is something else. *Chet! Don't lick your paws!* That's the kind of thing you hear when you turn up in a visible plumbing disaster. But forget about that. The point is we have lots of dive bars in the Valley where the hipsters like to go and this was the other kind of dive bar, not for hipsters but for the hombres who think they're tough and also the hombres, not nearly as many, who actually are tough. Bernie says the ones who think they are but aren't turn out to be more dangerous than the real ones, one of the many things in this life I don't understand. But I do understand a few things, important ones, like, for example, the fact that there's no one tougher than me and Bernie. We walk tall, but nice and easy at the same time. That's how you'll know us.

"Professional arsonists enjoy their work," Bernie said as we paused to recon the joint. "That's what to remember."

Enjoying work? I got it completely. Who enjoys work more than me? If an arsonist, whatever that was, ever came along we were going to get along great. As for reconning the place, there wasn't much going on. All we had was a bartender with hairy ears at the near end of the bar gazing at his phone, and two guys down at the far end, one in a business suit, the other in a sleeveless tee and jeans. They were drinking and talking in low voices, although not so low that I couldn't hear the sleeveless tee dude saying, "No way, Carlo. Double it." That made the business suit dude—Carlo, if I was following this right—laugh, perhaps a laugh of the in your face type, the only human laugh they could do without. Just my opinion.

The bartender glanced up at us.

"Yeah?" he said.

"We're looking for Werner Irons," Bernie said.

The dudes at the end of the bar turned our way.

"Never heard of him," the bartender said.

Bernie reached into his pocket, took out a bill with a picture of the thin-faced dude on it, a thin-faced dude name of Old Hickory, as I recalled from a conversation I'd heard between Charlie and Esmé, Esmé talking, Charlie perhaps not actually listening. The bartender held up his hands in the no way position, kind of strange, what with those Old Hickory bills being pretty popular in my experience.

"Word is he hangs out here," Bernie said.

Before the bartender could answer, the sleeveless tee dude rose. "Who's askin'?"

My, my, what a large fellow! And what large muscles! Plus tattoos, scars here and there, and a real aggressive look in his eyes. All in all an interesting sight. We moved toward him, side by side. I left out the smells coming off him, also aggressive, but none from any sort of gun, recently fired or not. We weren't carrying either, the .38 Special back in the safe at home next to the .45 and single shot .410. But Carlo was carrying, the gun somewhere out of sight. You can count on my nose for things like that, and lots more besides.

"Me, I'm asking," Bernie said. "Name's Bernie Little and this is Chet."

"What the hell?" said the sleeveless tee dude. "That sposta be a joke? Introducing me to a dog?" He stepped forward. Carlo rose, not a big guy, no visible tattoos or scars, but one of his hands was on the move, real slow and headed for his inside jacket pocket. My job was to watch that hand. Bernie's job was to do whatever he was planning to do. We're equal partners, in case I haven't yet made that clear.

"I'm missing the humor," Bernie said. "We both need to know what you look like in case we're unlucky enough to ever lay eyes on you again."

"Huh? Makin' fun of me, you wimp?"

Wimp? Bernie? Had I ever been more shocked?

"A promising idea," Bernie said. "But we haven't got all day."

Whatever that was, the sleeveless tee dude didn't get it at first, and when he did he didn't like it, not one little bit. He seemed to inflate like some balloon of muscles, and he bared his teeth in a way you see lots of times among me and my kind but not so often with humans. Carlo reached out and touched the sleeveless tee dude's arm.

"Easy, Werner," he said. "I've heard of this guy."

Werner shrugged off the business dude, shrugged him off so hard that Carlo staggered against the bar. Then he took another step toward Bernie.

Bernie didn't move, didn't get into a fighting stance, didn't do anything but say, "Got your wrench handy, Werner?"

Werner glared down at Bernie, his nostrils flaring. "Huh?" he said.

"The wrench for when you have to fight women," Bernie said.

"What the hell are you talking about?" Werner said. A vein in his neck started throbbing.

"No need for Freud to tell us what's wrong with you," Bernie said.

Freud? A new one on me. But Bernie was right—we didn't need Freud or anyone else to figure out the likes of Werner. He was clearly a perp of the worst kind.

"There's nothing wrong with me, you little shit." Werner's voice rose. "I do women how I want and they love it."

Right around then was the moment I knew I'd had enough of Werner, even though we'd just met. At the same time, I had to keep an eye on Carlo—a problem I still hadn't solved when Bernie said, "This time you picked the wrong one. You owe her an apology. In open court while you're pleading guilty would be best."

Werner didn't like that, although the meaning was unclear to me. He made a furious—bellow? Would that be it?—then roared and reared back and threw what we call a haymaker in this business, a tremendous hooking punch aimed right at Bernie's head.

I'd seen this kind of situation before, although maybe never involving a fist so huge. Bernie simply steps inside and delivers that sweet uppercut right on the chinny chinny chin where it lands with a click, followed by eyes rolling up and perps going down. But that wasn't what happened here inside this crummy bar, maybe the crummiest of all the crummy bars I'd known. Bernie delivered the uppercut, all right, but with some differences. First, it didn't land on the chin. Instead, it landed on the throat. Second it didn't make a click. It made a ripping sort of thud. And there were more differences, about which I had some . . . uneasiness, you might say, although whatever Bernie does is always right. There's no one righter than Bernie.

One difference was that Werner's eyes didn't roll up. They bulged instead. Then there was the fact that he didn't go down, not because he hadn't gone all rubbery, which he had for sure, but because Bernie was holding him up. With one hand. That was an important detail. It left Bernie's other hand free to do other things, and what it wanted to do was slap Werner across the face, making a sound like a screen door closing. Just the one slap and not particularly hard, but I found myself making a sound too, not a bark, not a whimper, somewhere in between. Bernie didn't hear. He seemed to have gone all rigid, like something very powerful loading up. I made the sound—certainly not a happy one—again. That changed things. The rigidity leaked out of him. I glanced around. Carlo and the bartender were gone. Bernie let Werner go. He slumped to the floor, his chest rising and falling, his eyes, hot and raging, on Bernie.

Bernie didn't notice. We walked outside. I could hear Bernie's heartbeat, way too loud, booming like a drum with horrible ideas of its own. I was never going back in that crummy bar.

Eight

We rode in silence for some time, me curled up in the shotgun seat with my head against the door, not at all my usual position which is the other way, head almost touching the stick shift. Why was I doing this? I had no idea and no desire to have an idea. As for Bernie . . . well, he's usually the most relaxed driver you'll ever see, sitting back, just one hand on the wheel and often only a finger or two. But not today. Today's Bernie was gripping the wheel real hard, like it was trying to get away from him, and his whole body was rigid again. He was staring straight ahead yet for some reason I didn't think his eyes were on the road at all, but on something else, far far distant.

Just from the sounds I could keep track of this little trip, from a freeway with heavy traffic to smooth two-lane blacktop with somewhat less, to rough two-lane blacktop with almost none. Bernie pulled over and got out of the car.

I sat up. We were in open country, parked by a pair of big red rocks, their tops just touching like they were leaning on each other. Not too far away rose a string of hills, smallest to biggest, a sort of hill family on the move. Of course, hills don't move but in the desert things that normally don't move can seem to, so you're never sure. Bernie put a hand on one of the big red rocks and then bent forward and puked.

Oh, no. Bernie puking? I'd never seen that, wasn't even aware he knew how. You see human puking from time to time and of course there's puking in my world, too, where we often— although not always—scarf it all right back up like it never happened. That part I'd never seen a human do and Bernie didn't do it now. Instead, he stood up straight, hands on hips, and breathed some deep breaths. After that he kicked some dirt over the pukey area and walked back to the car, no longer rigid but not quite my normal Bernie. He sat down and started us up, although he didn't shift into gear right away. Was there time for me to hop out and scarf up his puke? Or simply give it a lick? Or failing that the briefest of sniffs? Before I could make up my mind, Bernie turned to me and said, "Sorry, big guy."

Sorry? For what? I didn't get it. Humans say sorry to you when they've done something wrong—wasn't that how sorry worked? And Bernie had never done anything wrong to me, not today, not yesterday, not tomorrow. Had he ever done wrong to anyone? Only the ones who deserved it, which made it right, no? Wasn't that the MO for making wrong right? A bit on the tricky side perhaps, but weren't humans—not all of them and not all the time— tricky? Could you even say that trickiness was their thing? Maybe you could. But I couldn't. I like just about all the humans I've ever met, even most of the perps and gangbangers. Take, for example, Finley "Fine-Tuned" Finik, a thief who specialized in high end watches and when we nabbed him in the after-hours darkness of a jewelry store, he blinked his eyes real fast and said, "How the hell did I get here, Bernie? Do you think I was sleepwalking?" How Bernie had laughed at that, sometimes breaking into soft laughter days later. Was there any chance he'd start laughing now? I hoped so, but he did not. Instead, he shifted into gear and steered us onto the road, open country two-lane blacktop as I'd thought.

"Let's get back to work," he said.

Interesting. Were we on a case? If so, that was good news. We're at our best, me and Bernie, when we're on a case. I sat up my very straightest.

❁　❁　❁

We came over the top of a high pass and there down before us lay a city surrounded by mountains on all sides, kind of like the Valley but not going on forever.

"Gila City," Bernie said. He leaned forward. "And there's water in the river!" We started down the other side. "Just like when de Niza first came through. Maybe we're catching a break, Chet. Let's hope."

Let's hope. There you have it, Bernie's brilliance in a nutshell, although my advice on nutshells—and I've had a lot of experience—is don't bother. The rest of our ride down into Gila City went by in a happy blur, not the first happy blur of my life, not even close, and the next thing I knew we were rolling down a street with bars and restaurants and cowboy outfit stores that reminded me of the streets around the college back in the Valley, except a little more on the gritty side.

We parked by a store front with no cowboy boots in the window, just a picture of one human hand shaking another. Over the door hung a sign. "ProCon Resources," Bernie read. "From Darkness to Light. Billy Parsons, Director." We went inside. Oddly enough, it got darker, not what I'd been expecting at all. But you can't understand everything in this life. Why not, you might ask. I couldn't tell you.

We were in a big room with a few desk set-ups in front, and then ping pong tables, pool tables, easy chairs, bookshelves, and a small open kitchen at the back. As for people, we had two guys shooting pool, a woman with frizzy red hair and a purple bruise around one eye flipping through a magazine, and a man bun type man at one of the desks. He looked up.

"Welcome," he said, his breath arriving with the word, breath that carried the scent of gummy weed. But why even point that out? Gummy weed breath is everywhere these days. "How can I help you?"

"We're looking for Billy Parsons," Bernie said.

"He's not in. Anything I can do for you?"

"When is he expected?"

The man bun man gave us a closer look. "Can I ask the nature of your business?"

"We're friends of his parents. I'm Bernie Little and this is Chet."

"Ah," said the man bun man. "It's just you've got a cop vibe. We have strict protocols for how we deal with law enforcement. Protecting the rights of our clientele is our first priority."

"I get that," said Bernie. "When do you expect him?"

"So this is a social call?"

"Regarding his parents."

"Is there some problem?"

"I wouldn't say that."

The man bun man thought that over and then checked his watch. "Billy might be in later."

"Have you got his number?" Bernie said.

"We don't give that out."

"Can you call him then? Just to say we're here?"

The man bun man picked up a phone, turned away. Behind him pool balls clicked, a very nice sound in my opinion. The woman with the bruise around her eye was no longer checking out the magazine, but instead watching us.

The man bun man turned to us. "Billy's not picking up."

"Have you got his address?"

"We don't give that out. I'm sure you understand."

"Protocols." Bernie smiled, but only with his eyes, the lips not taking part. You see humans doing it the other way—possibly when they don't mean it, and then comes gunplay, at least in our business—but I'd actually never seen this particular smile from anyone, including Bernie. What did it mean? Gunplay? Yes? No? No was my take, what with the fact we weren't carrying, as I may have pointed out already. "Okay if we wait?" Bernie said.

"Everyone is welcome here." He gestured behind him. "Help yourself to coffee and snacks." He glanced at me, and I saw something in his expression I should have known from the first—he was a fan of me and my kind. "We've got doggie treats, too."

And just like that, things were looking up. Isn't that always the way, and if not exactly always then at least often, or possibly sometimes? I know what you're thinking: Good enough! Me, too.

Bernie had coffee. I had a biscuit, not from Rover and Company—where I'd once worked, I guess that's how to put it, in the test kitchen, all too briefly—but pretty good anyway, and then another and another and—well, no, somewhere in there Bernie said no mas. After that he sat gazing out a window, deep in a thought that seemed to darken his face. I curled up at his feet. From her chair not too far away, the woman with the bruise around her eye glanced our way from time to time. Late afternoon sunshine, gentle and reddish, flowed slowly across the floor. My eyelids began to feel heavy, and might even have shut down, but Bernie gave his head a quick shake—don't forget we're a lot alike in some ways—and rose. Then he made the chk chk sound and we were out of there.

"I'll tell him you were here," the man bun man called after us.

We walked over to the Beast and were about to get in when the woman with the bruise around her eye approached. We turned to her.

"You won't remember me," she said. "But I remember you."

"Oh?" said Bernie. Was he trying to keep his gaze on the unbruised side of her face? That was my take.

"You saved my brother's life," she said. "I saw the whole thing from the window upstairs."

"And your brother would be . . ."

"Ike Mooney," said the woman.

"Ah," said Bernie. "But I don't recall saving his life."

Ike Mooney? A gun smuggler? Cattle rustler? I wasn't sure. We've worked a lot of cases. All I really remembered about him was the expression on his face, called a sneer, I believe, one of my least favorite of the possible human looks.

"You don't remember him ambushing you from behind the trash cans?" the woman said. "You were about to eat an apple."

"Well, yes. He might have gotten off a shot or two, now that I think about it."

Gun smuggler. My very first guess. Were we about to go on a roll? I had that feeling.

"Three," the woman said. "But before he could empty the clip you threw that apple and knocked him out cold. Maybe the most amazing thing I've ever seen, hitting him square on the forehead like that, but later I found out you had a gun in your pocket the whole time and didn't use it. So to my way of thinking you saved his life." She held out her hand. "Mavis," she said. "Mavis Mooney. I . . . I've gone back to using my maiden name."

They shook hands. "Bernie Little," Bernie said.

"I know," said Mavis.

"And this is Chet."

"I know that, too."

She smiled. Bernie smiled back.

"What I'm saying is I admired your . . . I don't know what to call it. Self-control, I guess. There's not enough of it around, if you ask me."

Bernie's smile vanished. He almost looked upset, about what I had no idea.

"Oh dear," said Mavis. "Did I say something wrong?"

Bernie shook his head. "No, no, not at all. Um, how's Ike doing? He must have done his time by now."

"Ike's dead," Mavis said.

"I'm sorry to hear that. What happened?"

"He was a slow learner—that's what happened. It runs in the

family. But that's not why I followed you out here. Are you really friends with Billy's parents?"

"Yes."

"ProCon is big on confidentiality—one of the rules Billy's put in place, all good, in my opinion. Billy's turned this place around. But the point is he lives with his girlfriend at number eight Masterson Avenue—that's in the old Studio Village just south of town." Mavis headed back to the door.

"Thanks," Bernie said.

Mavis raised her hand but didn't look back at us.

"They shot some early silents here," Bernie said, pointing with his chin at what looked like the main street of a cowboy town in old movies he'd tried to get Charlie interested in—"Dad!"—with no success. This particular cowboy town was only half-standing, and two bulldozers were busy making sure there'd be nothing at all very soon. "Receivership," he went on, leaving me no wiser. "But back then some real cowboys from the wild west were still around and a few—like Wyatt Earp—acted as advisors. Wonder how that went down. It would be like having Moses on the set of the Ten Commandments."

Sometimes I'm a little lost. Once in a while, I'm lost completely. Right now, we had the once in a while kind—Moses? A perp? A cowboy?—but it didn't last long because soon we were on a quiet street lined with small adobe houses, some surrounded with shady trees and some not.

"Number eight," Bernie said, and we parked on the street in front of a shadeless one at the same time a buzzard with something in its mouth came circling down, spread its wings, and settled on the roof. Not a pleasant sight, which must have accounted for some sudden barking in our area.

"Chet? Something up, big guy?"

Not a thing. I put a stop to any barking that may or may not have been going on. We hopped out of the car, me actually hopping, and hopping big time. A shadeless house but maybe not shadeless forever: little trees were growing here and there in the yard. I was considering laying a mark on at least one of them when two kids came stumbling around from the back of the house. These were skinny kids, kind of tallish, perhaps the kind called teenagers. But I hardly noticed any of that. What caught my attention was what they wore on their faces, strange goggles that weren't at all like little windows, were in fact like little walls surrounding the top part of their heads. They were bobbing and ducking and dodging, throwing a punch or two and shouting, "nice try!" and "whoops!"

Bernie laughed. "VR, Chet," he said, which made no sense, and then he raised his voice and said, "Guys? Hey, guys!"

No response from the kids, who kept on doing whatever it was they were doing. Had I ever seen anything like this? Why, yes! Escaped hostages! I got ready for who knows what to emerge from behind the house, but before that could happen Bernie stepped forward and touched one of the kids on the shoulder.

The kid jumped right off the ground. Then he whipped off the gizmo. "Huh?" he said. "What the hell?" He got a good look at us and backed away. Meanwhile the other kid also took off his gizmo, also backed away. The first kid had a faint, fuzzy sort of mustache and a rat tail. The second kid had pimples but no mustache and no rat tail.

"It's all right," Bernie said. "I'm Bernie and this is Chet. Didn't mean to interrupt. We're looking for Billy Parsons."

"He's not home," said the pimply kid.

"Is he your dad?" Bernie said.

"Sort of," said the pimply kid. "Like stepdad."

"What's your name?"

"Felix," said the kid.

"Nice meeting you, Felix. Is your mom home?"

"Yeah."

"We'd like to talk to her."

Felix turned toward the house. "Mom! Someone's here! Mom!"

I heard footsteps in the house. The buzzard was out of sight from where we were, but I could smell what it was eating, namely a toad. Now it was my turn to feel a bit pukey. Meanwhile the rat tail kid was watching Bernie. Bernie noticed. The rat tail kid lowered the gizmo over his eyes.

Nine

The door to the small adobe house on Masterson Avenue opened and a barefoot woman wearing jeans and a denim jacket appeared in the doorway calling, "Felix? What's—" before noticing us and stepping back. "Whoa."

"No cause for alarm," Bernie said, which was totally true if she wasn't a perp. If she was we had a different and perhaps more exciting story coming real soon. "We're looking for Billy Parsons," Bernie went on. "I'm Bernie Little and this is Chet. We're friends of Billy's parents."

"Ah," said the woman. "The private eye?"

Bernie nodded.

"Billy's mentioned you," the woman said. "In a good way. I'm Gillian, his . . . well, we're a couple. He really appreciates how you look out for his parents."

"I don't do much," Bernie said. "And it's a pleasure. Is he around?"

Gillian shook her head. "Billy's at work."

"We tried that first. He wasn't there."

"Did they say where he'd gone?"

"It was more like he hadn't been in yet."

"No? Well, that can happen. Billy does a lot of outreach."

"What's that?"

"Like if he hears about some client maybe slipping a bit. He doesn't wait for them to call in. Billy believes in being—what's the word?"

"Proactive?"

"That's it. I'm a college graduate, believe it or not. Well disguised. My head wasn't in it. And for years after. Then Billy came along. And I got my head back, or at least some. I don't know why I'm telling you all this." Gillian glanced at me. "Maybe it's your dog. What's his name?"

"Chet."

"Nice," said Gillian. "There's something about him. Billy says Chet looks out for his parents' pup. Igloo, is it?"

Igloo? Yes, Gillian was aces, but at that moment I knew for sure that this case—if it was a case—was headed for the rocks.

"Iggy, actually," Bernie said. "But maybe Igloo would have worked out better."

"I don't understand," said Gillian. I was totally with her on that. So therefore . . . so therefore Gillian wasn't a perp! Because . . . because I was not a perp! Wow! I'd strayed—and I'm no stray, by the way, and if you see me wandering around it means I'm on the job!—into a so-therefore, which is Bernie's department, and not only that but I'd come up with a dazzler! Gillian was no perp because I, Chet the Jet was not a perp. We were off to the races. Was this a good time to leap right over her head and into the house? I went back and forth on that.

"Just a joke," Bernie was saying. "You'd have to know Iggy."

"I'd like to meet him. I did meet Mr. Parsons—he came down here for the day a few months ago. He loves his wife so much. You can just tell. Billy says she's not doing too well."

"She's a fighter," Bernie said.

Mrs. Parsons a fighter? Humans throwing punches, kicking, scratching—and even biting now and then, despite the tininess of their teeth—was a common sight in my life, what with my career and all, involving mostly men for sure, yet with a surprising number of women, although not a single one resembling Mrs. Parsons. Maybe Bernie would have gone into this a little deeper, but before he could the kids came running by, their gizmos in place and both of them chopping at the air like they were in a fight with somebody. Kids! I loved them.

"My son Felix," Gillian said, pointing. "The tall one's his half-brother Axel Junior—we call him Axie. Right now, they're in another universe."

Bernie watched the boys. They ran around the house and disappeared.

"Designed by Axie himself," Gillian said.

"Not following you," said Bernie.

"The VR set-up, the universe they're playing in, all that. Completely beyond me. The craziest part is that Axie's not a good student. He's not even reading at grade level. Billy says not to worry. Reading may be on the way out."

"Oh?" said Bernie.

"For a long time, there was no reading. Were we worse off then than now? That's Billy talking, not me. He's done a lot of thinking. He did some time, as you may know, but it's no secret of course since it's in the ProCon mission statement, and there's lots of time for thinking when you're locked up, and I should know. Most don't take advantage—they mostly cook up crappy schemes—but Billy . . . well, Billy figured out a lot of stuff."

"Like?" said Bernie.

"I hear your doubt," Gillian said. Bernie started to say something, but Gillian raised her hand—a fine little hand with a tattoo of moon and stars on the back—and went on. "Doubt is all right. That's part of what Billy came up with. You screw up and people are going to doubt you. Some are gonna doubt forever, but there's wiggle room with others. The big question is how you get them to wiggle."

"What's the answer?" Bernie said.

"That's the hardest part," said Gillian. "The hardest part for

Billy to figure out and the hardest part to put into your life. It's not in the mission statement—Billy didn't think it sounds business-like enough—but it's the core of everything." Gillian took a deep breath. "Put yourself second."

"Put yourself second?" Bernie said.

Gillian nodded. "Just not first, but being realistic at the same time—like come on, get real." She raised a finger. "But find one thing in this life to put before yourself. Billy has a whole story about how that came to him late one night in his cell."

"I'm listening," Bernie said.

"I wouldn't do it justice," said Gillian. "Get him to tell you."

"I'd like to," Bernie said.

A human sometimes searches the face of another human. For what, I have no clue, but it must be important because they look their very smartest when they're doing it, which was how Gillian looked now. "Is it bad?" she said. "Whatever you want to see Billy about?"

"More like touching base," Bernie said.

"About his parents?"

"That's right."

Gillian's whole body seemed to relax. She checked her watch. "Want me to tell him you're here?"

Bernie nodded.

She took out her phone, tapped the screen, put the phone to her ear. Then she laughed and shook her head. "Straight to voice-mail, only the voicemail is full. He's so bad! But he might be at Viva el Café—that's where he takes prospective clients."

"Where is it?"

"Right downtown, across from the bus station. But first let's see if he's there."

"How are you going to that?"

"Billy's truck got stolen so many times—an occupational

hazard, he calls it—that he ended up sticking one of those tags in a wheel well."

"A digital tracker?" Bernie said.

"I've got the app." Gillian did some more tapping at her phone. "That's funny. He's on Mule Kick Road. I didn't even know anyone lived there. But they must—it shows an address, number 1191."

"He drives a red pickup?" Bernie said.

"You thinking of driving out? It's a good twenty miles."

"Nice day for it."

Gillian nodded. "Yes, a red pickup—like just about half the guys in these parts. But with a vanity tag—2ND."

I missed all of that except for Mule Kick Road. Why couldn't I have missed that too?

When mules come up I think right away of Rummy. But even before I think of Rummy I smell him, smell him in my mind, if you're following me on this, and after a lot of time spent among humans, most of whom I've liked and some I've loved, with Bernie at the top, of course, somehow above love . . . I'm now pretty sure you're not following me. Rummy was a mule I got to know on a case involving a gold nugget, a real big one, the size of a golf ball. But on that same day I'd found the nugget I'd also had to persuade Rummy to come down off a high and narrow ridge. He turned out to be stubborn, even for a mule, and his smell was the purest and most powerful mulish scent I'd ever come across. How I'd rolled and rolled in the dirt to get it off my fur! The only reason I mention all this is to explain my confusion when Bernie pulled off a two-laner in pretty much open country and said, "Eleven ninety-one Mule Kick Road, big guy." And I smelled not a whiff of mule, not the least little . . . well, I don't want go there, but stink. So what was going on? I gazed at Bernie, waiting for him to start us back up.

"No red pickup," he said.

Then time to hit the road, wouldn't you think? I sure did. But instead he got out of the car—got out before me!—and said, "Let's sniff around."

But he didn't sniff, not even once. What he did do was give me an odd look. "Chet? You okay?" Fine, just fine. My tail, even though I was sitting on it, found a way to let him know. He smiled and made a sweeping gesture with his arm. "Thar's gold in them thar hills."

Ah. I got it. This was all about finding another golf-ball sized gold nugget, since we hadn't managed to hold onto that first one from the Rummy adventure, lost for reasons now unknown to me. Did I think, well, how about driving a little closer to the nearest hills, barely visible across a flat, scrubby plain? I did not. I simply hopped out of the car and began sniffing around in a professional manner.

"Attaboy," said Bernie, hustling to keep up.

Gold has a smell, very different from the smell of mules. I smelled not a whiff of either as I zigzagged back and forth, getting a tiny bit closer to the hills with every zig and zag. What I did smell were familiar desert smells, and I saw familiar desert sights, including weathered wooden stakes topped with tiny orange flags lying here and there on the ground, and cement blocks, some broken, some in lopsided little stacks.

"Another condo dream gone bad," said Bernie, somewhere behind me, and in that special voice he uses for musing to himself—and of course to me at the same time. "At least that's one thing we've never tried," he went on. "Although I wonder . . ." *Although I wonder?* Although I wonder what? I began to feel uneasy, but before I could figure out why, I picked up a faint but interesting smell. I followed it over to one of those broken cement blocks.

"That's enough, Chet," Bernie said. "Not here, obviously. Billy probably stopped for a nice, quick sandwich out in the wide open spaces. Let's go."

Sandwich? There was not a trace in the air. No mayo, no mustard, no butter, no ketchup, no BBQ sauce. No ham, no salami, no baloney, no roast beef, no meat of any kind. No lettuce, no tomato, no pickles. No PB, no J. No bread. What we did have was this interesting smell I mentioned, faint, yes, but leathery for sure. I sniffed around the broken cement block, a broken cement block with a red streak along the side—not blood but paint, the smells so different even—the smells different, let's leave it at that. I did some pawing, the ground crusty and dusty, and felt a little something half buried in the dust: a thin, round disc, hard and silvery, the size of a watch, although it wasn't a watch. But a human gadget for sure, although not in the best shape, dented and twisted. It hung on a short leather strap with a loop at the other end. I got that loop in my teeth and trotted over Bernie.

He smiled. "What you got there?" Bernie took the thing—maybe not immediately, on account of leather's special mouth feel, with which you may or may not be familiar—and gave it a look, casual at first and then close. "A digital tracker," he said. He went over to the broken cement block, ran his fingers over the red streak, shifted it then raised his head and looked all around. I saw nothing but the wide open spaces.

"How's this? He's driving around out here, bumps up against the block, loses the tracker?"

Fine with me, whatever it was. Then Bernie gave me a quick scratch between the ears and things were even finer.

Ten

Bernie pocketed the digital tracker. "Mystery doesn't mean conspiracy. Let's keep that in mind."

I'm sorry to admit I didn't even try. For one thing, my mind was on a sound coming from the sky, a sort of psst psst followed by a quick whirring, then back to the psst psst. In short, bird noises, or what humans call bird songs. Of all the ones I've heard, this was probably the least unpleasant, the most unpleasant being that of the crow. This particular song was incoming, but the sky seemed empty. And then a tiny dark blur appeared in the blue, on the way from those distant hills.

"Some people get that confused," Bernie was saying. "They jump from mystery to conspiracy. It leads to a lot of disruption, internal and external." Or something like that. Very bad of me, but I was listening more to this blur of a bird than to Bernie. To make up for that, I went right to him and sat on his foot. His hand came down—moving like it had a mind of its own, the human hand being a sort of substitute tail—and rested lightly on the back of my neck, where it could stay forever as far as I was concerned. "For example," he said. "Would I ever—no matter how old I was, no matter what—mistake someone else's voice for Charlie's? No. So why would Daniel be any different? It's a simple case. All that's left is finding out why Billy needed the money."

Charlie's voice was the subject? What a great idea! But that was Bernie—great ideas just came tumbling out of him! Any moment he might say, "In the mood for a snack?" or "How about a little fetch?" Wonderful subjects, as I'm sure you'll agree, and

Charlie's voice was in that league. Kids' voices—especially those of happy kids—are lovely to begin with, and Charlie's is at the tip top of lovely. All it takes is hearing him say, "Veggies, ick" and you'll know what I mean.

The bird had lost its blurriness, was now pure bird, circling down and down and landing on a thin bare branch of a dusty little bush, the branch not moving in the slightest. A small, chubby bird with a blackish head and a grayish neck. It watched me with its narrow sharp eyes and sang its song, psst psst, whirr whirr. Perhaps this was the moment for a deep rumbly bark, not to scare off the little critter, just simply to restore order. But before I could make up my mind Bernie, who can sometimes surprise me, surprised me again.

"Hey, Chet. Do you hear a bird?"

Have you ever noticed how in this life nothing much is happening and then all of a sudden it gets ramped up to way too much? Before I could even start to get a grip on what Bernie had just said—don't forget the bush this bird of ours was perched in was practically in our face, mine and Bernie's, and the bird was not at all a bird of the quiet type, if in fact that was even a thing—a fat-tire bike came zipping up the road, turned off the pavement and stopped near the Beast. This was one of those in-between bikes with a motor for when the rider didn't feel like pedaling, although this particular rider had been pedaling fast. Now, with a grunt, he got off the bike, took the biggest binoculars I'd ever seen from a saddlebag, and came toward us.

"Howdy, friend," he said. He was a tall old guy, thin and sun-baked, dressed in a T-shirt with holes in it, dusty sandals, cargo shorts with bulging pockets, and a straw sombrero with a bird dropping, quite small, on the brim. I'd seen this whole look before, other than the bird dropping. That was new and I like new things, meaning we were off to as good start.

"Hi," said Bernie.

"Nice day," said the old man. "But every day is nice when you're still above ground. I don't suppose you've heard, or maybe even spotted, a certain—" And then he saw my bird. Well, not really mine, of course, like I probably wouldn't be . . . taking him home, let's put it that way, but I'd come to feel somewhat close to him—in a way that seemed to involve my teeth! How interesting! But no time to get into that because the old guy had gotten very excited, watery eyes open wide, and his whole body trembling slightly. He placed a finger across his lips—that's the quiet sign, in case you don't know—and whispered, "Shh. Not a peep."

"What's up?" Bernie whispered.

"What's up?" the old guy whispered back. "I've been waiting all my life. That's what's up."

"For what?"

"Shh." With a shaking finger the old guy pointed to my—the—bird.

We all gazed at the bird. The bird gazed back, or possibly right through us, or possibly at nothing, at the same time singing away with the psst psst and the whirr whirr.

"Shh. For God's sake, shh."

That made total sense to me, but not to the bird, who ignored the old guy completely and went on pssting and whirring. That was bothersome, and then there was the fact that this was a bird and birds can fly. How annoying was that? Although the old guy was far from annoyed. He chuckled to himself and began going through his pockets. At the same time his legs were twitching like they wanted to dance. Out came a camera with which he snapped bird pictures, and some sort of box with a mic attached, a mic he pointed toward the bird like he was a TV reporter and the bird had just hit a homer, whatever that was, exactly.

"Hee hee, hee hee," went the old guy, and now he really was dancing for sure, a dance called a jig, I believe, usually danced in black-and-white movies Bernie and I sometimes watched, where an ancient prospector out in the desert strikes it rich. Yes, we were out in the desert, and yes, this was an ancient guy, but he was not a prospector and instead of gold we had this bird, so striking it rich was off the table. In short, I barked.

Perhaps not the right move, but it did shush the bird at once. No more psst, no more whirr. The chubby little dude flapped its wings and took off, darting up into the blue, veering in a wide turn, and headed for the hills.

Bernie turned to me. What an interesting expression he had on his face, like he was trying to look mad but wanted to laugh instead! "Um," he said. Bernie has a tough time being mad at me, and I'm the same way with him. Had he ever actually been mad at me? Had I ever actually been mad at him? No and no.

The old guy turned to us. He wasn't mad either. That was a bit of a surprise. "A red-letter day. You've brought me luck, sir. You and this amazing canine specimen of yours. A genetic mix—shepherd, border collie, just a dash of wolf, perhaps?—where the whole is better than the sum of the parts. But I'm out of my lane. Birds are my lane. Do you have any idea of what we just saw, of what I captured in picture and sound?"

"No," Bernie said.

"A buff-collared nightjar, my friend," said the old guy. "An adult male buff-collared nightjar, thriving and in the pink."

Buff? Pink? Wasn't buff about roided-up dudes, and pink about lipstick? I was a little lost.

"Are they rare?" Bernie said.

"Not particularly—in Central America! But north of the border? A very different story. I've been looking for upwards of forty years, have come to this very spot dozens of times. I could die today a happy man!" He dug through his cargo pockets, found a pen and a tattered notebook, flipped through, wrote something real quick, and brought the notebook to Bernie. "If you will please sign and date in this column headed witness."

"What am I witnessing?" Bernie said.

"Why, what you've just seen, of course! The fact that I, Arthur J. Revelstoke, on this day spotted a buff-collared nightjar on the east side of Mule Kick Road, Gila City, just south of the Desert Rose Coffee Shop at mile five."

Bernie wrote in the book, with Arthur J. Revelstoke watching over his shoulder.

"Why this spot?" he said, handing back the notebook.

"Excellent question." Arthur J. Revelstoke gazed at whatever Bernie had written and stuffed the notebook back in his pocket. "The long answer is that I've made a study of wind currents between the south side of Gila City and the border, factoring in seasonality, time of day, and oddball conditions such as the presence or absence of forest fires and the pineapple express we've just come out of, also taking into account those hills, and especially Buzzard's Peak—" He pointed. "—which bend the wind from Mexico and funnel it right to where we're standing. But the short answer is I become a buff-collared nightjar in my mind."

Whatever that last part was made me back away a bit, and I, Chet, am afraid of nothing. But if Arthur J. Revelstoke suddenly took off in the sky, well, I'd be close to afraid of that.

"When was the last time you were here?" Bernie said.

"At dawn this morning. I had a lucky feeling but an eagle was circling overhead so all the other birds were making themselves scarce."

"Did you see a red pickup?"

"Not today."

"But you have seen a red pickup here?"

"Not precisely here. More like out there." Arthur J. Revelstoke gestured toward the desert.

"When?" Bernie said.

"More than once, now that I think of it. Of course it might not be the same one, and I was never close. But always headed south." He made that gesture again.

"What's out there?" Bernie said.

"Open country, with a very rough track that comes and goes and after six or seven miles hooks up with the old highway ninety-seven, loop you back to town."

"When was the last time you saw the pickup?"

"I'd have to think. Last week, maybe?" He gave Bernie a close look. "Are you with the wildlife people?"

"Why would I be?"

"I'm hoping you are. I've called Wildlife repeatedly and you look like a cop of some sort."

"I'm not a cop," Bernie said. "Why are you calling Wildlife?"

"On account of the drones. Drone hobbyists like this spot. It's becoming an infestation. Drones are the enemy. They scare the birds."

"Ah," said Bernie.

"I've come up with a solution—if I can only cut through the red tape. Familiar with A.I.?"

"Heard of it," Bernie said.

"Same. That's what I meant. I couldn't tell you the first thing about it, not technically. But can anyone? What if we've created something that will enslave us all?"

"We'll never know," Bernie said.

"Ha!" said Arthur. Then he gave Bernie one of those second looks you sometimes see brainy types giving Bernie and he said, "Ha," again, only softer. He licked his lips, somewhat dried and cracked, the way human lips get in these parts. "But airplanes are using A.I. to avoid flocks of birds. I saw it on the news."

"So why couldn't the same thing work with drones?" Bernie said.

"Exactly! You, sir, are smarter than you—" He stopped himself, then gazed up at the sky, empty and blue. "The birds were here before us and they'll be here long after."

But they weren't here now, so we were good. That was my takeaway.

"I'm Drea, what can I getcha?" said the woman at Desert Rose Coffee Shop, a youngish woman with long green hair on one side of her head and none on the other. I knew right away I wasn't going to get past that. We sat at a table out back, a rusted-out tractor up close and all around us the enormous late-day sky, getting ready to do colorful things. "We do a totally awesome macchiato, Mexico City style."

"Just coffee," Bernie said. Drea turned to go but then Bernie added, "No, wait, I'll try that other, the Mexico thing."

Drea went off. This was a first. Bernie always drank just coffee, no milk, no sugar. I looked at him. He looked at me.

"Been thinking of mixing it up now and then, big guy," he said. "Not just coffee, but . . . well other things. For Weatherly's sake, if that makes sense." He looked down at his shoes. "Inflexibility— that was one of Leda's complaints. What if she was onto something? Women seem to like . . ."

His voice drifted off but that was more than enough. Leda was onto something about coffee? What could that possibly mean? But all at once I got it! This was simply Bernie's brilliance shining at its brightest, reaching the very top where he can't be understood. Is it any wonder I love him so much?

Drea returned with a large, steaming mug for Bernie and a water bowl for me. "Just in case he's thirsty."

"Thanks," Bernie said. "You never know."

What was this? Whether or not I was thirsty? Not really, but I could be. She set down the bowl. I moseyed over and gave it a sniff. She laughed—so something funny must have been going on—and said, "What's his name?"

"Chet."

"Nice," Drea said. "I had a dog named Choo Choo when I was a kid. I still miss her."

Had Choo Choo run off somewhere? I'm real good at finding runaways and hauling them back. I waited for Bernie to offer our services, but he did not.

"She wasn't like Chet, more of a lapdog," Drea said. "But she thought she was a giant."

Bernie laughed.

"Can I pet him?" she said.

"That's his kind of thing," said Bernie. "Actually one of his kind of things. He has many."

"Yeah?" she said. "Like what?"

And a whole lot of palaver started up, rather puzzling. Petting? Hello? In the nicest way possible I moved slightly closer to her, coming nowhere near an actual bumping situation, certainly not anything you'd call hard bumping.

Drea laughed, barely stumbling at all, and stroked my head. A very nice petter for sure, although not in the class of Tulip and Autumn, two friendly young ladies who worked in the More part of Livia's Friendly Coffee 'n' More place back in the Valley.

"He's so . . . so fearsome looking," she said. "But the expression in his eyes is . . ."

Her voice faded. There was a little silence and then she did some quick blinking, maybe a sign of changes going on inside. You can't help worrying about humans sometimes.

"Anything else I can get you?" she said.

"Maybe some help," said Bernie. "We're looking for a friend who might have stopped in here this morning—Billy Parsons."

She shook her head. "I don't know anyone of that name."

"He drives a red pickup."

"I don't remember any customers with red pickups, although . . ."

"What?" Bernie said.

"I did see one fly by on at the start of my shift. But whoever it was didn't stop in. And there are a lot of red pickups."

Bernie nodded. Drea gave him a close look. "Is something wrong?" she said.

"I wouldn't say that."

"Because if you like we could check the nest cam. The owner put in a whole security system, being so close to the border and all."

Not long after, they were looking at a laptop Drea had brought to the table, and I was looking at them. There's something I've always liked about two humans putting their heads together, hard to explain. Here's another hard to explain little fact. Remember me mentioning how I'd never get past her hairdo, long and green on one side and shaved on the other? I realized that I had passed it some time ago.

"Can you pause it there?" Bernie said.

Their heads bent closer to the screen. On it was a red pickup, quivering very slightly but the picture was clear, so clear I could make out a scrape along a front fender and also the driver, alone in the truck, leaning forward in an intense sort of way, like he needed to get somewhere fast.

"Is that him?" Drea said.

Bernie nodded.

"Do you want me to keep running it?"

"Yeah."

Drea glanced at me, then at Bernie. "Are you a cop?"

Bernie gave her our card. "A private investigator. But also Billy's friend."

"So you're wearing two hats?"

"At least."

Two hats? More than two hats? Bernie was wearing no hats

and never did. At that moment I knew this case—if it was a case—had taken a bad turn.

Drea touched a keyboard screen. The red pickup moved on, but not very far before it pulled over to the side of the road. The driver—yes, Billy for sure—got out, went around to the back, and lowered the tailgate. That was followed by a few moments of nothing, and then a small motorbike came putt-putting into view. It stopped behind the pickup. The rider, a tall thin dude wearing khaki pants, a short-sleeved white shirt, a black tie, and a helmet that kept most of his face from view, dismounted. He and Billy lifted the motorbike onto the truck bed and Billy closed the tailgate. They got into the pickup and drove out of the picture.

"Do you recognize that other guy?" Bernie said.

Drea shook her head. "Want me to call if I see either one?"

"Thanks."

Bernie took out some money. She shook her head again.

We got into the Beast and Bernie turned the key. The Beast started rumbling. The Beast has a few different kinds of rumbles, almost like . . . like the way I have different barks! Whoa! What a strange thought! And I got the feeling that even stranger ones might be lurking behind it, ready to come pouncing into my mind. For example, I've noticed that some humans can be a bit like machines at times. Not Bernie, of course, goes without mentioning. In fact, Bernie had to be the least machiney of any human I've known, just one more reason he's the greatest. But was it possible it could work the other way, with machines sometimes a bit like . . . no! Bad thought!

Bernie glanced at me. "Hey! What's that about?"

What was what about? Did I hear a distant barking? I listened my hardest. If there'd been any distant barking it vanished at once.

Bernie took the dented silvery disc from his pocket and gazed at it. "What's he doing out here? I kinda feel like doing some barking myself."

How wonderful! Just like me you're probably thinking, bark, Bernie, bark. Oh, how I wanted to hear Bernie bark. So much! Bark, Bernie, bark!

But he did not. Instead, he pocketed the disc and we hit the road, doubling back—just another one of our techniques at the Little Detective Agency—to the abandoned construction site where I'd found the disc. This time we didn't stop but bumped along a faint track toward the distant hills, hills that were distant at first and stayed distant and all at once were right on top of us. The desert has many tricks.

"Buzzard's Peak," Bernie said, staring up at what was either a tall hill or a short mountain. In the sky, all those colors that had been on the way had now arrived, somehow very energetic looking, like they were alive. Bernie slowed the car. "Actually two peaks, kind of angular, like wings." He tilted his head. "With the lower one shorter and the upper one bigger it is kind of like a buzzard swooping down in a sharp turn."

What was this? I saw no buzzard, no birds of any kind, nor did I hear the slightest flap flap of wings. I looked at Bernie. He looked at me. "No fan of buzzards, are you, big guy?"

True, but it had nothing to do with . . . with . . . whatever I'd been thinking about. But now, we seemed to be out of the car, strolling around, gazing up at Buzzard's Peak, and seeing no sign of anything human—no paths, no trails, no buildings of any kind—and also the ground, where there were no footprints, no tire tracks except our own, not even a single scrap of—whoa! A scrap? Well, no, more like a paper coffee cup, crushed and dusty. I grabbed it—yes, it still had a coffee smell, very faint—and trotted over to Bernie. He squatted down and read the faded writing on the cup.

"'Livia's Friendly Coffee 'n' More.'"

That was the place in Pottsdale where we got our coffee beans, as I may have mentioned. Livia herself is kind of a buddy of ours. The coffee part of the operation happened in the front, the 'n More part in the back. We did our business in the front, although we always liked running into Tulip and Autumn, two excellent petters, as I may also have mentioned, employed at the back but who occasionally came forward on a break.

Bernie smoothed out the cup, turned it in his hands.

"Whadya think?" he said.

This was the moment for him to say, "Good boy." That was my only thought.

He gave me a little smile. "Good boy."

A sudden breeze arose in the desert, but that was only my tail chiming in. Bernie stuck the coffee cup in his pocket and rose. We got in the car and drove off. In the distance I caught a glimpse of two-lane blacktop, and then for no reason at all turned my head and looked the other way, at the back side of Buzzard's Peak. The swooping buzzard thing Bernie talked about was suddenly clear from this angle and there was also something else not visible from the other side, namely a small whitish dome, mushroom-shaped but much bigger than a mushroom—in fact, a human-type building for sure, standing in the dip between the two wings.

I barked my low rumbly bark.

"I already said good boy," Bernie said.

I amped it up.

"But I'm happy to say it again. You're a good, good boy. The best."

How nice! I laid a paw on his knee. We sped up big time! And soon hit two-lane blacktop, where the Beast was at its best. I forgot about everything except the wind in my fur.

Eleven

First thing the next morning Bernie was on the phone. A man's voice—which I recognized at once, but that's just me—sounded on the other end.

"ProCon Resources." Yes, the man bun man. Somehow, I could smell his gummy weed breath over the phone. Life is full of good things if you pay attention, and even if you do it only partly.

"Bernie Little. We dropped by yesterday."

"With the dog?"

"Right, that's the we part. Is Billy there?"

"Nope."

"Has he called in?"

There was a pause. "You're what? His neighbor?"

"His parents' neighbor."

Another pause. "And where do they live again?"

"You tell me," said Bernie.

"Huh?"

"I thought we already passed your entrance exam."

The man bun man laughed a weak sort of laugh. "It's just the cop vibe. Not you so much. But the dog."

Me a cop? Was that what this was about? One thing was clear. The man bun man didn't know about me flunking out of K-9 school. Hey! Maybe lots of folks didn't know! All at once I felt tip top and I'd been feeling pretty good already.

"Mesquite Road in the Valley," Bernie said.

"All right, all right," said the man bun man. His voice got friendlier. "Billy's actually a little late for a meeting and his phone's broken or turned off or something. I'll make sure he calls you when he gets in."

"Instead you call me," Bernie said. "No need to—" At that moment his phone had a little . . . hiccup? Bernie checked the screen. "Got another call—I'll get back to you." He tapped the screen.

"Lou?" he said.

"Hey," said Lou Stine, his voice, never warm, now even less so than usual, but that was him, our hard-faced old buddy and Valley PD captain whose kid was named—or middle-named, I'd never been clear—after Bernie. "This call isn't happening."

Bernie sat up straighter. "Out with it."

"In a way I don't blame you," Lou said. "Not that I'd have done the same thing myself. But I'd have found some other way, the kind that wouldn't blow up in my face."

"What are you talking about?" Bernie said.

"That's a real question? You can't think of some action in your recent past that could have gone wrong?"

Bernie said nothing. But his heart did some talking of its own, and I'm a pretty good listener to the human heart, especially his, which now lost its steady boom boom boom and sped up.

"Bernie? Still with me?"

"I'm listening."

"This asshole—insignificant loser, scum, whatever you want to call him—turned up at the Valley General ER. Naturally they started asking questions about his injuries and what not."

"You're talking about Werner Irons?" Bernie said.

"Bingo!" said Lou. "Bottom line—Internal Affairs is opening an investigation and Weatherly is being suspended until further notice as we speak."

Next thing I knew we were swerving out of the driveway onto Mesquite Road, the phone falling out of the cup holder and onto the floor, and Lou still talking, his voice now tiny and squeaky, even a bit funny in a way, like the cartoons Charlie and I some-times watched on TV when we were doing his homework. Was the tiny, squeaky voice saying, "you forgot that even assholes have rights?" Something like that. Meanwhile there was nothing funny about the look on Bernie's face.

We crossed the Rio Calor bridge, passed the car wash with the big sign featuring lots of foam and a happy lady in a bathing suit, turned down a cross street that got quieter and quieter and ended at a canyon. But just before the end stood a small lemon-colored house with a lemon tree in the yard and a nice shady porch. We stopped in front of it. Trixie's scent—so annoyingly like mine except for the she-ness part and not being quite so pizzazzy, if you don't mind me mentioning that—was in the air, this being the house where she and Weatherly lived. A woman, dark-haired like Weatherly but older and smaller, was sitting on the porch, reading a book, but rose as we got out of the car. This was Tallula, Weatherly's mom, one of those humans who smiled a lot, although she wasn't smiling now.

She met us on the lawn. Tallula lived up in tribal territory, where I had many friends, and we hadn't seen her in some time. Her long ponytail was grayer now, pure white at the end. Ponytails are a great look, in my opinion. Do I have to explain why?

"Hey, Tallula," Bernie said.

She took both his hands in hers. Tallula was so much smaller than Bernie but somehow didn't seem it.

"What?" he said.

"Just that I'd have done the same," she said. "As a man, I mean, in your place."

Bernie gazed down at her, didn't speak.

"But I'm from a different generation and maybe you are too, even though you're so much young—" she began, and then

Weatherly was on the porch, dressed in jeans and a tee and holding a big paint brush.

"Mom? Could you come back inside please?"

Tallula let go of Bernie's hands, first giving them a slight squeeze, and headed for the house. Weatherly was already coming the other way. Tallula's eyes were on Weatherly, but Weatherly didn't see her. Her own eyes were on Bernie.

They gazed at each other. Bernie is not the nervous type, but he was nervous now. The scent of Bernie nervousness was so strange to me I almost didn't know what it was or where it was coming from. Meanwhile, scent-wise, Weatherly wasn't at all nervous. She was angry, very angry, instead. But when she spoke there wasn't a trace of it in her voice. Right there is one big difference between humans and the nation within. When we're angry, you know.

"I'm painting," she said, making a little gesture with the brush.

"Ah," said Bernie. "Sorry to . . . to interrupt."

"Actually repainting," she went on, almost as though she hadn't heard him. "I'm repainting the whole house."

Bernie thought about that, thought for too long, in my opinion. I got anxious to hear his voice. "It, um," he said at last, "doesn't need it."

When people are very angry and then get even angrier, they tend to amp up the loudness. I've heard some amazingly angry loudness in my career—comes with the territory—but nothing like that happened now. Instead, Weatherly got quieter, so much quieter. "It's my house," she said. "I'm repainting everything."

"Oh, sure, you're right, of course, no argument there," Bernie said. "I only wanted to save you from—"

Weatherly raised the paint brush, kind of like a stop sign.

Bernie's gaze went to it, and then to her face. "I get it," he said.

"Do you?"

"And I'm sorry. I'd never do anything that would even suggest that, well, that you couldn't fight your own, um, or just take care of yourself."

"But you did."

"I can see how you might—"

"IA is investigating, as you probably know from the old boy network."

"Aw, come on. You know I'm not part of any—"

"I'm not finished."

Bernie went silent.

"Until the investigation is over," Weatherly said, "we're not communicating, you and I."

"I really don't see why—" Bernie began.

"That's your problem."

"My problem?"

Hey! Was Bernie starting to get mad at Weatherly? How could something like that happen? All at once I was very thirsty. From inside the house came an odd sound from Trixie, close to whimpering, and Trixie's no whimperer. Was she thirsty, too?

"This isn't a negotiation," Weatherly said.

"But—" Bernie began, his voice rising. Yes, angry for sure. But he corralled it, yanked it back down. "The whole thing's crazy, Weatherly. It was me, not you. IA can be stupid but they won't miss that."

Weatherly gave him a long look, real complicated. So were the scents coming off both of them, strange, mixed-up combos. "And after," she said, "we'll see."

"We'll see?" said Bernie.

Weatherly said nothing. She just turned and walked back to the house, up the stairs, across the porch, and inside. I heard the click of her ring against the door as she pulled it closed. The ring was what I believe is called an engagement ring, but Weatherly called it the Desert Star on account of its yellowish glow. We'd bought the ring, me and Bernie, from Mr. Singh at his American Dream Pawnshop, and Weatherly loved it—her folks were desert folks going way back. But was it possible I'd gotten things wrong and she didn't love the Desert Star? I heard her mom start to say something, but Weatherly cut her off.

Twelve

We went for a long walk in the canyon behind our place on Mesquite Road, a strip of open country that runs all the way from the Rio Calor bridge to the airport. Bernie usually does some singing on our walks. He has a beautiful voice, which you've probably guessed already, and knows lots of fun songs, like "Death Don't Have No Mercy" and "God Walks These Dark Hills," but today he didn't seem to be in a singing mood. Instead, we just walked and walked. I did some—let's not call it harassing, more like just funnin'—with a javelina we came upon. Oh, how the playful dude wanted to sink those weird spiky teeth into ol' Chet, but that would take the kind of speed javelinas just don't have, and neither does anybody else if we're being honest. The point is we just walked in silence, me and Bernie, all the way to the last lookout, the one with the airport view.

Bernie leaned against a big red rock. He was sweating and had a water bottle, but he didn't drink. Instead, he filled my portable water bowl and then watched the planes coming and going. I slurped the bowl dry, licked my muzzle, getting it nice and wet, a feeling my muzzle likes quite a bit, and then sat and watched Bernie watch.

At last he made a little chin gesture toward all those planes and said, "Which one goes to Shangri-la?"

Shangri-la? A new one on me, but it had that south of the border sound and we've had adventures down there, often with a bit of gunplay toward the end. Bernie can shoot spinning dimes out of the air! The cartel dudes got a big kick out of that on our last visit. Until they didn't. Was this a good moment for shooting spinning dimes, sometimes even making them flat out disappear in the blue? That was my take, but we weren't carrying. When we weren't carrying, we weren't working, and when we weren't working, we weren't raking in the greenbacks, or even grabbing just a few. I almost came close to having a gloomy thought but it veered off like one of those clouds that wasn't coming your way after all.

Bernie took a deep breath and then reached for his phone.

"Hi, Lou," he said.

"Bernie. I didn't expect to hear your voice so soon."

Bernie laughed, a very strange laugh that had no fun in it at all.

"One thing about you," Lou said. "You never ask for favors. That's rare. Keep it up."

Then came a long silence, not the comfortable kind. "There are no absolutes," Bernie said at last.

Absolutes? At first, I was lost but then I remembered a case involving a big friendly gentleman named Olek who brought a bottle of clear booze from his far-off land and when we turned him down on whatever he wanted got somewhat less friendly, but what I'm getting at is the bottle—Absolut! And then everything was clear: Bernie had drunk so much of it that he'd forgotten. Otherwise, he'd have known there were absolutes, what with he and Olek polishing off a whole bottle. All at once I was on top of my game.

"Meaning you're asking for a favor," Lou said.

A favor? My guess would have been that Bernie was asking Lou out for drinks, perhaps at the Dry Gulch Steak House and Saloon, where we were buddies with the cooks, the waiters and the waitresses, and a bowl of steak tips appeared under the table at practically every visit. What was a favor? It came up from time to time, perhaps . . . perhaps something like a treat? Yes! That was it! Bernie wanted a treat. That was a first, but a good one. If

Bernie wanted treats then bring them on! Did anyone deserve treats more than Bernie? You know the answer to that.

Bernie looked my way. His eyes were as dark as I've ever seen them, but they lightened up just a little.

"Specifically," Lou went on, "you want me to put my thumb on the scale."

"I do not," Bernie said, which Lou should have known. Scales were all about fish. Perhaps, for example, a rather large fish somehow gets loose from a rich dude's enormous aquarium and starts thrashing around on the marble floor. You're sure to see some scales flying around, catching the light in a lovely way. But why, if in fact you had a thumb, would you want to put it on them? I was lost.

"All I want," Bernie said, "is the name of whoever's running the investigation."

Lou was silent for what seemed like a long time. Not totally silent, of course. I could hear him breathing, and also flipping through some pages.

"If I knew," Lou said, "and if I coughed it up, what would you do?"

"Depends," Bernie said.

"On what?"

"On whether whoever it is is straight up."

"Straight up as defined by who?" Lou said.

"You," Bernie said.

"Okeydoke," said Lou. "Straight up is her rep. Don't go near her."

"Huh?"

"I'm talking about the new DA."

"What's she got to do with Internal Affairs?"

"Orders from the governor. You haven't heard of his new broom initiative?"

"What's that?"

"His response to his lousy polls. Never mind that. Just stay clear of her."

Click.

Bernie gazed at his phone for a while. Didn't he realize Lou was gone? Wasn't that what the click meant? Lou was back to where he was and so were we, back at the lookout over the runways, me and Bernie. Should I be worried about him? I was wondering about that when he tucked the phone away and turned to me.

"I know Lou's voice, wouldn't mistake it for anyone else's," he said. "Is it particularly distinctive?" He gave me a close look. "Just once I'd like to hear the way you hear, big guy."

A stunner. Bernie had never said anything like that to me. But that wasn't the most stunning part, which was: just once. Why? Why would he only want to hear the way I hear just once? Why not always, what with how humans seem to miss a whole lot of the sound that's out there, almost all of it at times? Yes, I should be worried about him, for sure. I pressed against his leg, just letting him know, well, everything.

Bernie has excellent balance, barely stumbling, nowhere close to an actual fall. He laughed and said, "Hungry, huh? Let's go home."

We were in the kitchen—me curled up by the fridge and Bernie at the table, cleaning the .38 Special—when Mr. Parsons knocked on the front door. Different people have different knocks. I only have to hear you knock once and I know it's you forever. Mr. Parsons' knock is bony, with a pause just before the end and then one more. We went to the door side by side, me first.

"May I come in?" said Mr. Parsons. "I'm on a mission."

"Of course," said Bernie.

We led him into the kitchen, Bernie first, then Mr. Parsons, then me, which is how we lead people, even the good ones.

"Something to drink?" Bernie said.

"Well, that would be nice. I haven't had a drink in some time. We used to end every day with a little something, Edna and I. But only if you're having one, too."

Bernie got busy with glasses, ice cubes, bourbon. Mr. Parsons sat at the table and gazed at the .38 Special, in pieces, plus the cleaning tools, of which I only knew the name of one—the toothbrush.

"I've never owned a gun," Mr. Parsons said. "We had a houseful when I was a boy."

Bernie handed him a glass. "Cheers."

They clinked. Mr. Parsons took a sip. "Ah." Then he went back to looking at the gun. "I suppose it's basically an explosive device. Explosions happen in nature—volcanoes, for example. Do you think that provided the inspiration for the cavemen?"

Bernie laughed.

Mr. Parsons smacked his forehead. "But guns came way after the cavemen! Good God, Bernie. I was never the brightest but now I'm an idiot."

"Farthest thing from it," Bernie reached over and clinked Mr. Parsons' glass again.

Mr. Parsons reached out and touched the open barrel of the .38 Special, for a moment sticking his fingertip into the little slot where the bullet goes. That last part bothered me, although I couldn't think why. "So far gone that I confused the voice of some criminal with the voice of my own son. It's a fact I have to accept. I've been a fool."

Bernie opened his mouth to say something, closed it, and opened it again. But all he said was "Um," and he didn't look Mr. Parsons in the eye while he said it, which wasn't Bernie at all. Something was up. I waited to find out what it was.

Mr. Parsons took another sip, actually much more than a sip. "I saw Edna today. She was in good spirits, despite these new test re . . . but good spirits, that's the point. Naturally I didn't tell her about the whole scam business. Not urgent now in any case, thanks to Miss—Ms. Mendez and her special program. But speaking of that, Bernie, I'd like to make good use of that money." He rubbed his hands together, a human thing you sometimes see, maybe when they're about to start up on something new. "Namely," Mr. Parsons went on, "I want to hire your services."

"Oh?" said Bernie. "For what?"

"Why, to track down these horrible scammers." A fiery look, not particularly strong, more like embers in a fire from the night before, but still something I'd never seen from him, rose in his eyes. "Wring a confession out of them," he went on. "What if there's someone out there still thinking it could have been Billy himself? Can't have that, can we?"

What was this? Bernie doing that mouth opening and closing thing again, and so soon? This time he didn't even say "um," simply nodded his head. I'd seen many nods from Bernie, meaning all sorts of things, although never this one. Good or bad? Happy or sad? I wanted to think good and happy but couldn't quite get there.

"So what's your usual arrangement?" Mr. Parsons said. "Is there a . . . oh, what's the word? It's on the tip of my tongue."

The tip of Mr. Parsons' tongue happened to be visible at that moment. It was dry and yellowish but there was nothing on it. He was mistaken but that was fine with me. Mr. Parsons was a very good man.

"Retainer?" Bernie said.

"Retainer! Exactly!" He laughed. "I'd like to think it would have come to me anyway but that's the road to delusion. So how much is the retainer? Or do I sign a contract first? Or what? Just say. I'd like to get going on this."

"It's the mission you mentioned?" Bernie said.

"Mission?"

"You said something about being on a mission."

Mr. Parsons looked—well, maybe not confused, more like just blank.

"First thing when you came in."

Mr. Parsons snapped his old, twisted fingers, somehow making a surprisingly young-sounding snap, if that makes any sense. "Got it! The mission! Whew! Just so you know, it's not about hiring you or any of that."

"I'm all ears," Bernie said.

Oh, dear. How often have I heard that one from many, many humans, with different-size ears, but even the biggest human ears are not really what you'd want, certainly not compared to what we've got going in the nation within, and let's not even mention elephants. I know something about elephants, having worked a case involving a missing one name of Peanut, and her hearing came amazingly close to matching mine, if you can believe it. In fact, she was amazing in every way. She could knock down houses, for example, and when she peed, pools big enough to swim in appeared. I know that because, well, perhaps a story for another day. The point is humans are never all ears or even close. I won't say they're pretty much deaf as a post. That would not be nice.

Meanwhile, Mr. Parsons was giving Bernie one of those quick second looks. "Maybe I shouldn't have let on about the mission, left that part out completely, if you see what I mean."

"I don't," Bernie said.

"Meaning I should have executed the mission without actually identifying it as such. This calls for some finesse. Those were her very words."

"You're talking about Mrs. Parsons?"

Mr. Parsons nodded.

"She sent you on a mission?"

"Undercover," said Mr. Parsons. "And involving finesse. You're not supposed to be aware of it as it's happening." He took a quick gulp of his drink. "But now the cat seems to be out of the bag."

This conversation—about who knows what and uneasy from the get-go—was now completely off the rails. Once I'd seen a train leaving the rails, on a complicated case involving stolen peanut butter, but I'm pretty sure if I go there now there'll be no coming back. At times like these you stick to the facts or else and the facts were that there was no bag to be seen and no cat anywhere in smelling distance. And although the idea of a bagged cat might have its appeal, the sudden appearance of a cat escaping a bag would be . . . I don't want to say scary, since the Chetster doesn't scare easily, but . . . but it was a sight I hoped never to see, let's leave it at that. An angry cat, a furious cat, a cat looking for revenge—these are not what you're looking for in life. If you must see a cat, the sleeping kind is best.

"So," Mr. Parsons was saying, "if you don't mind, please pretend I used finesse to find this out."

"To find what out?" said Bernie.

"The gift," Mr. Parsons said.

"What gift?"

"The wedding gift. Edna and I are so happy about you and Weatherly and for a gift she—we—would like to give you something you actually want."

A sort of jagged groove appeared on Bernie's forehead, like something had gone wrong inside. Uh-oh. I started to move toward him. At the same time his phone buzzed. He took it from his pocket, checked the screen, then held it to his ear and said, "Hey, Trummy."

He listened. And so did I, what with how easily I can hear the other end of phone conversation.

"Hi, Bernie. Just checking in. Where are we?"

"In what respect?" Bernie said. He glanced at Mr. Parsons, who'd noticed that one of his shoelaces had come undone and was leaning down to tie it back up. But he couldn't get that far, not even close.

"Huh?" said Trummy. "In the respect of Billy Parsons, bringing him in, getting him to come clean. What else, for God's sake?"

"I'll get back to you on that."

"Bernie? What's up?"

"Nothing," said Bernie. "Bye." He tapped the phone, put it
away. Then he bent down and tied Mr. Parsons' shoelace, real
quick. Mr. Parsons didn't seem to notice.

He licked his lips. "Trummy's from the fraud squad?"

"Yes," Bernie said.

"Hate to pry but did he have any news?"

"You're not prying, And no."

Mr. Parsons picked up his glass—his hand quite steady—and
took a sip. "But it's early days still, isn't it, Bernie?"

"Early days for sure," said Bernie.

Mr. Parsons set the glass down carefully, like it might have
been planning moves of its own. Then he blinked a couple of
times and said, "Where were we?"

"What do you mean?" Bernie said.

"You and I. Before the phone."

"I don't remember."

"I hear you," Mr. Parsons said. "About not remembering. I've
become world class at not remembering. At the same time my
memory is working overtime, but just on its own, if you follow."

"It's flooding you with things from your past?" Bernie said.

"Flooding—that's it in a word. Edna says you would have
made a fine therapist."

"She's pulling your leg."

That had to be one of Bernie's jokes. He can be quite the
jokester, as I'm guessing you know by now. I didn't even bother
checking under the table. Mrs. Parsons wasn't pulling Mr. Parsons' leg. She wasn't even here!

Mr. Parsons didn't laugh. Maybe he didn't appreciate Bernie's
jokester side. No one's perfect, except for Bernie, of course, goes

without mentioning. He just shook his head and said, "These memories aren't even about me. I keep seeing the ending of Don Larsen's perfect game, where he jumped into Yogi Berra's arms." He reached for his glass and took a sip, a dry one, the glass being empty, although he smacked his lips like it tasted good. "In black and white and very small and fuzzy, which is how I saw it."

That all blew by me, except for the Yogi Berra part. Yogi Berra came up from time to time—quite possibly a perp of some kind so I hoped for his sake that he looked good in orange. But he'd said something that Bernie often repeated, usually when we were tracking bad dudes on desert roads, and that something was "when you come to a fork in the road take it." So it turned out I was in the picture after all! I felt pretty good about myself.

Mr. Parsons checked his watch. "Good grief! Iggy must be ravenous." He put his hands on the table and rose. Or tried to, but his legs just didn't have it in them at the moment. We helped him up—Bernie lifting on one side, me nudging in the other—and walked him home. Did things go smoothly after that? Perhaps not. For one thing, Iggy got loose. The worst part was that I knew he was going to make a run for it the instant the Parsonses' front door opened the tiniest crack. I was ready for that! I was in my crouch! But somehow—because of the enormous toilet paper tangle trailing behind him? Or was it the popcorn, popcorn all over the place? Or, well, it doesn't matter. The point was Iggy got loose in a sort of explosion of toilet paper and popcorn, his amazing tongue flapping wildly, his eyes filled with—what would you call it? Crazy glee? Close enough.

Is Iggy fast? When he takes off his little stubby legs are a blur but don't let that fool you. I can run circles around him. But that was the problem. Somehow, he kept dodging me inside those circles. I was beside myself, beside myself all the way down Mesquite Road to the little playground. There's a hydrant outside the playground. That's where Iggy made his first and only mistake.

Thirteen

Back home I lay down beside my water bowl, not because I was tired. Don't think that for one second, a second being not very long at all, unless I've gone wrong somewhere. I lay down for no reason. Bernie did some pushups. This happens sometimes, although never when anyone else is around, so the only one who knows is me. Normally when Bernie does pushups, I help out by hopping up on his back. Not now. And I know what you're thinking. Stop. It wasn't because I was tired. What kind of world would it be if the likes of Iggy could tire out the likes of me?

The phone buzzed from inside Bernie's pants pocket. Would what came next surprise you? Namely Bernie taking the phone from his pocket with one hand while still doing pushups with the other? He really is like a kid sometimes, a very strong kid.

"Bernie Little?" said a man on the other end, a voice I recognized at once the way I always do, one of the nice little things about me. In short, it was the man bun man from down in Gila City.

"Yes?" said Bernie, on his feet in one quick, smooth motion.

"Garth over at ProCon Resources. Just letting you know that Billy won't be in today."

"What about tomorrow?"

"That's all the info I've got. Enjoy the rest of your day." Click.

Bernie turned to me. "Do I have to? How about just having the rest of the day run smoothly, with no highs or lows?"

The meaning of that was unclear. Was Bernie suddenly tired and in need of a nap, possibly from the pushups? That was as far as I could take it on my own. But he made no move toward the bedroom. Instead, he tapped at the phone. It made that low, deep beep beep that comes before someone on the other end picks up. "Hi, Billy Parsons here. I can't take your call right now. Please leave a message and I'll get back to you as soon as I can, promise." Bernie lowered the phone and turned to me. "Didn't Gillian tell us his voicemail was full yesterday? I wonder . . ." He left the wondering part unsaid and put the phone to his ear. "Hey, Billy. Bernie Little here. We need to talk."

Bernie tucked the phone away, gave me a second look. "Something on your mind?"

Who, me? Why, nothing, nothing at all. Although it might have been nice to hear whatever Billy had said one more time. That little feathery thing his voice had going didn't seem to be there anymore, and in its place was an odd watery sound, very very faint, like distant liquidy ripples. In short, Billy didn't sound like himself. This was confusing. I put my mind to work. It worked hard, although nor for long. At times like this, humans sometimes say "rats!" I get that, get it big time.

"Frustrated, maybe?" Bernie said. "I know I am."

Frustrated was what, again? Before I could even get started on figuring that out, Bernie was on the phone again.

"Gillian?" he said.

"Speaking."

"It's me, Bernie Little. We dropped in on you today."

"Of course. You and Chet."

"Is Billy there? I called but he didn't pick up."

There was a pause. In the background a kid whose voice I knew, namely Felix, the one with the pimples, said, "I hate spinach."

"That's not spinach—it's simply lettuce," Gillian said. "Uh, sorry, Bernie. And no, Billy's not reachable. One of the ProCon clients is in some trouble out of state and Billy's gone to help him. He's going to be radio silent for a few days."

"You spoke to him?"

"He called a few hours ago, said not to worry. This kind of thing has happened before, Bernie."

"Where is he?"

"I didn't ask," Gillian said. "And he wouldn't have told me anyway. It's kind of like the doctor patient relationship."

"Because the patient's on the run?"

"That's not a very nice way of putting it."

"But has that part happened before? Aiding and abetting?"

"Aiding and abetting? Where are you getting that?"

"From the legal code," Bernie said.

"What the hell? You sound like a cop."

"I'm not a cop. I'm a private investigator but—"

"Working for the cops?" Gillian said.

There was a tiny pause. You would have missed it. No offense. "I'm a friend of the family," Bernie said.

Silence. "Okay," Gillian said. "His parents like you. That matters. But Billy knows what he's doing. You don't seem to realize that."

"We just want to help."

"He doesn't need help."

"Everyone does at one time or another."

Gillian said nothing.

"You mentioned out of state," Bernie said, his voice softening a bit. "Any idea where?"

"No."

Sometimes I feel a quick burst of power coming from Bernie. He doesn't need to be moving when it happens. He can even be asleep. But the point is I felt one now. And then, his voice still soft, on the friendly side, he said, "What does your tracking app say?"

Another silence. That happens in interviews. Was this an interview? Were we on a case? If so, who was paying? Mr. Parsons? I was suddenly in the mood for a little pacing, so I walked over to the fridge and came back.

"It's not working," Gillian said at last.

"How come?"

"I have no idea. I'm not an IT specialist."

Bernie took the bent disc out of his pocket, the bent disc, you might remember, dug up by me, Chet the Jet. There's a surprising amount of digging in this job, just one of the many fun things about it. He seemed a bit lost in thought, but before he found his way out I heard Felix's voice in the background.

"Lettuce sucks, too."

"Shh," said Gillian.

"Axie doesn't have to eat lettuce. He eats whatever he wants."

"No, he doesn't and even—"

"He has his own account at KFC."

"I don't care and—Bernie? Is there anything else right now? As soon as I hear from Billy I'll tell him to call you."

Bernie spun the broken disc in the air, like it was a spinning dime. "Okay," he said, tapping the screen. The disc came down and landed right smack in his other hand even though he wasn't even looking at it—kind of like the thing wanted to be caught.

Bernie awoke in the night. I was lying just inside the front door, where I can monitor all the smells and sounds of the night while I sleep. We sleep in very different ways, you and I, let's leave it at that. Bernie can be a very deep sleeper but some nights he's restless, tossing and turning, and even murmuring at times. Once I'd heard him murmur, "I'm afraid." I almost didn't believe I'd heard that, but my ears don't make mistakes. That night I'd hurried into his bedroom and stood beside the bed for a long time, just watching, but there was no more murmuring, and he lay quiet until morning, chest rising and falling, slow and easy.

Now I heard him on the move, his bare feet making soft plap plap sounds along the hall and into the kitchen. A light went on. Then came the scrape of a chair on the floor, a quiet grunt as he sat down, the rustling of paper. I lay on my side, still in darkness although I could see the little pool of light that had spread from the kitchen into the hall. I heard the point of a pen moving across paper. It sounded like very distant scratching. I rose and went into the kitchen.

Bernie was hunched over a pad of yellow paper. He knew I was there, but he didn't look at me. And I knew that he knew, so we were good. He wrote for a while, then sat up straight and said, "Damn it!" He ripped the top sheet off the pad, balled it up and got ready to fling it toward the trash, and into it, of course, Bernie's aim never off. But at that moment he glanced at me and paused.

"I decided on a letter," he said. "An old-fashioned handwritten letter, a real object. I was even going to mail it, with a stamp and everything, but it's not so easy. I don't mean the stamp. I mean . . ." His voice trailed off. What was going on? What was he talking about? Why was he up? I knew one thing for sure: my job was to herd him back to bed.

Meanwhile he was unballing the sheet of paper and smoothing it out on the table.

"Dear Weatherly—" He shook his head. "See, right there, wrong from the jump. Dear? Why dear? I've never called her dear, never called anyone dear in my life. How come letters start with dear? If we were talking we'd just start 'Hey, baby, what I did was wrong period end of story, I admit it, so can we just get back to where we . . .'"

Bernie turned to the yellow pad and began writing at the

top of the page. He did some muttering at the same time, like "wrong, period" and "yeah, I forgot to consider how you might" and "but it was way worse than if that jerk had done it to me" and "he's lucky I didn't . . ." The pen, which seemed so tiny in Bernie's hand, not at all up to the task, went still. Bernie sat up straight and gazed at the yellow pad, his eyes—beautiful, yes, but tired and even a bit . . . well, not crazy, that was impossible—moved back and forth, back and forth. Then he tore the top page off the pad, balled it up, and tossed it across the kitchen and into the trash barrel. But it missed! It didn't even come close!

I herded him back to bed.

At breakfast—bacon and eggs, coffee, half a grapefruit for Bernie, kibble for me, plus the tiniest scrap or two or more than two of bacon but absolutely no grapefruit, a once and once only adventure in my life—Bernie said, "The letter didn't come to anything. But you know what I realized?"

That fetch was a great game. That was my first and only thought.

"I'm going to light up a cigarette on my next try."

I never would have guessed that. For one thing, Bernie had quit smoking. He's an expert. How many times have I seen him toss away a practically full pack and say, "never again"?

He patted his pockets, perhaps seeking a smoke at that moment, but that wasn't going to work. There wasn't a single cigarette in the whole house—you can trust me on this kind of thing. There was one under the driver's seat in the Beast, but it had been there for a long time and the scent was starting to fade.

"The point is," he went on, sipping his coffee, "that saying what's on your mind is easy but putting it in writing is hard. And hand writing is the hardest. But maybe the best. What if the hardest way is always best?" He put down his mug. "That's why we're not making phone calls down to Gila City today. We're going in person. Flesh and blood." He rose.

Flesh and blood? A new one on me, but wouldn't this be a good time to put the .38 Special—still in pieces on the table— back together and take it with us? I went to the table and put my nose over the top, which in my case meant lowering my head a bit.

"Come on, big guy, bacon's all gone. Let's roll."

But it wasn't about bacon. It was about . . . Whoa! All gone? How had that happened? And what was this? Bernie was giving me one of those second looks? We ended up taking the .38 Special.

Fourteen

We walked up to the small adobe house on Masterson Avenue and Bernie knocked on the door. No sound came from inside, but I did hear wind chimes somewhere down the block. I liked that soft wind chime sound. Would wind chimes at our place on Mesquite Road be a nice touch? I thought so. What if I made a quick detour to perhaps grab those wind chimes from down the block and lay them at Bernie's feet? Would he get the idea of hanging them up back home? I was wondering about that when he turned to me and said, "I played it totally wrong."

What was that? Bernie wrong? It made no sense. Was he tired? How about we head back home and hit the sack? I myself wasn't the least bit tired but I'd be fine just watching him sleep.

He took a deep breath. "So clumsy. I was way too hard with Billy, threw a scare into him for no good reason. Well, for a good reason as it turns out, but too soon." He raised his hand to knock again and then paused, his clenched fist in the air. Very quietly he added: "And even clumsier with Weatherly." Then he did something I'd never seen him do, namely pound that fist into his open hand, real hard, like he was giving some bad dude what he had coming. I heard a high-pitched whimper. Bernie looked my way in surprise like . . . like maybe he thought I was the whimperer? Me? Impossible. I was just thinking that this day had taken a bad turn when the door opened.

I'd already known it wasn't Gillian, in case you were wondering. Smells have a way of leaking out of most doors—even the doors of safes, for example, a little fact that has served us well from time to time. So, not Gillian, not a woman at all, but a man—a meat-eating, cigar smoking, full-grown man with funky under-scents and shampooey over-scents. I had all that from the get-go, or actually before the get-go, if the get-go starts with the opening of the door. Is this a bit puzzling? Yes, for sure, at least to me. As for how he looked: a big broad-shouldered, deep-chested guy, kind of like Bernie, actually, but possibly bigger. Not by a lot! The teeniest bit! Forget I mentioned it. Also he was older, with a thick head of dark hair but also a silvery beard, trimmed short, and one of those deep tans you see around here sometimes, on the faces of golfers, for example, golfers being a huge subject which we have no time for now. And the ball itself, so interesting inside! And the feel of the putting green under your paws, so . . . so rippable! Was this man the golfing type? I hoped so.

Sometimes, by the way, a beard, even close-trimmed and silvery, can take over the rest of the face, but not with this dude. Strong nose, strong chin, broad forehead—all kind of Bernie-like, but without the beauty. There's no one like Bernie, and he's mine! Imagine waking up every morning and remembering that, first thing! That's my life.

He glanced at Bernie, then at me, and back to Bernie. Bernie's eyebrows are the best there are. You can't miss them. Plus they have a language all their own. This dude had hardly any eyebrows, just the narrowest little shadows! And yet, they too had a language all their own—something of a surprise—but I couldn't understand it.

"Hello?" he said, his voice deep and kind of friendly.

"Hello," said Bernie. Wow! The hello right back-atcha technique, one of our very best at the Little Detective Agency. I knew one thing for sure: if this was a case we were real close to clearing it, would be strolling away with a big fat check at any moment. Was this the guy who'd be writing it? I couldn't wait to find out, and when I'm in that sort mood I tend to ease my way closer to someone or other. I eased my way closer to him.

He saw me. When humans see me easing in on them their eyebrows—even the ones without a language all their own—rise up pretty damn quick. This dude's narrow shadows stayed put. He smiled. He had nice white teeth, big for a human.

"What can I do for you?" he said.

"We're looking for Gillian," Bernie told him.

"She's at work," the dude said. "Any message? I'm the baby-sitter."

"What about Billy?"

"Also at work. To the best of my knowledge."

"When will they be back?"

The babysitter smiled. Why? Because he was already enjoying Bernie's company? That was my take. "Which one?" he said.

"Either," said Bernie.

"Not sure. I can tell her—or him—you came by." His smile got a little bigger. "But I'd have to know who you are."

"Bernie Little, and this is Chet."

"I take it they know you?"

The babysitter still seemed to be having fun, but Bernie says things work better when we ask the questions, so maybe we had the beginnings of a problem. Questions have their own sound, of course, so I was pretty sure that this dude was asking most of them. So therefore . . . well, I didn't know, on account of the so-therefores being Bernie's department.

Before Bernie could say anything, someone else spoke, from back in the house.

"You're a jerk!"

And then a second voice. "Call me that again. I dare you."

A long pause, and then, quietly, "You're a jerk."

Had to be the two kids, first the rat-tail one, possibly named

Axie, followed by the pimply one, possibly Felix. I only need to hear your voice once to have it forever. Names are a little harder. Why? Because only two really count? Chet and Bernie? Well, that's not even true. How about Charlie and Weatherly and Esmé and even Trixie, and . . . I tapped the brakes on all of that.

Meanwhile, from back in the house came a sort of smacking thud. That's the sound of a punch landing somewhere on the human body, but not the face. There's a cracking that goes with the smacking and the thudding when the face is involved but I didn't hear it. What I did hear was an oomph and a cry of pain, that particular oomph usually coming right after a gut punch.

"Excuse me," said the babysitter. Still smiling he turned and headed back into the house, disappearing through a doorway. A small car rolled up the street and turned into the driveway. At the same time, more sounds came from inside the house, not loud but somehow real real quick, fleshy sort of smacks. Right away my mind went back to that moment, not long ago, when Bernie slapped Werner Irons across the face. My eyes happened to be on Bernie right now. Did he hear what I heard, or even close? Possibly not. In fact, it was for sure. I could tell by how closely he was watching the small car park in the driveway. Gillian, dressed in neat khaki pants and a white shirt, got out and came toward us.

"Bernie?" she said.

"Hi," said Bernie. "We just came by to—"

And suddenly the babysitting dude was back. I hadn't even heard him. How strange! All at once my teeth were feeling a strong urge to . . . well, I don't want to say it. Bite him. There. It got out. I'm sorry. Don't be mad.

"Hey, Gilly," said the babysitting dude, looking real happy to see her. "You're early. We haven't even gone yet."

"Two cancellations," Gillian said. "And it's Gillian," she added, maybe not quite as happy to see him.

"So sorry," the babysitting dude said. "Just a habit."

"Habits can be broken," Gillian said.

"Oh?" He gave her a great big smile. Then he turned and called into the house, "Boys! Get a move on!" He clapped his hands, very big hands that made a sound like thunder, but sharper. He turned back to us, shaking his head. "Kids," he said.

Gillian glanced at Bernie. "You've met Axel?"

"We're still meeting," Bernie said.

The babysitting man laughed.

"Bernie Little, Axel Sizemore," Gillian said.

They shook hands. Two big hands, Bernie's big, strong, and beautiful, Axel's perhaps bigger but certainly not stronger and in no way beautiful.

"Bernie's a friend of the family," Gillian said.

"Then he's a friend of mine," said Axel.

"Billy's family," Gillian added.

Axel smiled at her. "Can't see how that makes any difference." He glanced our way. "What do you do, Bernie?"

"Private investigations," Bernie said.

Axel's eyebrows rose. "Oh my goodness—did I hear your name on the live audio feed the other day?"

"What audio feed?" Gillian said.

"The Valley PD," Axel said. "Free entertainment—I often have it on when I'm working,"

Gillian turned to us. "Were you in the audio feed, Bernie?"

"Might have been."

"What about?"

Before Bernie could answer, Axel jumped in. "Doling out just deserts to some bad guy was the gist of it. Is that the story, Bernie?"

"I wouldn't put it exactly that way and these things get—" Bernie began, but at that moment Felix and Axie came running out carrying little airplane-type gizmos. Drones, of course. I'd dealt with them before, in fact once knocking one clear out of the sky with my paw, a fine moment in my career. The way it bounced across the pavement and came apart in twisted plastic pieces, one tiny prop still spinning in a jerky way that was just so . . . satisfying, would that be it? Something like that. In any case it was the kind of pretty sight you don't forget. There's nothing like the detective business when it comes to sights you don't forget. Wasn't that where we started? With Donnie the Docent in the cottonwood tree? My, my. Life is just so . . . so . . .

"Hey, guys!" Axel said, raising his hands high. "Let's fly those babies!"

The boys filed out past us. From where I was, I could see only one side of their faces, somewhat reddish in both cases, although Bernie says I have trouble with red, so forget this part. They followed Axel to a very long and wide black SUV and got in the back with their drones. Axel sat in the driver's seat and closed the door. He started up the engine and said something over his shoulder. What with the engine noise and the windows closed I couldn't be sure but it sounded like "One big happy family, correct gentlemen?" Whatever it was, the boys nodded yes.

Gillian watched them go. Bernie watched her watching. After not long at all, there was a quick narrowing of her eyes—you had to be a close observer of humans to have caught it, but of course I am—and she said, "You ask a lot of questions."

"I didn't say a thing," Bernie said.

"Your type doesn't have to." Gillian turned to him. "I can feel you nosing around for all the gory details."

Nosing around? The Little Detective Agency does plenty of nosing around, one of the big reasons for our success, except for the finances part, but the nosing around is done by me and me alone, Bernie bringing other things to the table. I shifted closer to Gillian and sniffed her feet. She was wearing sandals, and the smell of old leather mixed with old female human sweat—one of my favorites, the male variety a little too strong for the leather—was unmissable. Unmissable to me, that is. But the point I'm making is that here I was nosing around in no uncertain terms and Gillian had no clue while at the same time she could feel Bernie nosing around when he couldn't and wouldn't. Were we working a case? Was this an interview? I got the feeling things weren't going well. At the same time a plan started forming in my mind, all about taking possession of one—but why not both?—of those leather sandals and taking it—or them!—back to our place on Mesquite Road. All at once I knew for sure that we were rocking this case, rocking it but good. Please let it be a case!

Meanwhile, Gillian seemed to be waiting for Bernie to say something and he was keeping his mouth shut, right up there with nosing around as one of our best techniques. The Little Detective Agency, ladies and gentlemen!

Gillian took a deep breath, let it out slow. Something changes in a human after that. I had no idea what it was, but one thing for sure: once they're done with that last slow breath rough stuff is out of the picture. You can relax, although I couldn't at the moment, what with how hard my mind was working on the sandal—or sandals!—problem.

"I've made a ton of mistakes, but Billy wasn't one of them." Gillian gave Bernie a quick, sideways glance. "He says you're wonderful with his parents. Did I tell you that?"

Bernie nodded.

"I keep reminding myself of it because . . . well, just because. My history with law enforcement being what it is, and all."

"We're not law enforcement," Bernie said.

She shook her head. "Same mentality."

When Bernie's not buying something, I can feel it, whether he speaks or not. Whatever this was, he wasn't buying it, but that stayed just between him and me. Like many things that we don't have time for now.

"So here's my guess," Gillian said. "Billy's dad didn't like what he saw on his visit down here and he asked you to check out the set up. Or maybe just check out me."

Bernie gave her a look, not unfriendly, and said nothing.

"I'm right, aren't I?" Her voice rose. "I can see it on your face. Write this down if you can't remember—I love Billy and Billy loves me. We both screwed up in the past, in life and in love, if you want to call it that. His screw up was named Dee and mine was Axel. But we've found the right road, Billy and I. We found it together and God help me I'll . . . I'll murder anyone who tries to mess us up." She made a fist and held it in front of her.

Whoa! Didn't I just finish explaining that violence was off the table? Would I soon be grabbing Gillian by the pant leg? Those khaki pants ended up somewhere above the ankle, which was a bit confusing, but don't forget I'm a professional. I watched Bernie, waiting for a signal. It could be anything. That's how we operate.

But there was no signal. Instead, Bernie said, "What happened to Dee?"

Gillian blinked. "Why do you want to know that?"

"We met her, briefly."

"Who is we?"

"Me and Chet."

Gillian looked down at me. At that moment I happened to be rather close to her. Was one of my paws actually resting against the toe of one of her sandals? She drew back her foot in one swift and nifty move. Was any of that important? Maybe not. The important thing seemed to be Dee, who—have I mentioned this already?—we last saw near the end of the stolen saguaro case, zooming off on a motorcycle with Billy on the back.

"What happened to Dee is she turned Billy on to coke and then went off with a creep twice her age who owned a shipping line in Panama," Gillian said. "She's still there as far as we know."

"So she's no longer in the picture?"

Gillian backed up a step. "What are you saying?"

"Nothing. Has Billy said anything about his parents recently?"

"What kind of anything?"

"About how they're doing?"

"No. Is something wrong? Like the health problems? A turn for the worse?"

"They're hanging in." Bernie glanced down the road in the direction taken by the big black SUV. "What about Axel?" he said.

"How do you mean?" said Gillian.

Bernie shrugged. "You said Dee was Billy's mistake and Axel was yours."

"Mine's a little more complicated."

"How so?"

Gillian looked down at me and what do you know? My paw was right up against the toe of her sandal again!

"Might as well come in," she said.

Fifteen

"Axel's one of those larger-than-life people," Gillian said.

We were in her kitchen, Bernie and Gillian drinking coffee on barstools by the counter in front of a nice big window and me . . . actually not between them, where I was pretty sure I started, but over by the trash container in the corner. Was it possible that anyone could throw out left-over bacon? How could bacon be left over? Yet that was what it smelled like, and when it comes to smells you can count on me.

"Apologies if that sounds like an expert opinion," Gillian went on. "I'm no expert on any subject let alone this one, and Axel's the only larger than life person I've ever met, so I shouldn't generalize, but if he's typical then it's hard for them to shrink down to normal size when that's what will work best. For living the normal day-to-day, if that makes sense."

Bernie nodded. Have I mentioned what an ace nodder he is—with a whole bunch of different nods for this and that and even for nothing at all? This particular nod was all about being real interested. For a moment I could almost look through his eyes and see his fabulous mind.

"How did you meet?" he said.

"Interesting question," said Gillian.

No surprise there, at least not to me. Everything Bernie does is interesting. For example, once he built a house out of popsicle sticks! And the chimney was a popsicle stick with the popsicle still on it! Not a real house of course—there was no time for that—but a toy house when Charlie was little. He's still on the little side, but not quite so little now. That chimney! I still can't quite understand what made me—well, enough of that.

"One day he just walked into our store," Gillian said. "My boyfriend's and mine. Just a tiny place on the not-nice side of Tovar Square. We sold Western-style knick knacks, wall hangings, mobiles, that kind of thing, lots of it made by him. When he felt industrious, which wasn't often. I was the manager. Axel bought a mobile made from old horseshoes, the nicest thing in the store by far. Caleb—that was the boyfriend—said he saw it in a dream after a little session with mushrooms." She laughed one of those strange human laughs that have nothing to do with being happy. "'More shrooms!' I told him. Stupid me at my stupidest. Soon Axel hired me to run his office. Caleb encouraged me to take the job. Axel was paying me more per week than we were making in a month. But one thing led to another."

She sipped her iced tea, watching Bernie over the rim of the glass. Bernie was looking at the fridge. There was a photo of Billy and Felix on the door. Billy was smiling and Felix was laughing, his head thrown back, like maybe something real funny had just happened.

"What kind of work does Axel do?" he said.

Gillian put down her glass, the ice cubes tinkling softly. "Axel's brilliant. He dropped out of Cal Tech."

"But what does he do?" Bernie said.

"He's an investor."

"Investing in what?"

"Different things. Crypto something or other? Next-gen banking, maybe? He can see around corners. I don't know what he's into now, but back then it was shipping container arbitrage."

Shipping container arbitrage—a new one on me, and a complete mystery. But not to Bernie. He didn't ask a single question about it, just said "hmm." Wow! What doesn't he know?

"Arbitrage," Gillian went on, "is Axel's way of life in general.

I didn't realize that at first. It was only later when I had time to think. Lots and lots of time. Too much."

"When you were locked up?" Bernie said.

Whoa! Gillian locked up? Right now she looked just right in her white shirt, khaki pants—and those sandals. I tried to imagine her in an orange jump suit and could not.

"Ah, you like facts," she said. "Same with Axel. Billy's different."

"What does he like instead?"

"I wouldn't do justice to it," Gillian said. "I'm sure he'd be happy to explain when he gets back."

"When's that going to be?"

"I don't know. But these interventions—soft interventions, Billy calls them—never last long, just a few days."

"Do you know who he's intervening with?"

"Billy never violates client confidentiality."

"But doesn't he touch base with you when he's gone like this?"

"Sometimes yes, sometimes no," Gillian said. She gave Bernie a look. "Does the old man know I'm an ex-con?"

"What old man?"

"Billy's dad."

"If he does he never mentioned it to me. And it wouldn't bother him anyway, not in isolation."

"Good to hear," Gillian said. "Some people are wary of anyone who's done time. On the other hand, now we have a whole opposite group who think no one deserves being put behind bars. I deserved it."

"What did you do?"

"Caleb sourced a lot of his materials from Mexico, meaning he did the locating and I drove down, negotiated, brought the stuff back. After a while—this was at the little post near Sasabe—I knew all the agents and they just waved me through. You can probably figure out the rest."

"Weed?" Bernie said. He sounded kind of hopeful. I knew weed, of course. Anyone with a nose these days—even you!—knows weed. Was there something hopeful about it? I was a bit lost.

"Not only," Gillian said. "I sold to a dealer up in the Valley."

"Who?" Bernie said.

"It doesn't matter. He got stabbed to death at Central Correctional five or six years ago. But the point is they closed down the border post, a year or so before Axel came along, meaning that was the end of my smuggling career. But the past caught up. Axel and I had been together maybe six months when the dealer got busted. The dealer gave me up, plus a bunch of others, for a reduced sentence. That pretty much ended things with Axel. He doesn't like complications. That's the arbitrage mentality. The thing is it works with numbers but not with people." She smiled. "Felix was what I netted out of the deal."

"You were pregnant when you went to prison?" Bernie said.

"An unintentional blessing," said Gillian. "Axel and Cee-Cee, Axel's new wife or maybe previous-and-still-in-the-picture wife—I forgot to mention that Axel and I never tied the actual knot—took care of Felix till I got out. She had Axie soon after I went away—he's only five months younger than Felix. I thought going somewhere for a fresh start was the best move, but where Felix and I went was back home to Arkansas where my mom was living. Well, dying, as it turned out. I ended up taking care of her." Gillian blinked an odd sort of blink, the eyes staying closed for what seemed like a little too long. "After that I came back here, kind of out of ideas. But—saving grace—in prison I'd learned how to cut hair, actually turned out to be good at it—even the toughest gals were nice to me. So one lucky day I went to ProCon for referrals to the local salons. Which was how I met Billy. This was last year." She poked at an ice cube in her drink. "And we lived happily ever after."

Bernie smiled and started to rise. Then he paused. Wow! One of our very best techniques, hardly ever used. The almost-leaving-but-not-quite move. This case, whatever it was, had to be major. I tried to remember who was paying. No one came to mind.

"Did Billy say anything about the scam?" he said.

"Scam?"

"His dad was victimized by . . ." He paused and then went on. ". . . a phone scammer."

"Oh, how terrible!" Gillian said. "No, Billy didn't mention it. I hope they didn't lose a lot."

"TBD," Bernie said, losing me completely.

"I'm sure we could help them out, at least a little," Gillian said.

Bernie sat back down. Gillian blinked a couple of times, like maybe she'd thought we were about to vamoose. I was with her on that. But if Bernie wasn't vamoosing then neither was I. I sat back down myself. "How does ProCon work?" he said. "Where does the funding come from?"

"Grants—federal and state, mostly."

"So it's on stable footing?"

"No extras but yeah, stable. Plus there are some private contributions—the aerospace company, a few others."

"Including Axel?" Bernie said.

She nodded. "He may not be perfect when it comes to, say, marital fidelity, but he can be very generous. It wouldn't surprise me if the two are linked, in his mind at least."

Bernie gave her a look, friendly but close at the same time, one of his best. "Any contributions from Greta Analytics?"

Gillian shook her head. "Not that I know of. I've never heard of them."

Sometimes Bernie's face goes still like he's paying attention to something that isn't here. He had that look now, and he kept it the whole time they were saying goodbye and we were walking to the car. He didn't come back to normal until we were driving away and he happened to glance over at me, sitting tall in the shotgun seat.

"Hey! How did you get that?"

Get what? It took me a moment or two to connect to the seeming fact that I had a sandal hanging from the side of my mouth. How could that have happened? I hadn't the slightest idea! My mind was a complete blank on that subject. Perhaps I'd had nothing at all to do with it. Yes! I had my answer! Although there's one small correction I should add: I seemed to have only part of the sandal. You might almost think—judging only by the fraying—that the rest had been chewed away by something or other.

Bernie reached for the sandal, gave it a closer look, and changed his mind. "Good grief," he said. We get along great, me and Bernie, a point that hardly needs mentioning, but I like to mention it just the same.

Back in downtown Gila City—very different from downtown in the Valley, with no tall buildings and no one in a hurry—we drove along the street with bars and restaurants and cowboy outfit stores and came to the storefront with the picture of one human hand shaking another in the window. That would be the ProCon office, unless I was missing something. I got ready to hop out the moment we pulled over. But we did not. Instead, Bernie continued along the street almost to the end of the block, then hung a real quick U-ee, somehow noiseless, and parked between a van and a pickup on the other side. What I'm trying to get across is we were down the block from ProCon but still had it in our sights. Then we just sat. This technique is called sitting on a place. And that place had to be ProCon! Wow! Was I easing myself into the thinking department at the Little Detective

Agency? I glanced over at Bernie. Yes, he was thinking for sure. We were thinking together, side by side. What a moment in my career! It lasted until Bernie sighed and said, "Should I call her? Just say, come on, Weatherly, let's find a way to . . . to . . ."

Then all at once he had the phone to his ear. "Weatherly? Hi! Um. How about we find a way to—"

She cut him off. There really was something slicing in the sound of her voice, hard to describe. "Why can't you get this? Don't call."

Click.

Silence in the car. The phone rested on Bernie's knee, now doing nothing but at the same time somehow . . . active. I began to have strong feelings about the phone, most likely a machine of some sort. So was the Beast, of course. I liked the Beast better. In fact—and this hit me with some force—I didn't like the phone at all! Not one little bit. A plan, perhaps on the daring side, began taking shape in my mind.

But not fast enough. Before the plan emerged from shadows— shadows in my mind, if you see what I mean—the door to Pro-Con opened and a woman stepped out. This was the woman with the bruise around one eye, not visible at the moment because she was wearing sunglasses, but I recognized her right away on account of her frizzy red hair: Mavis Mooney, sister of Ike Mooney, an old acquaintance no longer with us, if I was recalling correctly. Bernie sat up straight and tucked the phone away.

Mavis unlocked a bike that was leaning against a parking meter, got on and started pedaling in our direction. She gazed straight ahead. There's something about the faces of bicycling humans I like, although I can't take it any further than that. As Mavis went by Bernie laid a hand on my neck, gently but sending a message. What was it? Jump out of the car, chase after the bike and topple it over? Or the opposite, no jumping, chasing, or toppling? How about keeping it to just the jumping and chasing, but leaving out the toppling, at least for now? I kept a close eye on Bernie, waiting for some sign. He gave me a nice big smile.

"Good boy," he said.

How nice to hear! So were we dealing with no jump, no chase, no topple? That was my best guess. Perhaps, in a perfect world, as humans liked to say, I'd have made a different choice. But— "good boy"? How do you top that? I suddenly got the picture. It is a perfect world! Just like this right here and right now! Wow. Kind of nice to know.

Bernie pulled another U-ee, this one again silent but also slow. Then real slow we rolled down the street, keeping plenty of distance between us and Mavis. We're real good at following, can follow from up close, far behind, many lanes over, even from in front, and once down in Mexico going backwards! So there was really nothing to this. We just had to go slow, meaning there was lots of honking behind us, and even some fist shaking as we got passed. Fist shaking is a real interesting subject, maybe for later.

Mavis turned a corner and headed up a side street, followed by a flatbed loaded with cement blocks and then us, the Beast rumbling the way it does when going slow, making sounds I felt more than I heard. Soon the flatbed was gone and we were in a hilly part of town, nice but nothing fancy, actually a bit like Mesquite Road. Mavis, never looking back, turned into the driveway of a small pink house and pedaled up and out of sight, disappearing behind some sort of shed. We parked a few houses away and walked up to the pink house. Hey! It had one of those brightly painted jockeys in the yard. What I like to do whenever I see one of those jockeys is—

"Ch—et?"

Instead, I gave that jockey a look as we passed by, a look he wouldn't soon forget. The next thing I knew we were behind the pink house, where there was a small pool with a big blow-up gator floating in the middle. I've had experience with an actual gator name of Iko. This was down in bayou country where we had a tricky case involving boats, oil wells, and a sort of midnight swim with me, Iko, and a tangled fishnet. Have I mentioned my collars yet? I have two, black for dress-up and gator skin for everyday. Was it actually Iko's skin? I didn't think so but at the same time couldn't remember why not, so let's say yes, Iko's. But meanwhile—and now I'm sure you'll understand—whenever I see a blow-up gator floating in a pool, I—

"Ch-et?"

That was when the door to the shed—which turned out to be a pool house, pool houses all having the same smell, like laundry rooms—opened and Mavis peered out. She looked surprised to see us even though we'd been seeing her for quite some time. We get that a lot in this business. It's just one of the perks, perks being a small treat, like the nub end of a Slim Jim that turns up on a picnic table when no one seems to be around.

"Bernie?" she said. "What's going on?"

"Still looking for Billy," he said.

She frowned, one frizzy red curl drooping down on her forehead. "You think he's here?"

Bernie smiled, a quick smile, mostly friendly, although it had a little—could you call it bite? A little bite to it? Oh my goodness! You sure could. But that was Bernie, the only human I knew who could bite with a smile, and when it comes to biting I'm something of an expert, if you don't mind me pointing that out. But don't worry. I don't do a whole lot of it and there'll never be any biting between you and me.

"Is he?" Bernie said.

"Of course not," said Mavis. "And how did you find me? Pro-Con never gives out addresses."

"And they didn't. Let's just say we followed our noses."

How puzzling! We often followed my nose, never Bernie's, and had followed neither of them this time. Hadn't we kept Mavis in sight the whole time? That was how I remembered it. But just then my nose got a little twitchy and I began to doubt. And the next thing I knew I was sneezing, a great big powerful sneeze. Wow! Did that feel good! I forgot about everything, just waiting and hoping for another sneeze to come along. But it did not. I tried to figure out how to make a sneeze happen and got nowhere.

Meanwhile, Mavis seemed to be puzzled just like me, but Bernie didn't notice. He looked around and said, "Nice place."

"It's not mine," Mavis said. "The owners spend most of their time in L.A. I just rent the pool house—there's a studio apartment at the back—and look out for things. But what do you want? I heard Billy was away on business. That's all I know."

"I just want to talk to him," Bernie said.

"Has he done something wrong?"

"Not that I know of. And we're not even here in a professional capacity. We're neighbors of Billy's parents up in the Valley and they're facing some challenges at the moment. I wanted to get Billy's take."

Mavis thought that over. "You were good to Ike," she said at last.

"Anyone would have done the same."

"You know that's not true."

Not long after that we were by the pool, Bernie and Mavis drinking ice water and me lying at the edge, doing nothing in particular. What a beautiful day: blue skies, not too hot, and a gentle breeze carrying desert scents and ruffling the water. The blow-up gator bobbed slowly around. I kept on doing nothing in particular, simply minding my own.

"Word is," Bernie said, "that Billy's away helping out some Pro-Con client who's having problems."

"I heard that," Mavis said.

"Any idea who it could be?"

Mavis shook her head.

Bernie smiled. And what was this? The bite-smile again? And so soon? But that was Bernie. Sometimes he latches onto something new and stays with it for a while. For example, there was the Thursday night Valley PD poker game, which was how we learned about something called a third mortgage. Or maybe fourth. But certainly more than two, meaning into mysterious territory for me.

"Maybe try a little harder," he said.

She set her glass on the table, very slowly. Was she thinking of bashing him with it? I kept a close eye on her from what seemed to be my new position, namely in the pool, drifting here and there in a pleasant manner.

"Excuse me?" Mavis said.

Bernie shrugged. "You could run through some of the clients in your mind, see if anyone pops."

That seemed to annoy her. "Pops?" she said. "Pops?"

And at that very moment there came an enormous pop from right in front of my face. Was it possible that while I'd been keeping watch on Mavis—security being a big part of my job— I'd also managed somehow to . . . to . . . All I can pass on is that the blow-up gator had lost its shape, becoming a flat plastic green thing that was sinking in and slowly fluttering way to the bottom.

I looked at Bernie and Mavis. They looked at me. How about diving down and retrieving what was left of the gator, retrieving being one of my best things? Or I could burst out of the pool and hop the back fence, fence-hopping also in my swing zone. Then there was simply racing crazily around the pool deck, zigzagging back and forth, back and forth. I still hadn't made up my mind when Mavis threw back her head and started laughing. She laughed and laughed, a lovely moment, somehow made lovelier by the fact she was missing a tooth or two toward the back. "I've always hated that damn gator," she said. "It gives me the creeps." She laughed some more, took off her sunglasses and wiped her eyes on the back of her hand, going gently on the bruised one. But it looked a lot better. That made me happy. She turned to Bernie. "No guarantees. But you could try Holger Niberg."

"Who's he?"

"The name who popped to mind."

"Tell me about him."

"I don't know anything. I saw him once or twice at ProCon. That was it."

"Did you ever talk to him?"

"No."

"What does he look like?"

"Normal-sized guy. Not big like you. More like Billy, kind of slight, but taller. He wears short-sleeve white shirts, like in the mission control room for the moon shots. In fact that's his look— techie. But with a crew cut, a techie from back in the day."

Bernie was silent for a moment or two. Then he said, "Any idea what sent him to prison?"

Mavis shook her head. "But that shouldn't take you long to find out." And now if she didn't smile with a bite of her own! "Meaning in your professional capacity."

"Does he wear a tie with that white shirt?" Bernie said. "And drive a motorbike?"

Mavis frowned. "If you know all this why ask?"

I was with her on that. But then I remembered—from out of nowhere!—the heart has its reasons. Suddenly—and for all time— everything was clear!

Sixteen

"Any theory of the case that depends on ProCon being in bad financial shape is out the window," Bernie said.

Theory of the case? Bernie often mentioned that. Theory of the case was important and maybe one day I'd find out . . . well, anything about it. For now it was enough to simply enjoy the pleasure of hearing him say "theory of the case," exciting and relaxing at the same time, a wonderful combo that comes around not often enough. We rolled away from Mavis' place, Bernie talking about the case, whatever it was exactly, and me listening to . . . what would you call it? The music of his voice? Close enough. But way too soon the phone buzzed.

"Bernard?"

Bernard? No one calls Bernie Bernard except for his mom. But no matter what she was saying I always recognized her voice at once, powerful and loud and with the suggestion below the surface that she was just getting started. She lives in Florida with her newish husband Tommy Trauble, owner of Tommy Trauble's Auto Mile Dealerships in Flamingo Beach. Tommy Trauble has the deepest tan I'd ever seen on a human face, tiny bleached-out eyes, and shoulder-length silvery hair that gleamed. He'd been sporting a white leather belt on their last visit and by now had had plenty of time to find a replacement.

"Hi, Mom," Bernie said. "How's it going?"

"Is there any point in complaining?"

"Um, well—"

"But the reason I'm calling is that Tommy and I had dinner the other night with an old friend of his who's in the advertising business. Platforms 'R Us—you can look him up. Anyway, we were discussing your situation and he's pretty sure he—meaning PJ, Tommy's friend—can help you out."

Then came something very unusual. Bernie seemed to squirm in his seat. It was over in a flash, but I didn't miss it. And for that brief moment how much he'd reminded me of Charlie! But why? What was going on? I was fine with Charlie squirming. He could squirm till the cows came home. Oh, no! Not the cows coming home thing again! I have some experience with cows, and one thing I know for sure—never mind! The point is I was not fine with Bernie squirming and never wanted to see it again.

"Situation, Mom? What situation are we talking about?"

"Bernard! Don't play games! Your financial situation. How many times have I told you you've got to toot your own horn? But you just won't. I said as much to PJ—in those exact words, he won't toot his own horn, and do you know what he told me?"

There was a long pause. Bernie said nothing.

"Bernard! Are you there?"

"Mom?" he said. "Do you remember when Dad used to take me to the batting cages?"

"Excuse me?"

"The batting cages off the old airport road. We went Saturday mornings in the spring."

"Vaguely, I suppose. But how do *you* remember that? You must have been—what? Seven? Eight?"

Bernie took a deep breath. "Apparently he liked my swing."

"You played on the swings?"

"No, no. It was the batting cages, Mom, for God's—" Had Bernie's voice gotten strangely loud? He cut himself off sharply and reloaded, much quieter this time. "Baseball swing, Mom. With the bat."

"No need to get shirty," said his mom.

I checked Bernie's shirt, Hawaiian, which was usually the case, this one being one of my very favorites, with its pattern of saxophone playing palm trees and dancing coconuts wearing short skirts and laughing their heads off. How could Bernie's mom not like it?

"I wasn't being—" He cut himself off again, this time taking a deep breath. "I was just wondering whether you remembered those days, that's all."

There was a long pause. "You're talking about the period just before he got diagnosed?"

"I guess so."

"Those weren't easy times."

"Because he wasn't feeling well?"

"He felt fine right up until the diagnosis."

"So you're saying?"

"Nothing," said his mom. "I'm saying nothing. And I didn't call to dig up ancient grievances."

Ah, too bad. You couldn't say Bernie's mom and I were close, but a little side-by-side digging is a good way to make friends with just about anyone. Maybe she'd feel like digging sometime down the road. That was my hope.

"Just remember," she went on, "that even hard-shelled people can be vulnerable."

"Sure, but—"

"And that closes the subject. What I'm trying to say—if you'll just let me finish the thought—PJ is standing by and ready to help. At no charge, by the way. It would be a favor to Tommy."

"PJ being . . . ?"

"For pity's sake, Bernard. Are you feeling all right? PJ Platt, who runs Platforms 'R Us. He very kindly offered to help you get sorted out."

"Sorted out how?"

"With your social media presence! With tooting your own

horn! He's going to—and I'm quoting now—custom design a horn just for you and show you how it works. All he needs is your go-ahead and some routine info. What's a good time?"

"For what?"

"For the call, Bernard! So his people can get started on this. What's your shoe size, by the way?"

"Why do you want to know that?"

"I don't, but PJ will. PJ believes you can wear anything you want these days as long as the shoes are super classy. He knows a guy in Milan."

Bernie gazed at his phone, almost like it was dangerous, maybe fixing to explode. I understood completely. "Mom? Got a call coming in I have to take. I'll get back to you."

"What can possibly be more—?"

Click. He dropped the phone in the cupholder, quite roughly, and turned to me. "Go ahead. Call me a coward."

A coward was what again? Most likely something not good, meaning it had nothing to do with Bernie. Just to make sure he got the picture I gave the side of his face a nice big lick, bringing the poor guy back to his senses.

Bernie stopped at the first convenience store we came to and bought cigarettes, which hadn't happened in some time. That meant soon he could quit again. Bernie was superb at quitting smoking. He'd done it many times. But for now we parked at a lookout just outside Gila City and Bernie lit up. He blew out a big ball of smoke. It drifted away on the breeze, grew long and thin and finally vanished. Bernie made a soft grunt, like something twisted inside him had gotten straightened out. I thought right away of . . . what would you call it? A misadventure? Close enough. A misadventure I'd had with a certain sweat sock. Funny how the mind works.

"They say the unexamined life isn't worth living," Bernie said. He gestured with his chin at some distant mountains. "But there's Mexico, big guy. We could ease on over and simply . . ." I never found out what simple thing we'd be doing in Mexico, because at that moment Bernie shook his head—rather sharply, as though trying to get rid of something inside—and picked up the phone. He tapped at the screen.

"Etta?" he said.

"Bernie. I didn't expect to hear from you so soon. Were you able to track down whatever his name was?"

"You know the name," Bernie said.

"Oh?"

"Plus, you know we found him and you probably know what went down."

Etta laughed. "I do have my sources. But why so feisty today?"

Bernie took another drag off the cigarette. "Who said the unexamined life isn't worth living?"

"Socrates."

"Did his dad die young?"

"I've never read anything about his dad." There was a rather long pause and then Etta said, "That's kind of a strange question. Something on your mind?"

Bernie said nothing, just sat and smoked, gazing at Mexico.

"Bernie? Out with it."

He opened his door, dropped what was left of the cigarette, crushed it under his heel.

"Did my mother know about you and my dad?" he said.

"I should have known this was coming," Etta said. "But what's the point after all these years?"

Bernie didn't answer. He watched another smoke ball thin out and waft away.

"Then there's the fact that all three of the players are gone. Only one dead and gone, but the other two now so far along that their younger selves might as well be goners, as you'll understand one day if you don't already."

Bernie remained silent, ordinarily a perp thing, but of course Bernie was no perp. I began to get uneasy.

Over on Etta's end I heard a little snick—the sound of a match getting struck. Was she lighting up a cigarette, too? Were they sort of smoking together? Humans could be very surprising, often when it came to the littlest things.

"We didn't discuss it much, Harry and I, but according to him she was unaware. On the other hand, love is blind. Never more blind than on a question like this. Is that good enough?"

"No," Bernie said.

"Then how about this?" Etta said. "The wife always knows."

Bernie nodded.

From the other end I heard Etta blowing smoke, one of those slow little streams. My ears can kind of picture things, if that makes any sense.

"Completely different if it's the husband getting cheated on," Etta said. "They never know. At the same time when they're not getting cheated on they can get very suspicious. That's why the cuckold is comedy and the betrayed wife is tragedy."

Bernie laughed.

"So we're still friends?" Etta said.

"Yeah," said Bernie.

"You really were a darling little boy. There was no hint of the inner propensity for . . . well, let's leave it at that."

"Propensity for what?"

"Do I have to spell it out? For what happened to Werner Irons."

Bernie's face hardened.

"I'm not being judgmental," Etta said. "In fact, I'm fine with it. The world needs good men to be tough—at least some of them." I heard her cigarette getting stubbed out. "Especially the ones who know how to minimize collateral damage."

"What does that mean?"

"I'm guessing you already know," Etta said. "Anything else I can do for you?"

There was a silence. Bernie's eyes got an inward look and didn't snap out of it for what seemed like a little too long. "Maybe," he said at last.

"Shoot."

"The name's Holger Niberg. That's pretty much all I've got."

"I've worked with less," Etta said.

"Here are two theories of the case." Bernie lit another cigarette. A cloud glided over the sun and Mexico darkened. "First, despite his denial and despite the lack of motive, Billy made the call to Mr. Parsons. That's where the evidence takes us. Second, someone impersonated Billy, exploiting the soft spots in the old man's heart. Was there a secondary goal of casting shade on Billy, either with his dad or with someone else, or even law enforcement? Did he have some sort of feud with one of the clients? Holger Niberg, for example? That could explain the bank account angle but it's not where the evidence takes us. Pure speculation, and yet . . ."

Bernie turned to me. Was he looking for input? We are a team, after all. I rolled over on my back—not so easy for a dude my size on the shotgun seat—and stuck my paws up in the air. Bernie scratched my belly. That got one of my paws started on some wild vibrations. Bernie laughed. He loved when that happened and so did I! We're willing to put in the work, me and Bernie, unlike other detective agencies I might name, except none of the names seemed to be coming to me at the moment.

And before they could, Etta was on the phone again.

"I cross-file all the A to Zs by occupation," she said. "Just for my own amusement. Did you know that line cooks lead the pack when it comes to assault with a shod foot?"

"Don't they usually wear clogs?" Bernie said.

"So?" said Etta. "What I'm getting at is that there are all these occupations that come up over and over—accountants, taxi drivers, club owners, florists, philosophy majors, but—"

"Philosophy majors?"

"—but I've never had a rocket scientist before. Holger Niberg is the first."

"Where does he work?" Bernie said.

"Now let's not get ahead of ourselves," Etta said.

Whoa! Why not? If you're the speedy type—and do I even have to remind you that I am?—then you're probably familiar with getting ahead of yourself. I'm not saying it happens all the time, but once in a while, on one of those perfect days where the wind seems to be blowing you along even if there's actually no wind at all, you take a glance back and what do you see? Nothing! Nada! Zip! You're not there. Why not? Because you're running so fast you've gotten ahead of yourself? What else could it be? So what I now knew for sure was that Etta was a slow runner, poor thing.

"Have you ever noticed there are ironies in this business?" Etta said.

"Maybe," said Bernie. "But I can't think of any."

"No? I sense that you're not quite yourself these days. Is something bothering you?"

One of Bernie's hands was resting on the steering wheel. Now it tightened, in fact gripping the wheel hard even though we were just sitting there gazing at Mexico while . . . while Mexico gazed back at us? What a strange thought! What was the point of having a mind in the first place? Do you ever think about that? If so, please pass on the answer when you get a chance.

"Nothing's bothering me," Bernie said.

"I withdraw the question since I already know," said Etta. "But here's your irony. Rocket science is all about numbers, so a rocket scientist is a wiz with numbers. With me so far?"

Bernie's hand stopped gripping the wheel. His fingers rose and then dropped back down, just how the hand says, I give up.

"I take your silence for assent," Etta said. "So by definition, numbers would be the last place you'd expect a rocket scientist to mess up. And yet, Holger Niberg, PhD in applied math from Cal Tech, served three years ending last September, at Northern State Correctional for getting the numbers wrong. How's them apples?"

I'd caught a break. Nothing Etta was going on about had come close to sticking with me until that very last bit about apples. I knew apples very well—the taste, the smell, the look, even the sound when they fall off a branch and go bumpity-bump on the ground. There were no apples in the picture right now, not a single one. I ended up feeling pretty good about our chances.

"Specifically, he misread the petty cash maximum single draw limit, taking a two for a three and therefore triggering an internal audit that revealed he'd stolen upwards of nine hundred thousand dollars from his employer, Lunar Imperial Enterprises. And counting."

"What was the single draw limit?"

"Twenty grand. He thought it was thirty."

"You're talking about petty cash?"

"Think big. Think the golden age of colonization. Think King Leopold in the Belgian Congo."

"But there's nobody indigenous on the moon."

"Which makes all these tech bros even more untethered," Etta said. "Dr. Niberg's current address hasn't turned up, but Lunar Imperial's HQ is just east of Empty Wells—if you're looking for a place to start. And don't bother thanking me."

"Why not?"

"I'll let you guess."

* * *

Empty Wells was a crossroads with a single rusted-out gas pump, an RV park with a leafless tree in the center, and a giant tumbleweed wobbling by the side of the road. In short, our kind of place. Bernie read a faded sign. "'Twenty thousand acres for sale or rent. Will subdivide. Reasonable!'" He smiled. "What's a reasonable price for no water?"

Wow! What did that even mean? All I knew was it had to be brilliant. What else could it possibly be? But that was Bernie. Just when you think he's done amazing you he amazes you again. We drove on. The tumbleweed followed us for a short distance and then gave up. High above a strange bird did not give up. Not that it was following us, more like simply moving in the same direction. Birds did do some following out in the desert, but only when some creature down below was in trouble and the creatures down below were me and Bernie who were not in trouble. And even if we were we could take care of it no problem. But I barked at that strange high-up bird anyway. It rose even higher and gleamed in the sunshine, gleamed like no bird I'd ever seen. Could I bark it up still higher? Any harm in trying?

"Chet?"

I kept my mouth shut, or perhaps shut it and then kept it that way. The road, single-lane blacktop with lots of potholes, got worse and worse and then all of a sudden much better, as wide as the airport freeway back home in the Valley, just as smooth and black, but with no traffic at all, except for us. We rounded a bend and saw a building that seemed to be made all of glass, tucked into a hillside—not a tall building, but very long, and somehow rising and falling as though it was a sort of hillside itself. Also it had a strange way of sometimes gleaming and sometimes vanishing completely, like it wasn't there at all. But when it was there it was full of tiny people, hunched over at their workstations.

We stopped at a guardhouse. The guard stepped out.

"Welcome to Lunar Imperial," he said. "Do you have—?" Then he noticed me. "Ah, the dog," he said. "Drive on in."

He waved us through. We drove up to the glass building, which grew and grew the closer we got. Bernie parked. The front door, also glass, was enormous, but there was a normal-size door within it, and that was what opened. A barefoot man in a suit came hurrying out, a big white smile on his face, the same shade of white as the moon on the brightest of nights.

Seventeen

The barefoot man in the suit hurried toward us. At first, I'd taken him for a big guy, maybe even Bernie's size, but the closer he got the more he shrank. The big white smile stayed the same, maybe even growing. Was he one of those dudes who ended up seeming bigger than he was? I tried to think of another dude like that and could not.

"Welcome, Mr. Breeze!" He shook Bernie's hand real fast, the blurriest handshake I'd ever seen. "I'm Meelo Morster, founder." He turned to me. "And this must be Crispy! I hadn't realized he was quite so sizeable, but I'm sure our outfitting department will be up to the task. In fact, I'll alert them he's coming—we can take Crispy's metrics while the paperwork gets drawn up." Meelo Morster put his hand on Bernie's shoulder, possibly directing him toward the entrance.

But Bernie didn't let himself be directed.

"There's a misunderstanding," he said. "I'm Bernie Little and this is Chet. Not Crispy."

I knew that, of course. I was Chet, not Crispy. Nothing could have been clearer in my mind. Still, it was nice to hear Bernie say so out loud.

Meelo Morster got busy with his phone. "That's odd. I don't see you down here at all."

"Down for what?" Bernie said.

"Why, the auditions, of course. They've gone viral."

"Auditions for what?"

The smile seemed to separate from Meelo Morster's face, a

very odd moment that passed not quite quickly enough. His eyes—
which maybe hadn't been part of the smile from the get-go—
took a real good look at Bernie. They didn't seem to like what
they saw or not like what they saw. They just simply saw, if that
makes sense. Probably not. What if I add there was something
machine-like in the way they were seeing? Does that help? No?
I give up.

"Really?" said Meelo Morster. "You're unaware of the Moondog contest?"

Bernie nodded.

Meelo Morster shook his head. "There's no end to human . . .
variability. Let's just call it that and put value judgments aside."
He gestured toward the glass building. "Do you know what
this is?"

"Lunar something or other," Bernie said.

Meelo Morster laughed. "And now I know you're pulling my
leg."

He couldn't have been more wrong about that. First, leg pulling was my job, not Bernie's. Second, pulling Meelo's leg hadn't
even occurred to me. True, the idea was now on the table.

"But I'll spell it out anyway," Meelo went on. "My media
people make a religion of spelling it out. You're looking at the
world headquarters of Lunar Imperial Enterprises. Just beyond that hill is our launch pad. In—" He checked his watch.
"Twenty-one months, eight days, three hours and twenty-nine
minutes Nina One will be blasting off with a crew of three plus
our first fourteen colonists and the winner of our Moondog
contest."

"You're colonizing the moon?"

"Let's call it setting up shop."

"What sort of shop?"

"Mining, of course. The moon is simply and eternally one giant potential mine, the mother lode of all mother lodes."

Bernie glanced up at the sky, blue and cloudless. You can sometimes see the moon by day, but not now. I had the crazy idea that the moon was hiding out.

"What are you going to mine?" Bernie said.

"Water, Mr.—what was it again?"

"Little."

"Water, Mr. Little. There's water on the moon, some in the form of ice at the poles, but vastly more locked up in various compounds. Lunar Imperial already owns the technology to unlock those compounds, and after that, why, le deluge!"

Meelo slapped his knee and laughed and laughed. I had the strangest idea about him, an idea I've never had about any human: he needed to lie down and take a rest. Instead, he was looking at me.

"I've never actually had a dog, but now that all these Moondog photos are rolling in, I've become quite the canine connoisseur. And this fellow—Chet, correct? I never forget a name—this fellow has the goods. Any thoughts on the fair market value?"

"Excuse me?"

"Lunar Imperial will retain all rights to any income streams generated by Chet, but in return we're prepared to be generous. Name your price."

Streams generated by me? Splashing down on hydrants, for example? Was Meelo saying that my streams were not mine but . . . but his? I gazed at his bare feet. At this very moment I was fully capable of generating a generous stream on one or both of those feet, and up and down his suit pants if necessary. I was inching my way a little closer when Bernie took out our license and handed it to him.

Meelo glanced at it. Well, that wasn't quite what happened. Instead, it was a matter of those eyes again, changing from human to machine, sort of taking possession of our license, and then becoming human once more. At least partly.

"You're here as a private investigator?"

"Correct," Bernie said.

"Nothing to do with the Moondog program?"

"We're looking for a former employee of yours."

"I'll put you in touch with security." Meelo began tapping on his phone.

"Maybe we can skip all that," Bernie said. "His name's Holger Niberg."

Meelo's fingers, rather small, pale and smooth, almost like they were new and hadn't been used a whole lot—what a strange idea! I hoped it was the one-and-done type—went still.

"What's he done?" Meelo said.

"Nothing that we know of," Bernie said. "Other than the original expense padding or whatever it was. He may know the whereabouts of someone else we're looking for. That's our only interest in him."

"Who's this someone else?"

"Billy Parsons. He runs a support agency for ex-cons in Gila City."

"Never heard of him or it," Meelo said.

"The word is Billy goes the extra mile for his clients. I'm speculating that Holger's in some sort of trouble right now and Billy's trying to help."

"I don't find any of this interesting," said Meelo.

Bernie smiled. "Maybe you can spice things up. Any idea what sort of trouble Holger could be in?"

"Spice things up—I like that," Meelo said.

"Is it true Holger stole over nine hundred grand from you?"

"Something like that. But the important thing was the breaking of trust, not the money."

"Any idea what he did with it?"

"Gambling debts, I believe. Poker?" He waved his hand at the building. "My people love poker. You can figure out why. What's your IQ by the way?"

"No idea."

"You've forgotten? You were never told? Never tested?"

"Pick one."

"Amazing," Meelo said. "Is there a more important metric when it comes to human beings?" He waved his . . . ghostly? Why would that have popped into my mind, Halloween being my least favorite of all the holidays? But still, wasn't there something about that pale little hand that reminded me of kids in ghost costumes? If I hadn't been able to smell the kids inside the costumes, I'd have gone crazy every single Halloween. I sort of did anyway. But forget all that. Meelo waved his—yes—ghostly hand at the glass building, which was changing shape now, all the hunched over workers coming into view, and said, "I know the IQ of each and every Lunar Imperial employee, from the zenith to the nadir, the nadir currently occupied by Leo Ramirez, IQ 112."

"That's the lowest?" Bernie said.

"But perfectly adequate for Mr. Ramirez's job as an assistant in the shipping department. At the zenith we have me at 199. That's no secret. It's been on the front page of the New York Times. The IQ of the reporter of that piece—I have access to the IQ's of over two billion earthlings, with my database expanding at the rate of ten thousand per hour—was 107." Meelo shook his head. "Journalistic IQs are shocking. But they do explain so much. Holger Niberg's IQ is 166, by the way. Let's say that your own is 115, and I'm being generous. Do you see what you're up against?"

"How could I?" Bernie said.

Meelo's mouth opened, closed, opened again. No sound came out, like the TV when the cord gets unplugged, say when someone who may have had one too many trips on it. Kind of an odd thought, since no cord dangled from anywhere on Meelo's body and there was nowhere out here to plug him in.

Bernie reached out and put his hand on Meelo's shoulder. What a hand! The whole world did a little quiver and started making sense. "Let's not over-complicate things," he said. "We're just looking for solid little facts, like a home address for Holger, or failing that something that will help find him—any special interest he may have, the identity of any friends."

He let go of Meelo's shoulder. Meelo brushed it off with the back of his hand.

"I have no solid little facts, as you put it. I don't think in those terms."

"Ah," said Bernie. "I'm jealous."

Meelo nodded like that made sense. But—Bernie jealous of Meelo? That had to be Bernie's sense of humor. He can be quite the jokester, the jokester side of him sometimes emerging when you'd least expect.

"I understand your jealousy," Meelo said. "I know I've got to lower—to adjust my sights at times. My wives—past, present, and future—all tell me that. They can be so damn entertaining! But, look, how about I throw you a bone? I have no idea where Holger could be living, but I can tell you about his special interest. It's photography, specifically the photography of deep space. His goal, perfectly reasonable—he's a reasonable human being, setting aside his material greediness—is to eventually produce images of the big bang itself." He raised a finger and touched the tip of his rather pointy little nose. "God, if you will," he added.

"Is that what he did here?" Bernie said. "Space photography?"

"Oh, no—that's just his hobby. Or was. Holger's specialty was A.I., with an emphasis on deep fakes. The moon—I'm talking about our new moon, the moon going forward, the useful moon of the future, will first be built on A.I. virtual platforms from the ground up here on earth so preparational dead-on deep fakery of every conceivable lunar detail is essential. I hear you—hard to imagine anything more exciting than that."

Bernie nodded. He has many nods but I'd never seen one like this. It seemed to take a lot of effort, like his head didn't want to move. "Did he have a studio for the photography?"

"More like a small observatory, way out there." Meelo gestured toward some distant hills.

"Where, precisely?"

"Precisely? Like the coordinates?"

"Just a nearby place name will do."

Meelo scrunched up his face. Some faces—Charlie's, for example—look good scrunched up, but Meelo's wasn't one of them. "I have a photographic memory, of course, so if I ever heard a name it will be there."

"Take your time," Bernie said.

Silence.

"A lot of place names out here have old Indian or Spanish names," Bernie said.

More silence.

"Or they come from some geographical feature."

Still more silence.

"Then there are the animal names."

Meelo stood there thinking. What a thinker he was! I could feel the power of his mind. Not quite up there in Bernie territory, but . . . just not quite up there. I'm sticking with that.

"Nope," he said at last. "Holger must not have told me. Otherwise I would have remembered. Simple logic."

Was Bernie about to smile? For a moment I thought so, but no smile came. "Here's our card, in case the information comes your way."

Meelo glanced at the card. "Flowers?" he said.

This was the card designed by Suzie, who'd been with Bernie in what seemed like a long time ago. She'd ended up marrying Jacques Smallian, a dude we liked, who, same as Bernie, had played college baseball, although not as well. None of that was the point. It had all happened in the time before Weatherly. Which also was not the point.

"I'd have expected something with a little more oomph," Meelo said. "Like a gun, for example."

That was the point.

They shook hands. We walked away. "If you change your mind about Chet, get in touch," Meelo called after us.

Bernie didn't answer. We got in the car.

"I'll make it worth your while." Meelo laughed. "You could buy a whole kennel!"

We zoomed away, the Beast never louder. Had I made a big impression on Meelo? That was my takeaway. Nevertheless, my teeth kind of wanted to—well, let's leave it at that. As for the bone he'd promised to throw us? That never happened. I should have known.

The strange bird, now looking silvery, the wings kind of complicated, dipped down low over us and then zoomed away, maybe the fastest bird I'd ever seen. Whoa! I knew what that was. But before the word came to me, Bernie said, "I like the flowers."

Whoa! That was a stunner.

He glanced at me. "I like them a lot."

Eighteen

We stopped at a little roadside place and chowed down, burger and a beer for Bernie, burger—no bun but a bacon bit or two—and water for me. Once or twice Bernie took out our card and gave it a quick glance. The sky darkened, seemed to be darkening way faster than usual. The phone buzzed.

"Bernie? Meelo here. I remembered where Holger's got that observatory. Knew I would, of course. It's south of Gila City, partway up Buzzard's Peak."

Bernie's voice rose. "Buzzard's Peak?"

"Yeah, one of those animal place names, like the Canary Islands or Pigeon Forge."

Bernie said something after that but I missed it. My mind was on the sound of Meelo's voice, a liquidy sort of voice like any moment now he'd be clearing his throat. Which he never got around to when we had that little meet and greet outside his strange glass building in Empty Wells, at least not that I remembered. The point was that sometime in between then and now his voice had wettened up quite a bit. Had the same thing happened to someone else's voice recently, going very, very slightly liquidy? I took a swing at remembering whose and did not connect. That's called whiffing in baseball, the sound of the whiff—like a sudden powerful but brief and tiny storm—my favorite part of the game. Except the ball itself, of course, which is aces.

✿　✿　✿

With a slight wobble, the moon rose, orange at first, but soon shrinking and turning white. We followed it in the Beast, on two-lane blacktop and then into the desert on a track that was nothing more than an occasional rut. Everything's different at night, of course, but I remembered it.

"The moon doesn't know what's coming," Bernie said.

I thought about that. What was coming to the moon? Us? If so, it was going to take a long time. We didn't seem to be getting any closer. In fact, it was possible the moon was actually running away from us. Not running, exactly, since it had no legs, but more like a drifting balloon when a kid lets go of the string.

"I'm not saying we don't need water," Bernie said. "We do. And a whole big water bonanza—to say nothing of all the other bonanzas Meelo has in mind—well, what's the argument against? Something poetic? That's not going to cut it. Am I just jealous? Is it as simple as that? Are all our rational beliefs built on a pile of emotions that we can never—?"

He paused, leaned forward, peering into the distance. I saw a line of hills, blacker than the night sky and gently rounded, except for that one double-jagged peak. From this angle the buzzard was swooping down for sure, meaning we were coming from the back side.

Bernie leaned forward. "Is that a light?"

I saw no light. Then I did. Then I didn't. Meanwhile Bernie cut our own lights and the night came flowing in close around us. And now I did see a tiny flickering light between those two wings. Then I didn't. Then I did. Then I—

"Easy there, big guy."

Whoa! Had something uneasy been going down? Something not unlike growling? If so, I did what I could to put a stop to it. I'm not saying it was me. I'm not saying anything one way or another. But I'm a team player. Let's leave it at that.

We drove. Sometimes nighttime drives are just drives at night.

But in this business there are other night time drives where we, me and Bernie, are bringing the night. This particular night was feeling like one of those. At the same time I heard the flapping of wings and smelled the scent of snakes I couldn't see. We were in charge of all that and more. It's hard to explain.

For what seemed like a long time we bumped slowly along, the moon rising and drifting toward Buzzard's Peak and Buzzard's Peak keeping its distance. Then all at once it was right there, looming above us. Now I could make out that mushroom head white dome I'd seen before, set between the two wings. A light shone in a small round window on the side of the dome. Bernie stopped the car.

"How did I miss this?" Bernie said. "What's wrong with me?"

That was easy: nothing, nada, zip. We stepped outside—me silently and Bernie silently for him—and started toward the base of Buzzard's Peak. Then Bernie stopped, went back to the car, opened the glove box, took out the .38 Special, and stuck it in his belt. I was already feeling tip top. Now I dialed it up a little more, reaching a mood where I might not have been able to contain myself. I lifted my leg against the first bush we came to. And just like that I went back to containing myself, no problem. We're professionals, don't forget, me and Bernie.

A little cactus forest grew at the base of Buzzard's Peak, but after we made our way through it—me out front where I belong—we came upon a sort of trail. This was not a trail that got a lot of action, was mostly just rocks, pebbles, dirt. A man had passed this way, a man I didn't know. Ah, but more recently another man had been by. And more recently than that—maybe even tonight—there'd been another. How many did that make in all? I couldn't tell you. Did I know these jaspers? Not all of them. Some? I thought so.

The trail, what there was of it, wound up around a big rock, then steepened and started zigzagging up and up, sometimes in dark shadow, sometimes in patches of moonlight. I caught a glimpse or two of the dome with the light shining in the small round window, and once a shadow passed across it. Meanwhile I heard some huffing and puffing behind me, and stopped to let Bernie catch up. From somewhere above, up beyond the dome toward the higher wing, came a soft crunch, very faint. Soft, yes, but also strong and on the sneaky side. I sniffed the air for the catty scent of a mountain lion, and there it was, but faint, and not recent. I've dealt with mountain lions before. I'm afraid of nothing—goes without mentioning—but if the possibility of not dealing with them again anytime soon was out there, then I was taking that.

Bernie came up beside me. "We good?" he said, his voice soft, almost like a little breeze. I pressed against his leg. We moved on.

Up and up, the dome vanishing and appearing, each time a little closer. I smelled coffee and also heard music, and someone humming along, all of that rather pleasant and relaxing. Would Bernie and I soon be joining whoever it was? Would there be snacks? My mind was running along those lines when we rounded the last bend and stepped onto a shadowy plateau with the dome looking kind of small in the little space between the buzzard's wings.

We moved toward the dome, side by side, slow and easy. This was reconning the joint, just one of our specialties. Coffee, music, humming: what a peaceful recon! I sniffed the air, my nose on the lookout for snacks, but smelling none. Here's an odd fact: if snacks were in the fridge I sometimes couldn't smell them! How amazing was that? Was it a sure thing that snacks were waiting in the fridge inside the dome? I couldn't think why not. And now we were out of the shadows and at the door of the dome. Was Bernie was going to turn to me and say, "Snack time, big guy!" Before he could there came another one of those soft crunches from up above.

I looked up, way, way up, and there on a ledge not far below the highest point of Buzzard's Peak, stood a figure, framed by the moon. Not a mountain lion: this was a man. He seemed to be reaching into his pocket. Then he was holding some shadowy object, not a gun, more like a TV remote. Yes, all this was happening quite far away, but with the moon right there behind the man everything was clear: the man, the remote, the strangeness—and the fact that he was now pointing that remote straight at us. For a long moment nothing happened, and I even had the thought that nothing was going to happen. Can you imagine that? And me a professional? Then I remembered just that very thing—a professional! Me!—and did my job. In short, I barked, loud and savage, at the same time driving my whole body at Bernie, trying to push him into the shadows.

"Chet! What—"

Then something did happen. First, a flash, not a big one, nothing like you'd see from a gun at night. Also, there was no sound. Just a small, pale flash. Then nothing. Nothing, nothing, nothing, followed by the whole dome trembling, almost like it was afraid—whoa! What a strange thought!—and then . . . KA-BOOM!

The top of the dome rose right up into the night and a blast of hot blue-white light blew me into the air, too, and next I was rolling and rolling across the little plateau and back down the trail. I bumped up against a pile of stones and then something big and strong came bumping up against me. It was Bernie! He sat up, turned and touched my shoulder.

"You okay?" he said. He patted me all over.

I was fine, especially now that we were together. I could have been finer, if his eyes hadn't been open quite so wide, and hadn't been so brightly blue-white.

There was another boom, this one not so loud. We rose together and made our way back up the trail and onto the plateau.

The dome was burning and melting at the same time, blue-white flames shooting up and a thick smoke plume darkening the face of the moon. We moved toward the fire, bent forward, heads down, but the heat warned us away, and in no uncertain terms. We didn't go away. That wouldn't have been us. At the same time, we didn't go closer. We just stood there, our hearts beating together. So loud: I could hear them easily. And then, in all that heat and smoke and noise, something moved—a shadow, a form, a man.

Yes, a man. A man on fire. His hair, especially, was on fire. A horrible sight.

We hurried toward him, forgetting about the heat, the smoke, the noise. He turned toward us. He saw us, for sure. I could see it in his eyes. His eyes were maybe the only part of him that weren't on fire. He opened his mouth like he was going to speak, but only smoke came out. Then he twisted around and slumped down.

We ran to him. Bernie whipped off his shirt and pressed it against him, pressed it against him over and over, smothering the flames. When they were finally out, each and every one, the man lay on his back. In the darkness, what with the moon still hidden by smoke, he actually looked much better, like he might soon wake up and . . . and go on living. It was Billy Parsons. Him going on living was not in the cards. When the door closes on that there's a new smell right away, and I was smelling it now.

Bernie touched the side of Billy's neck. He sat back on his haunches. "Billy," he said. He smoothed what was left of Billy's hair, sweeping the singed ends out of Billy's eyes. Was Bernie about to say something? I thought so, but before he could I heard another soft crunch from somewhere above.

I barked, a bark that echoed around us. What an angry bark! The sound made me feel—well, not good, there was no feeling good right now—but at least a little better.

Bernie rose right away. He looked all around—sideways,

back down the trail, at the dome, now mostly gone with just a few flames popping up here and there, and up, up toward higher peaks. Way up there but lower now than he'd been before and silhouetted against the smoky moon, a man was on the move.

And so were we, with me in the lead. How did I know where to find the trail that led off this plateau and up? Don't ask me. I just knew, and Bernie knew I'd know. I could feel him right behind me, moving very fast for him, as we made our way up a narrow sort of chute—hands and knees for Bernie, two long leaps for me—and then onto some stony zigzags that took us around a bend and onto a sort of backside hill where the trail from above met the trail we were on. The man had already gone by. I heard a brief tumble of loose rocks from somewhere below.

We sped down, my paws hardly touching the earth, but soon the path leveled out and we were following the edge of a cliff. Down below—and not as far as I would have thought, the night maybe playing one of its tricks—I could see an ATV, parked by some bushes and gleaming in the moonlight. At the same time I heard the man speeding up, the sound of scattering pebbles now almost constant. Was he heading for the ATV? What if he got there first? I was wondering about all that when I felt Bernie slowing down behind me.

I glanced back. Bernie was no longer moving and now had the .38 Special in his hand. That was always an exciting sight, especially if some bad dude had drawn down on us first, and rounds were plinking around through the scenery. Nothing like that was happening now but I knew it could at any moment. I've been around, in case you haven't noticed.

Bernie stepped in front of me, a move I didn't like one little bit, and went right to the edge of the cliff, where a soft warm breeze that smelled of daytime was flowing straight up into our faces. Not fast, not slow, his grip not particularly tight, he pointed the .38 Special over the side. Then came a gentle squeeze and

POP. A *POP* followed by a *PING* down below, a *PING* off that ATV. Somehow that was quite satisfying, and so was the next *POP* and *PING*. But the last one—no PING this time—was best of all. *POP!* And then *BOOM*. Well, more like just a small boom, with no *KA* part at all, as in *KA-BOOM*, so the sound wasn't anything to write home about, as humans say, a complete mystery there's no time for now. What mattered was the sight: a lovely jet of flame that rose quite high off the ATV, bringing the smell of a cookout when there's trouble getting the charcoal going and some guest who's maybe had one too many has an idea involving more lighter fluid. After that came burning rubber smells, a few more flames waving around over the ATV, puffballs of smoke, and finally silence.

Bernie looked at me. I looked at him. I was feeling pretty delighted, but I saw no delight in his eyes. Then I remembered: Billy. I stamped out the delight inside me, stamped it out but good. We moved on, the path sloping down, with a row of big and lumpy round rocks on one side and the cliff edge on the other. My delight, turning out not to be completely stamped out, began to stir, even threatening to spring back up. Meanwhile Bernie was somehow in the lead. How had that happened? It was flat out wrong. I moved to correct things at once, and that was when all sorts of activity broke out, which I may or may not get in the right order.

First, out from behind one of those round lumpy rocks, with a sort of furious roar, came charging a big dude, crouched low like a bull, but with his two meaty hands, unlike a bull, of course, out front. He hit Bernie from the side, hit him with a tremendous thud that made Bernie go oomph. His eyes rolled up, white under the light of the moon. Oh, what a terrible thing to see! I felt kind of sick, and at the same time I saw heat. Makes no sense but that was what I saw, hot heat bursting in my mind.

And now Bernie was on the ground, actually at the very edge, with one arm hanging over, into nothing. The big dude strode forward, drew back his leg, and launched a kick, hard and horrible, right at Bernie's head. But that kick never landed. How could I ever allow something like that to happen? It was an impossibility, like . . . like nothing else I could think of. The point was that I, too, was launched, launched at the big dude's leg.

Thump! I hit him with the loudest thump you'll ever hear. At the same time I clamped down on his leg good and hard. In fact, my hardest. He got the message right away. I could tell by his scream. But somehow, even screaming, he managed to get an arm free and punch me right in the face. The next thing I knew he and I were rolling, rolling right over the cliff edge and into nothing.

That was when Bernie grabbed me from behind, grabbed one of my back legs, down low, near the paw. Then he was sort of sliding toward the edge himself. So this was the situation, but what with how quick things were changing I might be getting a detail or two wrong. One thing for sure: Bernie had me by the back leg, had his hand, so strong and lovely, wrapped around it good and tight. I myself was dangling in midair, and it was a long, long way down. I'd had some doubts about that. Now they were gone. Also dangling, and somewhat below me, was the big dude, dangling, if you'll remember, on account of the fact that I'd clamped down on his leg good and hard and was still clamping down on it. And meanwhile Bernie was slip slip slipping toward the edge. I wasn't sure what was going to happen next but I got the idea it wouldn't be good.

"Chet," Bernie said, not loudly, just sort of normal. "Let go."

Let go? But then this dude—a perp, unless I was missing something—was going to get away. Could that happen on my watch? Never!

Around then was when the dude glanced up at Bernie and I saw his face good and clear. It was Werner Irons, the arson guy, if I was remembering right, and maybe the cause of all the problems with Weatherly. He gave Bernie the look of someone who was winning—how odd!—and said, "I'll see you in hell."

Then I felt something amazing. Bernie's hand, always so strong, now took it up a notch, and not just one notch—whatever notches were, exactly—but many many.

"Not so fast," he said, and with more than the mightiest move you can imagine, no offense, he hauled me up to safety, and not just me, but Werner, too, since I still had him in my grasp. Also pretty mighty, if you don't mind me sticking that in here.

Werner sat up, breathing hard. We stood over him, also breathing hard. His face was as white and stony as the moon.

"Who paid you to kill Billy?" Bernie said.

"Billy?" said Werner.

"Billy Parsons."

"Don't know any Billy Parsons."

"No? He just burned to death up there. Didn't you see?"

Werner nodded the slightest nod. "I thought it was you."

"Was that the plan?"

Werner shrugged. Humans have lots of different shrugs. Unless I was missing something, this one meant "so what?"

"Who's paying? Bernie said. "Who hired you?"

Werner clamped his mouth shut.

"Was it Meelo?" Bernie said.

"Never heard of no Meelo," said Werner.

"Meelo Morster. Come on—everybody's heard of him."

"I'm not everybody." Werner glared at Bernie, a scary look. Bernie gave him an empty look back, even scarier, in my opinion.

"Hands behind your back," he said, taking a set of plastic cuffs from his pocket, the red, white, and blue plastic cuffs featured by the Little Detective Agency, just another one of those things that makes it what it is.

Werner put his hands behind his back. Bernie moved around

behind him and bent down with the cuffs. At that moment Werner got an idea. I could see him getting it from where I was, but Bernie could not. With a real quick and powerful corkscrew motion, Werner sprang up. Yes, like a huge spring made of muscle, and at the end of the spring a giant fist uppercutting—but not sweetly, like Bernie's uppercut, Werner's uppercut being all about nastiness—right at Bernie's face, a face, you might remember, in easy striking distance and impossible to miss, what with Bernie bent forward and busy with the cuffs.

But we were dealing with Bernie here, who even when you think is done with amazing you can amaze you again. He ducked. Not much of a duck—and why call it ducking in the first place? But no time for that now. Bernie ducked just enough. That was the point. And the force of all that nasty corkscrewing violence hitting nothing but air took over, as though Werner's huge hard fist was now leading the charge, and he spun around, lost his balance and flew off the cliff, this time on his own. There was a scream, growing faint, and not too long after that a thud, even fainter.

Bernie sat down, lowered his head between his knees. How strange! Like he was the loser. I poked his shoulder, perking him up.

Nineteen

A lot of lawmen and lawwomen showed up during the night, and crime scene tape got strung up all over the desert. They searched all around, finding a red pickup parked on the other side of Buzzard's Peak, but there were no more bodies. Then came pats on the back for Bernie and treats for me. What a fine mood I was in, until I noticed how quiet Bernie was. Then I remembered about Billy and came close to refusing the next chewy that came my way. I mean I came close in my mind. You might not have noticed any difference when the actual chewy transfer went down.

At dawn the DA arrived, riding in a trailer towed by a huge pickup with flashing lights. We were buddies with the old DA— now doing time at Central State Correctional for reasons I'd forgotten or may never heard in the first place—but this was our first time meeting the new DA. The old DA always sent Bernie a fine bottle of bourbon at Christmas, bourbon, now that I think of it, that had been seized from hijackers, an interesting fact I'm recalling just now, and may help explain . . . something or other. Oh, I'd come so close to . . . to putting it all together. Wow. Certainly, close enough to feel pretty good about myself. So I did!

One other thing about the old DA: he was a buddy of me and my kind, and an expert belly rubber. He happened to have a rather big belly himself. I've noticed that big-bellied types make good belly rubbers. There are little clues in life that sometimes pop up along the way. But you have to notice. Otherwise, they might as well not pop up! Whoa! My mind was on fire, even though I'd had no shuteye since I couldn't remember when. What if I never slept at all? Right away I knew I didn't want to go there. So I didn't. Simple as that!

We entered the trailer. The new DA sat behind a desk. She was not the big-bellied type. Her hands were long and thin, with pointy red fingernails that went on and on. I ruled out belly-rubbing. She made a pointy-red gesture at a chair opposite the desk. Bernie sat down. I sat beside him. She didn't seem to notice me at all. Neither was she paying much attention to Bernie. Instead she was turning pages in a file, her eyes going back and forth. Her phone pinged a few times but she ignored it. Some time passed before she closed the file and gazed at Bernie.

"I'd heard of you," she said, "but I hadn't done my research. You turn out to be a colorful character."

Bernie sat there and said nothing.

"Don't get me wrong," the DA said. "I enjoy colorful characters. Just not professionally. My professional goals are monochromatic. So although there's probably been plenty of back-slapping in the last few hours, there won't be any from me. Any questions?"

Bernie shook his head.

"Nothing on your mind?" the DA said.

"That's not what you asked," Bernie said. "You asked if I had any questions."

The DA picked up a pen, opened the file, and wrote something. "Let's start with how you came to be here last night. What was your purpose?"

"That didn't turn up in your research?" Bernie said.

The DA sat back. "You're a dinosaur. That's what turned up in my research."

Bernie a dinosaur? I knew dinosaurs on account of the T-shirt Charlie wore every day for the longest time, a T-shirt that came out of the drier that last time as just a few shreds, finally getting rid of itself. But the point is there were dinosaurs on that T-shirt and Charlie had lots of questions about them that he asked over and over, and over and over Bernie gave him the answers. So I knew a lot about dinosaurs and the DA couldn't have been wronger. Bernie was no dinosaur. Just check out his teeth for starters. Were we done here?

"Meaning," the DA went on, "your days are numbered. I'm not saying it's a low number. Think of how long the old west has been fading away. But look around. The future is here."

"And you're it?" Bernie said.

The DA smiled, a happy smile she seemed to hold for a long time, like someone was taking her picture. "One thing about the future that's already clear—it's all about narrative. So, just for practice, let's hear last night's narrative. It's a three character story—Billy Parsons, Werner Irons, Bernie Little. Shape it for me."

Bernie glanced over at me. What were characters again? Was I one? I'll leave that to you.

"We've been looking for Billy Parsons," Bernie said. "That's no secret."

The DA's smile hadn't completely faded when she said, "Who's we?"

"Chet and I."

Now she looked at me for the first time. "You and the dog?"

"Chet and I, yes."

The DA blinked, a very rapid flutter and then it was gone. So was the last of her smile. "Looks like you were a big success," she said. "You found Billy."

Bernie gazed at her and said nothing. She gazed right back.

"So what comes next?" she said.

"We'll be telling Billy's parents," Bernie said. Then came a change in his tone, very slight, but somehow on the scary side. "That will be us doing it. Not you, not any of your people, no one from Valley PD or Gila PD."

"They're your clients?" the DA said.

"Our neighbors," Bernie said.

"Neighbors," said the DA. She sounded a bit confused. What was confusing about neighbors? Neighbors lived next door, or maybe across the street. She lived somewhere with no neighbors? That was as far as I could take it on my own.

"Correct," Bernie said.

The DA leaned forward a bit. "What about Werner Irons' parents? Are you going to tell them, too?"

Bernie rose.

"What are you doing?" said the DA.

"We're done here," Bernie said.

Wow! Had I known that before him? Strange days often followed strange nights—that's the kind of thing you learn in this business.

The DA rose and pointed a red-tipped finger at Bernie. "I can't keep you—not at this stage—but do you imagine I'm going to simply ignore the fact that a guy you've been feuding with, a feud that screwed up your romantic life, ends up—I won't say gets lured, not at this stage—in some sort of struggle on the edge of a cliff on a dark night? You're a sharp guy. It says so right here." She tapped the file. "What would you do in my place?"

"Find another line of work," Bernie said.

It turned into a fine morning, warm but not hot, with a gentle breeze carrying lots of different flower smells. This was the best time of year for flower smells in these parts. We walked up to the Parsonses' front door. I could hear Mr. Parsons whistling inside, and the swish swish of a broom. Was he enjoying the flower smells, too? Bernie raised his hand to knock but then paused, and we had a strange and longish moment with him just standing, fist in the air, and me beside him, and suddenly panting for no reason I knew. It wasn't hot, as I've already mentioned, and I wasn't tired, having slept curled up on the shotgun seat the whole way from Gila City.

Bernie knocked on the Parsonses' door. The whistling stopped. Then came footsteps, not fast but on the light side, making the soft swish swish of slippers. Slippers are a particular interest of mine, which maybe we can get to a little later.

The door opened and there was Mrs. Parsons, not Mr. Parsons. Well, he was in sight as well, but farther back in the hall, leaning on a broom. Mrs. Parsons held a dustpan. She wore slippers, but otherwise was dressed for daytime, in jeans and a checked shirt, perhaps Mr. Parsons' shirt on account of its being too big for her. Mrs. Parsons had rolled up the sleeves and knotted the shirt at the bottom instead of buttoning it and tucking it in. I hadn't seen her in some time. What I'm getting at is that she seemed kind of . . . stylish. Would that be the word? Once we'd had a case involving a model who'd mixed up the names of her husband and boyfriend, plus there was the girlfriend, whose name happened to . . . but forget all that. My point was that the model had worn—this was the morning of the gunplay part of the story—a too-big checked shirt in this exact same way. Maybe I should add that Mrs. Parsons' face was rosy, her hair was pulled back in a tight bun, and her eyes were just finishing up a smile. She looked good! At the same time whatever was wrong inside her was still wrong, or maybe even more so. My nose doesn't get fooled by things like that. Or by much, if anything.

"Bernie!" she said. "You must be a mind reader!"

"Oh?" said Bernie.

"Daniel? Weren't we just saying let's have Bernie over for coffee?"

"We sure were!"

Mr. Parsons beamed like having Bernie over for coffee was the best idea ever. He left out the part about having Chet over for water and possible treats, maybe thinking the idea couldn't be improved on.

"They sent Edna home," Daniel said. "There's been a remarkable turn of events."

"Now you know that's not what they said, Daniel." Mrs. Parsons turned to Bernie. "It's just that the thingamajigs have stabilized for the moment."

"I'm glad to hear that," Bernie said.

"Bless you," said Mrs. Parsons. "It's like this . . . this . . ."

"Low pressure zone," said Mr. Parsons.

"Oh, perfect!" Mrs. Parsons said. "It's like this low pressure zone has suddenly lifted and the light is shining in. But come in, come in. We may even be able to scare up some snacks."

Whoa! Snacks got scared? Of what? Getting eaten? I'd never thought about that before and didn't want to think of it again. Was Bernie wondering along the same lines? For whatever reason, he was lingering in the doorway, showing no interest in going inside.

"Um, where's Iggy?" he said.

Good question. Had there ever been a time when the Parsonses' door was open and Iggy wasn't right there, trying to flee the coop? And right now he wasn't even yip-yip-yipping? But he was home, all right. I could hear him breathing, slow and steady, somewhere upstairs.

"So interesting," Edna said. "We've been talking about it all morning. How would you put it, Daniel?"

"It's like what you said about the low pressure zone and the light shining in," Mr. Parsons said. "I think something of the same's going on with the little guy. He's kind of a—" He turned to Mrs. Parsons.

"Maniac," she said.

Mr. Parsons laughed and laughed. Mrs. Parsons joined in.

"Our little maniac!" said Mr. Parsons. "But—"

"But he's also very sensitive."

"Exactly. And when you came home the light shone away all the tension he's been under and he just went right to sleep."

"On our bed," Mr. Parsons said.

"On our bed," said Mrs. Parsons.

"And I swear he has a smile on his face."

"But come in, come in. The moment he senses Chet's in the house he'll be up and at 'em." Mrs. Parsons stepped aside to let us in, making a little welcome gesture with the dustpan.

Bernie leaned in a bit like he was about to move, but his feet stayed planted on the ground. His face went from normal to the paleness of bone just like that.

Mrs. Parsons gave Bernie a close look. Her eyes narrowed. She turned back toward Mr. Parsons. His face was going white.

"Dead?" he said.

Mrs. Parsons cried out something, maybe not words, just a terrible sound. She thumped her chest so hard I thought she'd crush it. The broom slipped from his hands and started to fall in a strangely slow way. Mr. Parsons was falling, too, also slowly, so slowly, in fact, that Bernie was able to get over there and catch him before he hit the floor.

Bernie, kneeling, held Mr. Parsons, keeping his head raised. All at once Mrs. Parsons was there, taking over, rocking Mr. Parsons gently. Tears dripped from her eyes but she didn't make a sound. The tears themselves did make a sound, like the very faintest rain landing on Mr. Parsons' face. His eyes opened. A tear of hers landed in one of his open eyes. He didn't seem to feel it. His mouth opened and he licked his lips, lips and tongue so dry.

"I need to die now, Edna," he said.

Mrs. Parsons shook her head. "Not now, Daniel."

"But—"

"No buts. This is about . . ." For what seemed like the longest time she couldn't come up with whatever she wanted to say. Then, very softly, so softly that even I almost missed it, she said, "Billy." She glanced over at Bernie, kneeling on the other side of Mr. Parsons, and found her normal voice, not a strong one to begin with. "We need to do what's right for him, don't we, Bernie?"

Bernie gazed at her. His eyes seemed rather damp. Was that a tear pooling over one lower eyelid and running down his cheek? Had I ever seen such a thing? Well, yes, but from my Bernie? I searched my memory but before I came across anything Mr. Parsons suddenly sat up straight and stared right at Bernie.

"I didn't know the voice of my own son?" he said. "Is that the final end?"

Mrs. Parsons began to shake. She shook and shook, couldn't stop. Bernie laid a hand on her shoulder. She shook him off, or did the shakes themselves shake him off? Maybe that makes no sense, but it did at the time.

From upstairs came sounds from Iggy. He was whimpering.

Twenty

"What the hell's going on?" said Captain Stine.

Lou Stine's an old buddy, as I'm sure I've pointed out already. We were parked cop style, driver's side to driver's side, at Donut Heaven. I was in the shotgun seat, busy with a cruller. Normally Lou and Bernie would be munching on doughnuts or perhaps bear claws, but not now. That was odd, especially since Lou had asked to meet us here, if I'd gotten things right. What was Donut Heaven without doughnuts? Or bear claws? Or crullers, of course. True, it was a nice-sized parking lot with nice smelling freshly painted straight white lines and plenty of trash barrels, but with no doughnuts or bear claws or crullers what was the point? I just didn't get it.

"You tell me," Bernie said.

Lou's face went a dark red. Hey! Was he angry? How could he be angry at us? Wasn't his kid named Bernie? Or possibly middle named, whatever that may be? I myself am Chet, pure and simple. Is that a better way to go? I went back and forth, but I ended up at forth. That's often the case with me.

Lou's voice rose. "That's how you're going to ruin yourself, right there. Don't you know what you're up against?"

"Spell it out."

"The DA, for chrissake! Now you're on her radar."

"So?"

Lou shook his head. "You're like a child," he said.

Wow! I could sort of see that. Kids had something they all seemed to lose along the way. Maybe when they got so big, it leaked out of them, whatever it was. But it hadn't leaked out of Bernie! Just one more reason to love him, although Lou didn't seem to be getting that.

"And she's no child, believe me," Lou went on. "She is about power. Period. Meaning her own power—growing it and wielding it. But the wielding is secondary. It's just the demonstration that she has it. Following me so far?" He gave Bernie a look and then said, "Didn't think so. I'll make it easy for you—she's going to pull your license."

"How can she do that?" Bernie said.

"Just watch," said Lou. "Or you can try to head her off."

"How?"

"I don't know but I'll help you figure it out. That's if you didn't do what she thinks you did."

"Which is what?"

"Billy Parsons was on the run from you. You hired Werner Irons to take him out, planning on taking out Werner yourself after he was done, on account of this feud you had going on with him. That's about it."

Bernie laughed, the kind of laugh called laughing in someone's face, a laugh I'd never seen from him, and never wanted to again.

"I take it that's a denial," Lou said.

"For God's sake, Lou!"

"Can you prove you didn't do any of that?"

"I don't have to. I'm presumed innocent. America—remember?"

Lou sighed.

Bernie made a call.

"Hey!" said Meelo on the other end. "I was just going to call you."

"What about?"

"All this . . . this violence that seems to have gone down last night. Are you okay?"

"Yup."

"And Chet?"

"He's fine, too."

"Good, good."

"Meelo? I appreciate it, but is this about the Moondog contest?"

"Oh, no. Well, always, until you say yes. But I just wanted to see if you were all right."

"With the hope that I'd be on the shelf for a while? And Chet would not?"

"Ha ha! I'm not denying that the thought occurred. But it wasn't top of mind. I wanted to talk about Holger. Where is he?"

"I don't know."

"What's going on?"

"I don't know that either."

"Are you in the Valley?"

"Yes."

"Do you know the Lab of Tomorrow?"

"No."

"It's a little research center of mine, near the college. I'm there right now."

The college is downtown, not far from the towers although not like them at all, the buildings much smaller but also more solid, mostly made of desert-type reddish stone and looking like they'd been around a long time and would be around for a long time more. But the best part was the college kids. And there they were, so many of them out in the sunshine on what I believe was called the quad, hitting the books. Books that perhaps today had been forgotten, so instead they didn't waste a moment but got busy with frisbee tossing, beer ponging, and spliff passing arounding. College kids knew what was what. That had always been my takeaway.

The Lab of Tomorrow was on the next block. The lobby was dark with little pools of light. There was nothing in it but a small screen that seemed to be drifting around in midair. It spoke: "Second door on the left."

I wanted to be out of there at once, but instead I followed Bernie, followed him from behind, which wasn't me at all. A door opened in front of us and we entered a white room with a small pool inside and soft music playing. Meelo, wearing a white bathrobe, sat on the edge of the pool, busy on his phone.

"Welcome," he said. "I'll be right with you. This will only take two minutes and twenty-seven seconds."

"Huh?" said Bernie.

Meelo gestured at the pool. "My daily session."

"You're taking a bath?"

"Ha," said Meelo. "Ha ha ha. I'm talking about my daily session of ultra-cold immersive therapeutic decalcification."

"Sounds scary," Bernie said.

Meelo wagged one of his soft, white fingers. "Not as scary as death. Do you realize that all of our thinking—I'm talking about each human being and the whole history of human thought—is warped by the fear of death?"

"I don't know much about the history of human thought," Bernie said.

"It's never too late to learn."

"No?" said Bernie. "Didn't you just get through saying it's always too late?"

"Ha," said Meelo, but this time he didn't go on with more ha-ha-haing. Instead he gave Bernie a quick glance and said, "So you're one of those rare types who's smarter than he looks. In my world I'm constantly dealing with the reverse. It's a real problem."

"Is Holger Niberg one of those?"

"Oh, no. Holger's just as smart as he looks. That's not his issue."

"What is?" Bernie said.

"A lack of imagination," said Meelo. "Can you believe it? He didn't see the point of what we're doing here."

"You mean going to the moon?"

"No. He gets that. I'm talking about our work at the lab. It's not just the ultra-cold. That's one tiny aspect. We're into everything you can think of and more—cellular redesign, pre-proteinization, mitochondrial metabolic hibernation—you name it."

"I don't understand a word you're saying," Bernie said, which had to be his sense of humor, often popping up at unexpected times. Bernie understands everything, which I'm sure you know by now.

"But I just spelled it out in black and white, so even the meanest intel—". Meelo cut himself off and took a long breath. "We're deep-sixing death," he went on. "That doesn't mean simply extending human longevity. It means extending human longevity infinitely."

Bernie was silent. Meelo watched him. He had a waiting look that reminded me of cats, specifically how they wait for a bird to take that one more little step.

"What about dogs?" Bernie said at last.

"Dogs?" said Meelo, sounding confused. But what was there to be confused about? Wasn't that the perfect answer to cats? I myself have known that from the get-go.

"Yeah, dogs," Bernie said. "What about eternal life for them?"

"I hadn't thought of that," he said. "Do you mean as a sort of experiment, trying things out on them first?" That one zipped right by me. But Meelo sounded kind of excited about it, whatever it was.

"No," Bernie said. "I do not."

Meelo nodded. "Probably wise from a cross-species cost benefit point of view." He glanced at his watch and . . . and seemed to speak to it. "Two twenty-seven." Then he slipped off his fluffy white robe—revealing that he was wearing what I believe is called a Speedo, perhaps not the best choice in his case—and lowered himself into the pool. "Oooh," he said. "Whoa oooh whoa. Ah." He looked up at Bernie. "It takes getting used to."

"What's the temp in there?" Bernie said.

"Twenty-eight degrees. And I know what you're thinking. How do we keep it from freezing. Answer: the addition of three ounces of a proprietorial fluid."

"That wasn't what I was thinking," Bernie said.

"No?"

"I was wondering why twenty-eight degrees."

"Ah. That was the water temp the night the Titanic went down."

"What's the connection?"

"You don't see it?"

Bernie shook his head.

"It's not really a scientific connection." Meelo shivered. "It's more of a zeitgeisty thing. The idea wasn't actually mine. Well, all ideas generated by, at, and for Lunar Imperial are mine under the terms of our company charter, but I meant more in the everyday common man sense."

"Whose idea was it?" Bernie said.

"Holger's," said Meelo. "This was before the discovery of his transgression. But I don't bear him any bad will. Once he'd done his time, that is. In fact, I even offered him his job back. He didn't want it."

"What was his job?"

"A.I. Didn't I already tell you?"

Or something like that. Meelo's voice was back to its non-liquidy self. Did it have something to do with this ice bath, or whatever it was? Meanwhile his lips were turning blue, and his heart was beating very fast, although no one else seemed to hear it. I began to worry about him.

"Yes," Bernie said. "But specifically."

"Specifically everything—that's the point." Meelo checked his watch. "Three two one—blast off!" He rose from the pool— actually seeming to leap right out of there, although no real leaping could be managed by a human of such a body type. He wrapped himself in his robe and danced around, pounding himself all over. "I feel great! Greater than great! Greatest!"

He high fived Bernie. Bernie high-fived him back, perhaps a little too enthusiastically, what with how Meelo came close to tipping right over. But he didn't seem to mind. "I've done the calculations. Or had them done—by Holger, now that I think of it. Every session in the pool turns the clock back four hours and eleven minutes."

"How did Holger come up with that figure?"

"With A.I.," said Meelo. "He can apply A.I. to anything. Jeez, Bernie, for the umpteenth time."

"How does A.I. handle umpteenth?" Bernie said.

"Ha!" said Meelo. And then, with a sideways look, "Ha," again, but more quietly. He patted himself a few more times, but the dancing had come to an end.

"Why didn't Holger take his job back?"

"He'd evolved. His word. Seen the light."

"In prison?"

"Exactly. He heard a visiting speaker who'd made a big impression on him. How to live a good life, all that."

"Who was the speaker?"

"Why, that Billy fellow. The one who burned to death up on that mountain. Incidentally, I was wondering how you found your way up there so fast."

"Excuse me?" said Bernie.

"I told you about Holger's observatory but I didn't know the location. How did you nail that down?"

Bernie backed up a step. "Are you okay?"

"What do you mean?"

Bernie tilted his chin toward the pool. "From the ice bath."

"Okay? Better than okay. Didn't I just go through all that?"

"Does it affect your memory?"

"Sharpens it like you wouldn't believe."

"Then you remember that you called me with the Buzzard's Peak info, less than twenty minutes after we left here."

"Called you?"

"You said it had come to you like you knew it would."

Meelo shook his head slowly from side to side. His forehead wrinkled up and he looked quite a bit older. This was an odd moment. Everything seemed strange in that dreamlike way that sometimes seems to fall on you even when you're awake. It's a problem but I've found that action is always the answer. So therefore—wow! So-therefores were normally Bernie's department—I jumped right in the pool! And the whole dreamlike thing went poof, as I knew it would.

The water felt great. I'm a good swimmer, in case you didn't know. Swimming is trotting through water. That's all there is to it. Can you trot? Then you can swim! I swam around and around Meelo's little pool, throwing in some back and forth. The water felt great! Was there supposed to be something especially great about it? If so I missed that part.

Twenty-one

What was this? Bernie putting on his suit and tie? When had that last happened? Not that he didn't look good in a suit and tie. Let's be real, as humans like to say. Although not Bernie. He never says let's be real to anybody. Also he never calls anybody chief, or throws the first punch. He does say make it a double.

Uh-oh. I'm off track. The problem, when you've got a nose like mine, is why bother to stay on track? You can always pick it up again, no problem. But back to Bernie's suit, a very dark gray, perhaps even black at one point, and now beautifully faded. He has two ties, one blue, the other with a pattern of lights that flashed if he remembered to put in a new battery. I was hoping for the flashing lights tie—probably goes without mentioning—but he went with the blue. Then came the tying. Bernie used the mirror for that. How nice to see two Bernies! But whoa! Who was this tough-looking hombre standing right next to him? No one gets away with—

"Chet! For God's sake! Keep it down!"

The tough-looking hombre, who'd suddenly gotten into a barking mood—kind of a ferocious barking, even scary, although nothing scares me—went silent. Was . . . was there something about mirrors? Something I'd learned but not completely remembered? While I was rooting around in my mind, finding not much at the moment, Bernie said, "Windsor knot, big guy. Kind of complicated but the only one I know. My dad taught me how to—"

He went silent and didn't say another word until we were

halfway out the door, when he glanced at me and said, "Let's change that collar."

Have I mentioned my collars? My everyday one, which I was wearing at that moment, was gator skin, meaning I always carried, very faintly, the scent of gator. My other collar is black leather. It's for dress-up. Bernie switched my collars, hung the gator skin one on a hook by the door. Now I was carrying, very faintly, the scent of cattle. No need to go any further with that. Which would you rather smell like—gators or cattle? Exactly. But if Bernie said this was a time for dress-up then that was that.

Not much later, we were in the part of Pottsdale where the fancy stores peter out and the golf courses begin, pulling into a parking lot outside a small adobe church—churches always easy to spot on account of the steeple with the cross on top. As for what went on inside, that was a bit of a mystery. True, I'd been in one once, but the place had somehow put me to sleep right away. Was that what churches were for? Catching Zs? I couldn't take it farther on my own.

Bernie glanced around. The parking lot was pretty much empty. "We're early." We got out, neither of us hopping, Bernie probably because he hardly ever did, and me because, well, I just didn't feel like it. Why not? I didn't go there, my go-to when why-nots were suddenly in the picture.

We walked around the church, Bernie giving it a careful look. "The old Spanish mission," he said. "Deconsecrated now, but this was where the old-timers got buried when I was a kid."

Something about Bernie when he was a kid? Wow! That by itself was so interesting. Bernie had been a kid—just imagine!

There was a graveyard behind the mission. Ah! Old-timers getting buried—that fit right in. I knew something about graves, having dug up a couple in the course of my career. The way it's done is that first Bernie tips over the stone and then we dig, me taking care of most of the digging. Once it turned out the wrong body was down there. The second time there was no one at all. That was all I remembered about those cases, except for the fact that we didn't get paid for either one. But the fun of digging! Who's luckier than me? Was Bernie about to start tipping over gravestones? If I had to get out of the car all over again, I'd be hopping now! You can bet the ranch! I've actually seen that done, and more than once, maybe stories for later.

Bernie stopped in front of one of the stones, maybe not as old as those around it, what with not being so worn and faded. This stone was about as high as my head, squarish, and made of desert-type red rock. Bernie bent down before it, but no tipping happened. Instead, he cleared away a few twigs and straightened a small cactus that was growing at the bottom. The cactus— the kind with the little red flowers—slumped back over. Bernie straightened it again, this time in no uncertain terms. The cactus straightened up again, this time looking like it would stay that way. But maybe not. Should I just dig the thing right up and take care of things? I was going back and forth on that when I realized we were not alone.

I turned, and there, coming around the church were Weatherly and Trixie. The sun shone on Weatherly's glossy black hair and on Trixie's glossy black hair as well. I've probably mentioned that Trixie has one white ear and so do I, a fact that's led to some complications in my life. But I wasn't going to get into that now. Instead, I gave Bernie a low rumbly bark. And wouldn't you know it? Trixie gave Weatherly a low rumbly bark, sounding identical—no, out of the question—but perhaps similar to mine. Right there, by the way, was the kind of complication I meant.

Bernie rose and turned. Weatherly was turning our way at the same time. He looked at her and she looked at him. Nobody moved. The red-flowered cactus slumped over. Then Weatherly started walking, not fast, in our direction, Trixie right beside her. I actually thought Trixie took the first step, but I might have been wrong. I was distracted by a very unusual smell, coming off Bernie, namely human nervousness. There's nothing unusual about human nervousness. It's out there all the time—on the street, in office buildings, in bars and restaurants. But from Bernie? Maybe once or twice in the past when we'd been in—no, when you, an outsider, might have thought we were in real trouble. How could we be in any sort of trouble right now?

They came up to us. Weatherly didn't speak and neither did Bernie. Trixie and I sniffed each other, no avoiding that, but we got it over and done with in a hurry. Weatherly glanced at the writing on the gravestone, then took a second look.

"Your dad?" she said.

Hey! It was nice to hear her voice. I'd missed it, even if it wasn't as lively as usual, actually not lively at all.

Bernie nodded.

"Harry," she said. "You never mentioned his name."

Bernie shrugged.

Weatherly took another look. "Just the name and the dates."

Bernie nodded.

She turned, facing him for the first time. She was nervous, too. The scents of their nervousness rose and merged in the air.

"Lots of times there's an inscription," Weatherly said.

"Yeah," Bernie said. He glanced down, noticed that the cactus had slumped. Then he frowned and said, "My mom would have been in charge of that."

"I haven't met her y—" Weatherly cut herself off and started again. "I never got to meet her."

Bernie winced, just the tiniest bit, like he'd felt a sudden pain inside, "No," he said. "She lives in Florida."

"I know that."

"Right. Sorry."

Weatherly gestured toward the gravestone. "Do you remember the funeral?"

"No."

"How old were you again?"

"I'm not sure I ever told you."

"You did. You were young, that's all I remember."

"Eight," Bernie said.

"So maybe you didn't come."

"Maybe not."

She checked the gravestone again. "He didn't live that long. Comparatively, I mean."

"Smoke and drank," Bernie said.

Weatherly smiled a very slight, very quick smile, hardly happening at all. "There's your inscription," she said.

Now Bernie smiled, too, a longer lasting one than hers. "He gave me one piece of advice."

"You have my attention," Weatherly said. I got the feeling that this confab was taking a turn for the better.

"Always piss downwind and downhill and you won't go wrong," said Bernie.

Wow. Had I ever heard anything more important? It explained . . . well, everything, the whole wide world. Weatherly's eyes opened slightly wider, like she was about to burst out laughing. But then they clouded over, like bad weather storming in.

"Is that where I'm standing?" she said.

Bernie rocked back slightly, like he'd been hit. "Huh?"

"Downhill from you?"

What was going on? The ground here in this graveyard was level and flat. I didn't get it. But maybe Bernie did. He raised his hands, palms up, like . . . like he was getting busted.

Weatherly's voice sharpened. "I didn't come to see you. It was for that lovely old couple. I knew you'd be here, of course. I came in spite of that."

Bernie lowered his hands, held them stiffly at his side. "What can I do? I was wrong. And you know I know that."

Weatherly was silent.

"Say you know," Bernie.

Her voice rose. "No one makes me say anything. As for what you can do, how about nothing? You're like a bull. What the hell's going on? What happened on that goddam mountain? Did you set Irons up?"

"What are you talking about?"

"Did you lure him up there? That's what they're saying."

"Who's saying that?"

Weatherly slashed the air with her hand, like she was cutting down what Bernie had just said.

Now his voice also rose. "We didn't set up anybody. We got set up."

Weatherly glanced at me. When she spoke again there was way less anger in her tone. "By who?"

Bernie didn't answer, just shook his head.

"Is someone trying to kill you? Who, Bernie?"

Bernie didn't answer. Maybe he would have, except before he could the steeple bell tolled, just once and quite softly for a steeple bell, but it was enough to change everything. We walked around the mission in single file—kind of strange since we had plenty of room—with Weatherly first, then Trixie, then Bernie, and me last, although by the time we got out front, where there were now lots of people, I was in the lead. So things were looking up. That was my takeaway. Also anyone who was trying to kill Bernie—or hurt him in any way, or even muss his hair—was a goner.

The mission was small on the outside and even smaller on the inside. It was packed with humans, plus not two but one more than two—oh, what did they call it again? I was so close!—members of the nation within, namely me, Trixie, and Iggy. Did I include me? Me. There. Your mind has to go backward and forward at tho same time in this life, and also keep tabs, whatever those are exactly, on the here and now. Ever noticed that? Not so easy, amigo.

The mission was downstairs with rows of benches, where most everybody was, and a sort of upstairs wraparound with a single row of folding chairs set behind a stone railing built on stone pillars, all this stone old and worn, almost soft to the touch. We were upstairs—Bernie, me, Trixie, Weatherly, with the mailman who delivered on Mesquite Street on one side of us and a tall, thin blond woman I didn't know on the other side, and next to her Axie, wearing a shirt and tie, his rat tail the same color as the blond woman's hair, and beside him, Axel—his dad, if I had all this under control. With my muzzle resting on the floor between the pillars, I could look down below, where Mr. and Mrs. Parsons sat right up front, she in a wheelchair and Iggy on her lap. Next to her was Gillian, dressed all in black, and Felix, dressed in white pants and a white shirt, all that white catching my attention for some reason. A guitarist sat at one side of the little stage, one of those stages barely raised above the floor, playing soft music.

Axel leaned toward us. He was dressed sort of like Bernie, in a dark suit and dark tie, but also he had heavy gold cuff links while Bernie's sleeves just had buttons. Gold has a smell by the way— not nearly as strong as copper, which surely even—which I have every confidence you can smell—but more pleasant, with just the faintest hint of honey. The truth is I love the smell of gold. And the taste! Have I mentioned the fat gold nugget—golf ball size—I once held in my mouth? Not between my teeth, but right on my tongue where I could taste it. I believe I did mention it. But no harm in mentioning it again. I could almost taste it now.

"Bernie," Axel said in a low voice, although not a whisper. I could feel it through the stone floor. "Meet my wife, CeeCee. And you know my son, Axie. Axie, say hi to Mr. Little."

Axie didn't turn to look at Bernie, but he did say, "Hi."

"Hi, Mr. Little," said Axel.

"Hi, Mr. Little," Axie said.

Bernie smiled. "Hi, Axie," he said. "Hi, CeeCee."

"Hi, there," she said. Then she glanced at Axel and sort of started over, saying, "Hi, Mr. Little."

"Bernie," Bernie said.

"Okay," said CeeCee, "Bernie." She threw another glance Axel's way. He didn't seem to notice, instead was gazing down at the guitarist on the stage, still softly playing. CeeCee leaned a little closer to Bernie. "It's so awful," she said.

Bernie nodded. Was she a woman of a certain type? Bernie tends to run into problems with women of a certain type. I was pretty sure CeeCee belonged in that group, until I picked up her smell. There was the add-on floral part coming from little bottles, of course, and beneath that strong human female scents—a certain one way down deep making me think she was noticing Bernie in a big way—but my nose was also picking up a lot of anxiety. Women of a certain type didn't get anxious. Bernie was not going to run into problems with CeeCee.

Axel turned back to us and smiled. He patted CeeCee's knee, one of those friendly human gestures you see from time to time. The anxious smell got stronger. She pressed her legs closer together.

"This is a lucky break, Bernie, sitting beside you like this," Axel said. "CeeCee was just saying we should find a way to thank you, weren't you CeeCee?"

CeeCee nodded, at the same time blinking in what seemed like confusion. Had I ever seen that combo before? I searched my memory and found not a whole lot at the moment.

"For what?" Bernie said.

"Good question," said Axel, coming very close to a laugh. "The news stories weren't very informative. But for whatever you did up on that mountain—Buzzard something?—thank you."

"Buzzard's Peak," Bernie said. "But we got there too late. And Chet is the one who deserves any thanks."

Then all eyes were on me. Did I happen to be in the middle of a yawn right then? Perhaps. "Well, well," said Axel. "Interesting." And he appeared to be on the verge of saying more, but down below, Garth, the man-bun dude from ProCon, was stepping onto the stage, microphone in hand. His gaze swept slowly over all the folks. He took a deep breath.

"Three words," he said. "Put yourself second. Those three words changed my life and the lives of many others, including some of you."

That brought tears to the eyes of just about everyone. I didn't know what was going on in their minds, but I sure knew what was going on in mine: three! Wasn't that what I'd been trying to think of, and not so long ago? Three, three, three! I wasn't going to forget it now, not ever, no sirree! Three, three, three.

Meanwhile I seemed to be missing Garth's little talk, or whatever this was. Did a screen get lowered at the back of the stage? Did a sort of movie with Billy Parsons in it get shown? Don't rely on me for the details. Remember that yawn I mentioned? Some yawns are for no reason, just a sort of mouth stretching that feels good. Other yawns can mean you're sleepy. It turned out that my yawn was that kind.

Afterwards there was some hugging and some crying out in front of the mission.

A lot to keep track of but I have a clear picture in my mind of Weatherly bent over Mrs. Parsons' wheelchair, and Mrs. Parsons holding Weatherly's hand in both of hers. Also there was a moment when Gillian, her eyes dark, and dried-up tear tracks on her cheeks, said, "Oh, Bernie, I just don't understand. Can we talk?"

"Of course."

"Maybe out at my place? Or Axel's? I'd like him to be there."

"Why?"

"He's such an organized thinker and I'm so scatterbrained."

"I disagree."

"Maybe not always, but now for sure."

"Okay," Bernie said. "Let me know when."

Gillian squeezed Bernie's hand, her own hand bearing that moon and stars tattoo, which seemed a bit sad at the moment. How strange! Meanwhile a lot of hand squeezing was going on, like all these human hands had a job of their own to do. Maybe not so hard to understand. Think of us in the nation within, specifically think of our tails. Iggy's, by the way, a strange loopy little thing, was still at the moment, an unusual sight. Iggy himself lay in the shade of a bush, his eyes open. Trixie pawed at him to get him up and moving—an excellent idea I wished I'd had myself—but Iggy just lay there. Was harder pawing the answer? I tried some of that. Iggy just lay there, gazing at the sky.

"Here, Trixie," Weatherly said.

Trixie, who was about to try pawing Iggy again, hurried over to Weatherly. That bothered me—I wanted Trixie to play some more, maybe do some chasing around—but I couldn't think what to about it. Bernie went closer to them. He was within touching distance of Weatherly. There was no touching.

"We're leaving," she said.

"I'll walk you to your car," Bernie said.

"That's all right."

"Okay."

"Bye," she said. She turned and walked toward the street, Trixie beside her.

"For now," Bernie said, his voice quiet, the voice he uses just for talking to him and me. Did Weatherly hear? I didn't know but without turning back she made a little gesture with one of her hands, like a plane wagging its wings. Wagging: you had to love Weatherly, and I did.

As she and Trixie got into their car I noticed another car, black with tinted windows, not a cop car but what Bernie called coppish. One of the rear windows was rolled down and a woman in the back seat was watching Weatherly. I recognized her right away, from her pointy red fingernails, even though they weren't in view. Kind of strange, maybe, but it was the DA, for sure.

I barked my low, rumbly bark. Bernie's head came up and he looked around right away. The tinted window was closed.

We ended up being the last ones out there. And even then we didn't leave right away. Instead we walked around to the back of the old Spanish mission, Bernie leading and me following, not our usual MO at all.

We moved through the graveyard, stopped in front of the squarish red stone with the floppy cactus at its base. Bernie made no attempt to straighten it back up. Instead he just touched the stone, a quick touch, not at all lingering. Then we were out of there.

Twenty-two

Bernie's phone buzzed. He glanced at the screen. "Hi, Leda," he said.

But it wasn't Leda. "Dad?" said Charlie.

"Charlie?" Bernie said.

"I'm calling you," Charlie said. "On Mom's phone. Hi."

"Hi," Bernie said. "This is a first. Is she there?"

"Who?"

"Mom."

"She's in the Jacuzzi."

"Where are you?"

"In the kitchen. Her phone's on the thing. By the fruit bowl. I picked it up."

"And figured out how to call me?" Bernie said.

"Hi," said Charlie.

"Well, this is great. How're things?"

"What things?"

"Like school."

"I hate school."

"How come?"

"I'm immature."

"Who told you that?"

"Esmé."

"What does it mean, immature?"

"You don't know?"

Bernie smiled. Whatever was going on was making him very happy. So: more, more, more.

"I don't think you're immature," he said.

"No?"

"You're just right for your age. Which is what again?"

"Dad!"

Then they were both laughing, even with the same sort of timing, although the sounds they made were very different, of course, Bernie's voice being so deep and powerful and Charlie's so high and light.

"My team's the Sharks," Charlie said.

"What team?"

"Soccer. Our first game's today."

"No one told me."

"I did."

"When."

"Now. We got a game today."

"When?"

"Later. I'm the goalie."

"I thought you were a forward."

"Now I'm the goalie. The goalie plays goal."

"We'll be there. In fact, we can pick you up if that's okay with your mom."

Silence.

"Charlie?"

Bernie checked the phone, glanced at me. "Looks like he hung up." He laughed again, this time softly, to himself. Then he took off his suit and tie and everything else he'd worn to the Spanish mission, and took a shower, on the longish side. I started getting excited, for reasons unknown.

I'd had experience with many different kinds of balls, but not soccer balls. Why was that? I'd never even thought much about soccer balls. But why not? One thing for sure, I'd been missing out, which I discovered during the warm-up before the game, when I managed to—well, perhaps a story for another time. Right now, Bernie had his hand resting lightly on my back and we were sitting in the first row of a small set of metal bleachers.

Meanwhile out on the field we had a lot of fun going on. There were all these kids—some in green jerseys, some in yellow—chasing a soccer ball all over the place, a soccer ball that never seemed to do what the kids wanted it to do, but to be fair to the ball the kids had forgotten how to pick it up so whenever they got close all they could manage to do was kick it with their feet and off would go the ball again, bouncy bouncy and free. Wow! What a game! You could even say it was right up my alley, like I was born to—

"Ch-et?"

Something about me? I was simply sitting quietly, a very good boy. Meanwhile a man in a green cap up on the bench behind us glanced down at me, and then at Bernie. I liked him from the get-go. Why? I had no idea. Was it because he seemed—from the look in his eyes—to be the wide awake type, at the same time having one of those gentle faces, a combo you didn't see every day? I had no idea.

At that moment there was some excitement in the stands, not a whole lot of excitement on account of the crowd being on the smallish or very smallish side, but at least some. Out on the field a big kid in a yellow jersey had gotten loose from the others and was zooming toward a sort of netted something or other—whoa! Possibly the goal?—at the same time kicking the ball forward like he could make it obey, at least a little. And in front of the goal, just finishing up with a bit of nose picking, stood Charlie, all alone. Was he even paying attention? I had the feeling that paying attention was the best idea right about now.

The big kid came closer, closer, drew back one foot and kicked the ball—thump, a lovely sound—and the ball went sizzling—oh, yes, I could hear that sizzle—toward the far corner of the goal. But what was this? Charlie like I'd never seen him, diving in the direction of the ball, his skinny arms outstretched? Yes it was! And Charlie like I'd never seen him caught the ball in his two hands, snatching it right out of the air! That was a big moment in my life, the moment I realized that in fact Charlie was primo in the brains department, the only kid who'd figured out that hands were way better than feet when it came to playing ball.

And I wasn't the only one who'd noticed that the kid turned out to have a head on his shoulders. Why else would there be all this cheering? Although not from Bernie. He looked shocked. I didn't get that at all. Then, mouth hanging open—not a Bernie-type expression at all—he clapped his hands, just once and softly. At the same time I could hear his heart suddenly pounding, like . . . like it wanted to take off and fly. Crazy idea, of course, but no time for it anyway, since Charlie like I'd never seen him wasn't done. He flew through the air, hit the ground, rolled and bounced up, the ball still in his hands, and kicked it downfield. And what a kick! Long and high and soaring, a thing of beauty. It landed way way down there, bouncing alone on the grass, but all at once a kid in green came swooping over, corralled the ball—hey! With her feet, yes, but that turned out to be a lot like herding some difficult goats into a pen, something I've done from time to time, and hoped never comes up again—and took off toward the other goal, where a kid in yellow, the other goalie, if I was getting this right, was waiting, highly alert, not picking his nose. Was there something I should have been noticing about the kid in green? Yes! She had a top knot. It was Esmé! Boom! She kicked that ball so hard! It started in low but rose and rose like a plane taking off, out of the reach of the leaping goalie—not quite the leaper my Charlie was, just pointing that out—and into the top of the goal.

Cheers from the crowd. "Yay, Esmé!" Bernie yelled.

The man in the green cap cleared his throat and leaned forward. At the first sound of his voice I remembered him. "Charlie's dad, right? We met at that Christmas party."

"Um," said Bernie. "Uh, I am. Charlie's dad, that is. Bernie Little."

"That was quite some party," the man said. "Esmé never stops talking about you. And Chet. I'm her dad—Malachi Carter."

"Of course!" Bernie said. "You played the trumpet, and so well." Excellent! Now Bernie and I were on the same page, as humans say. We belong on the same page—that's one of my core beliefs.

They shook hands, and then Bernie said, "Care to—" at the same time Malachi was saying, "Mind if—" and then Malachi was sitting beside us.

"And that was quite some goal," Bernie said.

"Thanks," said Malachi. "Although I never know if that's what to say. I mean I didn't do anything."

Bernie laughed. "But it rubs off on you."

Malachi gave Bernie one of those second looks and nodded slightly. Then he turned toward the field, where the kids seemed to be on a break, snacking on orange slices along the sideline. Charlie ate a slice and stuck another behind his ear.

Malachi laughed. "He's such a funny kid. His perspective— it's just so original."

"Who are you talking about?" Bernie said.

Malachi's eyebrows—unmissable, although not as unmissable as Bernie's—rose. "Seriously?"

"Charlie?"

"Yes, Charlie. For example, Kristina over there—" Malachi pointed to a tall, square-shouldered woman in a green track suit, slicing oranges for the kids. "—she's the coach, asked him, last practice this was, when he made a couple of saves just like the one you saw, 'How come you enjoy playing goal so much?' And you know what he told her?"

Bernie shook his head.

"'I like getting in the way.' Pretty cool, huh?"

Bernie nodded, just a tiny nod, hardly any movement at all. He glanced over at Charlie. A chubby kid was playing that armpit flapping kids' game—a boys' only game, in my experience—to make farting sounds. Farting is a huge subject, one of the very hugest, so there's no time for it now. The point is Charlie was laughing his head off. Bernie blinked a couple of times, looked very close to being confused, which also was not a Bernie expression.

"Kristina told him, 'me, too,'" Malachi went on. "She was the back up goalie for Greece, a few World Cups ago."

"Huh," said Bernie.

The ref blew her whistle and the kids ran back out on the field. Malachi got busy with his phone, taking pictures. I know taking pictures on account of how some folks like taking pictures of me, even some of the perps. What a life! But meanwhile Bernie's eyes weren't on the field. He was watching Malachi, and I could feel him thinking.

"You played Roy Eldridge's trumpet solo from 'If You Were Mine'?" he said.

"At your request," Malachi said. "And you handled Billie Holiday's vocal."

"Good grief," said Bernie, meaning he must have forgotten how well he'd done. "But you played great, if I remember."

"Not disgraceful," Malachi said. "For an amateur. I've got no illusions about that. But I've always loved music. Not to sound too pompous—one of my failings, recently pointed out by Esmé but my wife agreed immediately—it's my belief that music reveals the beauty of math even to folks who hate it."

Bernie thought that over. "Esmé was saying something about this. You're a mathematician?"

"Applied," said Malachi, losing me completely, although I was already there.

"You work in tech?"

"I've got a small consulting company, smaller than yours."

"Smaller than mine?"

Malachi glanced at me. "I don't have a Chet." He smiled. "I do have a fish named Buttercup."

Right away I was looking forward to meeting Buttercup. That's how I roll. Was Buttercup one of those fish that live in a bowl high up on a shelf, perhaps, although never impossibly high? Life just keeps passing around opportunities. And all you have to do is be there! Who came up with all this?

Was Bernie feeling the same excitement? Maybe, because at that moment he snapped his fingers, a real loud snap, like a gun shot. "Toasters are going to be smarter than us!"

"Excuse me?" said Malachi.

"That's what Esmé said. She was talking about your work. You're in A.I., correct?"

"True," Malachi said. "But I never said that about toasters. Esmé—" He stopped and shook his head. "Do you ever get the feeling that your work is other people's play?"

"No," Bernie said.

"Maybe not yours," said Malachi.

They glanced at each other and looked away. Silence fell. Then came the thump of the soccer ball, and Bernie said, "A.I. came up in a case we're working on."

"Is that the one about the missing reindeer?"

"That's all wrapped up."

"You found the reindeer?"

"Chet did."

My tail wagged but I was sitting on it, so maybe not noticeably.

"Sorry I missed that," Malachi said. "The truth is I don't follow much that's going on out there." He raised a hand. "I'm not proud of it. It's a liability, for sure. But tell me about this case.

Does it involve patents? There's a lot of patent litigation in my world right now."

"I don't think it does," Bernie said. "But I can't rule it out. Does the name Billy Parsons mean anything to you?"

"No."

"Werner Irons?"

Malachi shook his head.

"What about Holger Niberg?"

"Holger? I know Holger. Or knew him, at least. I haven't seen him since . . . well, in a number of years."

"Meaning since he went to prison?" Bernie said.

"That's right," Malachi said. "Excuse me for being euphemistic. I wouldn't want to gossip about him."

"Holger Niberg is linked to a murder," Bernie said. "So we're beyond gossip." He spoke quietly but somehow with even more power in his voice. I loved that one!

Malachi sat up straight. "He killed someone?"

"I didn't say that," Bernie said.

"Then involved in what way?"

"Did you know he had an observatory?"

"Observatory?"

"For taking astronomy photos."

"I knew that was one of his hobbies," Malachi said. "I didn't know about the observatory. Maybe it's new."

"Maybe," Bernie said. "It's up on Buzzard's Peak."

"Where's that?"

"South of Gila City. What can you tell me about Holger?"

"Have you met him?"

"No."

"I can show you a picture."

Malachi got busy with his phone, turned the screen toward us. Malachi and a thin-face guy with a crew cut seemed to be riding in . . . the truth was I had no idea what I was looking at.

"That's us on the Colossos in Heide Park," he said.

"You like roller coasters?" said Bernie.

"Not me. That was my first and only time. We were in Germany for a conference. Roller coasters are another one of his hobbies—wooden only."

"What was the conference about?" Bernie said.

"All things A.I.," said Malachi. "Only six years ago but practically every word that was spoken is dated already. I was there to talk about some particular coding ambiguities. Holger gave a talk on what alien A.I. would look like."

"You lost me," Bernie said, but that was probably just his sense of humor, popping up out of nowhere.

"With the coding ambiguities or alien A.I?" Malachi said.

"Both," said Bernie. "What's alien A.I.?"

"A concept of Holger's. Our A.I. is an artificial replica of our human intelligence, en masse. But what would A.I. be like if it was created by alien beings with their own intelligence?"

"Like Martians?" Bernie said.

"Well, we know there are no Martians. But that's the idea. Let's imagine some planet—" He glanced at the field, where the game had stopped while some kid's shoes got put back on. "—call it Messi, with intelligent creatures who come up with their own A.I."

"You're saying if they were smarter than us then their A.I. would be better?" Bernie said.

"Sort of," Malachi said. "The title of Holger's talk was Garbage I. In, Garbage A.I. Out. He did this thought experiment, the upshot of which was that alien A.I., if confronted with human A.I., would know at once that it was only a machine and not human, whereas we ourselves are already at the point of being easily fooled in that department."

Bernie thought about that. I could feel him going deep down in his mind. Malachi watched him think. At that moment, for some reason, it hit me that they were friends.

"Why did you ask if I knew those other people—Billy, was it? And Werner?—before you asked about Holger?" Malachi said.

Bernie came up from wherever he'd gone. "Occupational hazard," he said. "But since we're on the subject of who you know, what about Meelo Morster?"

"I know of him—who doesn't?—but we've never met. That's where Holger got himself in trouble, stealing from the company. Have you tried Meelo?"

Bernie nodded. "He thought Holger might have been trying to cover some gambling debts."

"Poker was another one of Holger's hobbies. But it's hard to imagine him losing. He was a brilliant poker player, or so I've heard. I don't gamble, myself."

"I'd have bet the ranch on that," Bernie said.

Malachi laughed. He got Bernie's sense of humor, knew right away we had no ranch. They were friends for sure.

"Any idea where he played poker?" Bernie said.

"None."

"Did he go to Vegas?"

"Not that he mentioned."

"Is he married? Does he have kids?"

"No kids that I know of. He was divorced—I believe his ex-wife was Estonian, and lives over there. Was there a second divorce? I'm not sure. When I knew him there was no romantic partner. I . . ."

"Go on."

"Just between us?"

"Okay."

"I suspect he was seeing, you know, hookers."

"What makes you think that?"

"Nothing certain. And it might make you think that he's uncentered somehow. I wouldn't want to leave that impression."

"Uncentered?" Bernie said.

"Not in control. Lost in life."

"There are lots of guys in prison like that."

Malachi raised a finger. "Not all."

"Lots," Bernie said again.

Malachi looked down. "There was this one time—" He stopped himself and started over. "There's this coffee place I go to in Pottsdale. And the craziest thing, like right out of the Wild West, hidden away in the back part is a, well, a brothel. And one day, when I was picking up some beans, who came strolling out of the back part but Holger! I actually ducked behind a fern."

Bernie looked at Malachi sort of . . . fondly. For one weird moment I thought he was going to pat Malachi's shoulder. "What kind of beans do you get there?" he said.

"Desert Dark," said Malachi.

"Me, too," Bernie said.

Malachi's mouth opened in surprise, but before he could say anything, Charlie and Esmé were with us.

"You guys weren't even watching," Esmé said.

"What's a fern?" said Charlie.

"Hey!" said Malachi. "We saw the whole thing!"

"Then what was the score?" Esmé said.

Twenty-three

The Beast rumbled beneath us. If I squirmed a little bit closer to the gear shift, it got even rumblier. I squirmed a little bit closer. Bernie glanced over, then glanced over again.

"Um, Chet? Where'd you get that?"

I lay still, took a swing at pretending I wasn't even there.

"I guess the where of this isn't really the question. But how did I not notice?"

I had no answers to any of this, whatever it was. The truth was my attention was elsewhere, namely on these . . . remains . . . was that the name? Close enough. In any case, what a wonderful mouth feel! The soccer ball—now flattened and floppy and totally herdable, if that makes any sense—had a wonderful mouth feel but the insides were the best, really special. When was the next soccer game? I waited for Bernie to tell me, but he didn't say anything, just gave me a scratch between the ears. A quick scratch scratch, one two over and done, and oh so nice. Would this drive be going on forever? That was my hope.

Meanwhile we crossed the Rio Calor bridge and entered Pottsdale, one of nicest parts of the whole Valley. Soon we were passing Pepe's Mandarin, best Chinese food around, according to Bernie. He always orders tequila chicken balls but right now we rolled on by and parked a few blocks down in front of a store with a big coffee cup sign hanging over the sidewalk. This would be Livia's Friendly Coffee 'n' More. Had coffee just come up with Esmé's dad? Sometimes everything suddenly makes sense. Other times it goes the other way. I'm good with either!

Bernie opened the heavy wooden door, the kind you see on old ranches in these parts. Right away we were in a world of coffee smells, little scent streams, all a bit different, swirling around, coming together, drifting apart. Coffee smells are one of the great human inventions, the drink itself, sampled only a few times by me—how could you not, what with part-full paper cups practically in every gutter?—not my favorite. Water's the drink for me, cold and clear being better than warm and muddy, but I'm really not fussy.

There was no one around except a somewhat older woman wearing a dark pantsuit and a string of pearls. Livia Moon, of course, but what was she doing working the counter out front? I'd only ever seen her in her office in back, in the 'n More part of the business.

"Bernie!" She hurried out from behind the counter, a big woman, big and curvy, and gave Bernie a tight tight hug that went on and on, at one point involving some squeezing of his upper arms. "You look great."

"Uh, well, right back at—"

"Stop! Don't even try. Look at the size of me!" She twirled around. Did she move very gracefully, like a dancer? That was my takeaway.

"Well, there's no one single, ah, standard," Bernie said, "like ah, for example, what was his name?"

"What are you trying to say?"

"The painter guy, you know."

"A house painter?" Livia said. Her eyes were twinkling. Livia was one of those humans that's ready for fun at just about any time, not unlike us in the nation within. "Because I'm big as a house?" she went on.

"No, no," Bernie said, "what I meant was . . . was Rubens! That's it—Rubens!"

"Oh, Bernie!" Livia threw herself around him again, this time giving him a kiss on the mouth, a big, long one. Right about then is when the door to the kitchen opened and a young apron-wearing man came in.

"Thanks for filling in, boss. I—"

"No problem, Ricky, but don't make it a habit." Livia stepped away from Bernie. "Meet my old friend Bernie. We go way back to my early days when I had a teensy weensy establishment near Fort Hood and Bernie was protecting all of us from the bad guys. I'm very patriotic, as you know."

"Yes, boss."

"So please get Bernie here whatever he wants—on the house."

"A pound of Desert Dark, Ricky," Bernie said. "And I'll pay."

"Bernie's pigheaded in case you hadn't noticed," Livia said. "Anything else you need around here, Bernie, also on the house?"

"How about a few minutes of your time?" Bernie said.

"As long as you like, sweetie pie," said Livia.

Ricky's mouth fell open. The reason was obvious. Bernie had the finest human head I'd ever seen, nothing at all like a pig. I knew pigs, by the way. You don't want them in your life.

"Holger Niberg," Bernie said. "A client or former client."

"What's he done?" Livia said. "Or do I not want to know?"

We were in Livia's office in the 'n More part of her operation, which did have a desk but was more like a nice living room with a soft rug, some puffy-looking sofas and chairs, and a small bar, where Livia was now pouring a beer for Bernie, a glass of white wine for herself, and a bowl of water for me.

"His name keeps coming up in a case we're working," Bernie said.

"So the answer's B, I don't want to know." Livia served the drinks, then went to her desk and flipped open her laptop. "N-I-B-E-R-G, first name initial H." She gazed at the screen. "Hasn't been here for some time." She reached for her phone. "Tulip? Got a minute?"

A door opened and almost at once in came Tulip, wearing a little black dress and bedroom slippers. Human eyes sometimes light up. It's lovely to see. Tulip's eyes lit up now and she hurried over to me. "Chet! How's my big buddy?" Then she gave my head a pat pat. No one pat pats like Tulip. Well, Autumn, a pal of hers, was maybe just as good, but Autumn no longer worked here, had moved on to something else, perhaps with our help, if memory serves, although it doesn't always serve very well, like now, for example.

"Bernie here is interested in one of our clients," Livia said.

The pat patting came to an all too soon end. "Oh, hi, Bernie," Tulip said. "Who's the client?"

"Holger Niberg," Bernie said.

"He's not a client anymore," said Tulip.

"Oh?" Livia said. She closed the laptop, softly and firmly at the same time.

"Holger had a—what did he call it?—awakening? Reawakening? One of the two. Last fall, this was, after he got out of jail."

"Back up, please," Livia said.

"Kind of shocking, right?" Tulip said. "I mean someone like him doing time. All the jailbirds I know are kinda dumb. Holger's real smart, the smartest guy I ever met. There was this one night with a full moon right out the window—" She pointed toward the upstairs. "—and he just lay there and explained the whole universe. And, boss! I understood it, at least for a moment."

Livia smiled. "There's a perk."

Bernie smiled, a tiny little smile. Was something just a tiny bit funny? That was as far as I could take it on my own.

"What did he go to jail for?" Livia said.

Was that a question? Was this an interview? Normally Bernie

says interviews go better when we're asking the questions, but this time he did not.

"For being self-damaging." Tulip held up her hand. "I know, I know. But that's what he told me. The actual crime was some kind of theft—embezzling, maybe?"

"So someone else got damaged," Livia said.

"Should I have told him that? I didn't even think of it at the time."

"Nah," said Livia. "How long was he in for?"

"Three years. He got out in September. I saw him the very day."

"Here?" Livia said.

Tulip shook her head. "He took me out for coffee."

Livia frowned. "We have coffee. It's what we do. Partly."

"Which part brings in more revenue?" Bernie said.

Livia turned slowly and gave Bernie a long long stare, so long he ended up looking quite a bit like Charlie in the end. "Are we friends, Bernie?"

He nodded.

"Do friends nose around in each other's beeswax?"

"Never again," Bernie said, the perfect answer if bees were in the picture, but that was Bernie every time.

"Right answer," Livia said, meaning she and I were like this, as humans say. "My point, Tulip, is that we have rules around this place. Safety rules."

"It was just coffee," said Tulip.

"Where?" Livia said.

"Pecos Pete's."

Livia thought that over. "What did you have?"

"My usual—goat milk macchiato."

"And?"

"Nothing like ours, boss. Not even close."

"Um," Bernie said.

Livia turned to him. "Goat milk's good for a lady's skin," she said. "You wouldn't understand."

"I won't even ask," Bernie said. "I was just wondering what got talked about at Pecos Pete's."

"That was the funny part," Tulip said. "But I didn't realize till later. It was basically a dear john letter from a john!"

"Ha!" said Livia. "Who wouldn't love my job? You see new things every day!"

Wow! What a stunner, although I couldn't quite figure out why.

"You're talking about his reawakening?" Bernie said.

"Exactly," said Tulip. "But before he got to that he asked if I'd consider marriage."

"To him?" said Livia.

Tulip nodded. "I told him what I tell all the others—I'm not that kind of girl."

Bernie started to laugh but he cut himself off and said, "Whoa! This happens?"

"You can be so naïve, Bernie," Livia said. "It's just one of the things I love about you."

"Maybe you should marry Bernie, boss!"

"I believe he's engaged," Livia said. "Isn't that right, Bernie?"

"I believe so," said Bernie, but very quietly and with an inward look.

Then they were both watching him. He didn't seem to notice.

"Even some of the married ones," Tulip said. "But Holger's proposal, if that's what you want to call it, was different. If marrying him was out of the question then this was the last time we'd see each other. That was when he got to the awakening part. He'd gone to a talk at the prison. The speaker had been an inmate there himself, and maybe now ran some sort of outreach thing, I didn't get the deets. But that talk changed Holger's life, or at least that's what he told me."

"Who was the speaker?" Bernie said.

"Billy something. I'm not sure he mentioned the last name. Holger just called him Billy."

"How did the talk change his life?" Livia said. "From what to what?"

Bernie nodded, hardly any movement at all, but if you knew Bernie you knew it meant he was a big fan of Livia. I know Bernie.

"At first I just thought it was that—oh, who were those guys again? With the tall hats?"

"The Puritans?" Bernie said.

"Yeah," said Tulip, "that Puritan thing, taking all the fun out of life. But Holger had an answer. This Billy character says there's a difference between fun in life and pleasure in life. Fun is like the waves. Pleasure is like the tide."

"Are you buying this, Bernie?" Livia said.

"Renting with an option," said Bernie.

Livia laughed, so that must have been Bernie's sense of humor again. We were really getting along great, this little group. I could have done with a snack long about now, nothing major, just the butt end of a Slim Jim, but no complaints.

"Did Holger say anything about putting yourself second?" Bernie said.

"Hey!" said Tulip. "You know about this?"

"Not nearly enough."

"But that's the key, putting yourself second. Holger was actually thinking of getting a tattoo—2ND. As if he was the tattoo type! But he rejected it because that would have been cultish. He'd made up his mind to reject many things."

"Like?" Bernie said.

"Well, a lot of his old life."

"His job?"

"Uh-huh. He's brilliant with tech and all that. You know the guy down in Gila City with the moon rocket thing? Holger was high up in that. He's not going back there, of course—it's where he got in trouble. Plus he's not going back to the tech world at all."

"What's he going to do?"

"Something human. That's how he put it."

"Like what?"

"I asked him that. He said he didn't know but would figure it out."

"How?"

"By watching the stars."

"Watching the stars?" Livia said.

"He has—he had an observatory on Buzzard's Peak," Bernie said. "Did he mention that?"

Tulip shook her head.

"What was he going to do for money?" Bernie said.

"He wasn't going to need much," said Tulip. "The big problem was the money he still owed."

"To who?"

"He didn't say. The gamblers, I think, where he got in trouble in the first place."

"The money he stole wasn't enough to repay them?" Bernie said.

"No."

"How much more did he need?"

"He didn't say."

"Gambler or gamblers?"

"Maybe just gambler."

"Where is this gambler?"

"I don't know. Was the gambling online? I can't remember if he said that but it was poker, for sure."

"Did he mention online?"

"A lot. And offline. Holger's going offline for the rest of his life. 'I'm a human being,' he said. 'And human beings can't be quantified.'"

There was a long silence. I realized that yes, I was definitely hungry. But still no complaints.

Tulip turned to Livia. "I didn't love him or anything like that but I was kind of fond of him. What if I'd said yes?"

Livia shook her head.

Twenty-four

Bernie always drank his coffee black, but as we pulled away from Livia's Friendly Coffee 'n' More he was sipping cream-colored coffee from a little paper cup. He shot me a quick glance and raised the cup.

"Actually not bad at all. How's my complexion?"

I had no idea what he was talking about. Anyone can get tired, of course. I gave him a close look. Yes, perhaps he needed a quick nap. I curled up on the shotgun seat to give him the idea.

"I'll order it the next time Weatherly and I . . ."

What was this? Something about coffee, perhaps? I kept a close watch on him. After a while he said, "That's if there's ever . . ." And then he went silent again. I yawned a huge yawn. He didn't seem to notice, but then maybe he did. Something certainly happened, although not about naps, because all at once he sat up straight, wide awake and spilling a few drops from the paper cup. They fell on the console, right in front of my nose. Normally I'd quickly lick them up, but before I could I picked up an odd smell—drifting inside the coffee smell, but a much fainter scent, although not so faint I couldn't place it. That would have taken some doing. But back to this faint scent, clearly goatish. I left those drops where they lay, slowly drying on the console.

"Do you remember what she said? It was in the graveyard. 'By who?' She was giving me my marching orders, big guy, but I was too dumb to pick up on it."

I'd been right the first time. He needed a nap. I rolled over and stretched a big long stretch. No reaction from Bernie, no "let's swing by the house and grab some shuteye." Instead he got on the phone.

"Etta? Bernie here."

"My, my. We're becoming soul mates."

Bernie was silent.

"Bernie? Still there?"

"I actually wasn't going to ask you this, but . . ." He went silent again.

"Spill it," Etta said. She had one of those voices that have lots of smoking and drinking in them. If it hadn't been for the goat smell I might have been able to pick up the booze and smoke right over the phone.

Bernie cleared his throat. "Have you ever been to the old Spanish mission?"

"There's a question. I didn't go to Harry's funeral, if that's what you're asking."

"It wasn't."

"But once I went to stand by the stone. I told him I missed him. No one lies when they're speaking to the dead. Ever spoken to the dead, Bernie?"

Bernie got a very faraway look in his eyes but said nothing.

"Don't tell me," Etta said. "You spoke to him, too?"

"No."

"'Kay," she said. "'Kay.' But this is a detour. What did you call about?"

"Werner Irons."

"We're not done with him? It was on the news by the way. Somehow your name didn't come up. I wouldn't have taken you for an éminence grise"

"A lucky break since I don't have a clue what that is," Bernie said. Etta laughed. "But," he went on, "I need to know more about him. Any contacts—professional, familial, romantic."

"Don't you have sources at Valley PD?"

"I'll pay you, of course," Bernie said.

Etta laughed again. "Just yankin' your chain. I know what's going on, young man. The new DA's something else, ain't she?"

You don't need me to point out that Bernie was not chained at that moment. We'd both been chained in our career, once each. You can imagine what happened to the chainers in the end.

"Don't want your money," Etta went on. "When this is over you give me an exclusive on the whole story."

"Why?"

"I've been doing some writing, that's why."

"You want to be a writer?"

"I am a writer, blockhead. I've been a journalist for fifty years."

"Sorry."

"And also I know someone."

"Who?"

"You wouldn't know. He's high up at Netflix. I'll get back to you." Click.

Bernie turned to me, about to say something very important. But before he could the phone beeped again.

"Bernie? Gillian here. That talk I mentioned. When would be a good time?"

"Now?"

"How about in a couple hours?"

"Your place?"

"Axel's," she said. "I'll text you the address."

"All this astronomy has gotten into my thinking," Bernie said, as we drove into Gila City.

Astronomy? Whatever that might have been we didn't need it, Bernie's thinking being one of our strengths at the Little Detective Agency just the way it was.

"It's like we're in an expanding universe where the more we

find out the less we know. For example, Meelo calls us with the location of Holger's place up on Buzzard's Peak, and then when we ask him about that call he goes blank. What's that about? Meelo's name meant nothing to Werner. And why would I be Meelo's target? Because I'm not enthusiastic about you going to the moon?"

What was that? Maybe the strangest thing I'd ever heard, certainly from Berrnie. I counted on my mind to forget it as soon as possible.

"And what was Billy's motive for stealing the forty-seven K?" Bernie went on. "Was it for Holger? So he could pay Meelo back some of what he'd stolen? But Meelo didn't care—he offered Holger his job back. Or was it a payment to the gamblers? Did Billy think he could somehow recover the money before anyone noticed? Wasn't he too smart for that? But Heisenberg says we can't simultaneously measure . . ."

He went silent. A good thing. Heisenberg—a perp for sure, and I hope he looks good in orange—has popped up before, never leading to anything good. I needed a vigorous shake but there was no room, so I held that shake inside as we drove through a nice neighborhood in Gila City, into a nicer one, and then another even nicer—meaning we were going up and up—and finally came to a wall with a tall gate in the middle. It opened all by itself and we followed a tree lined lane to a Spanish-style house that didn't seem very big. We parked in front and hopped out, me actually hopping, hopping somewhat urgently. The instant my paws touched down I gave myself a tremendous shake. Did a moth fly off me? That had to be my imagination.

"Chet? You all right?"

Never better. We walked to the front door. Bernie raised his hand to knock, at the same time saying, "Don't be fooled, Chet— it's one of those places that turns its back to the road."

From somewhere above, came the kind of laugh that I believe is called a chuckle. This was a man's chuckle, deep—and also barrel-chested, if that makes any sense. I looked up and saw what looked like a gold bar set in the wall above the door, the sort of place you might see a horseshoe or a painted sun. Was it possible this thing that looked like a gold bar also smelled like a gold bar? Yes it was. As for where the laughter had come from I had no clue. Gold bars are silent, of course. And then I remembered something I'd heard many times, both from good guys and bad: Money talks.

Perhaps some follow-up thought might have occurred to me, but before it could the door opened—another one of those by-itself openings—and a voice, this one a woman's, and what was more a woman I knew, namely Gillian, spoke. "Hi, Bernie. We're on the upper deck. Down the hall, second left."

Yes, a voice I knew, but now it had lost all its oomph. We walked down a wide hall lined with big brightly colored pictures, all of playing cards. I knew about playing cards from our one and only visit to the Thursday night Valley PD poker game a while back, where I may or may not have chewed up or possibly completely eaten something called the joker. You might think that was a bit on the naughty side and so did I, at least a little, until on the way home Bernie said, "I wish you'd done that sooner." Have I already mentioned that night? It was when we found out that there were mortgages beyond two. Nothing to do with me, of course, since two is almost always the end of the line numbers-wise for me.

Meanwhile we were stepping into the sky. Well, not really, but it felt like that. We were on a deck jutting out from the house, which turned out to be set on the edge of a mountain, which I'd never have guessed from the road. And down below was another deck jutting farther out and below that another and maybe even one more. In short, the house—whose was it again?—turned out to be a mansion. Had Bernie said something about that right from the jump? My Bernie.

Over on one side of the deck was a pool. Felix and Axie were in it, both floating on blow-up rafts, Felix with his eyes closed and Axie open-eyed and watching us. CeeCee sat nearby under an umbrella, her eyes hidden behind big sunglasses. A long glass table stood on the other side of the deck, a table with a very nice spread laid out, a spread that included deviled eggs, which Bernie is a big fan of, for some reason, and a heaping bowl of those little cocktail hotdogs. The name hotdog is bothersome but so far in this life I've gotten past it every time. Gillian and Axel sat at the table, not close to each other, and not eating. Oops. Just then Axel popped a cocktail hotdog into his mouth, the toothpick looking tiny in his hand. Things change all the time in this business. I got ready for anything.

Gillian and Axel rose, but only Gillian came toward us. Her face was puffy, her eyes were red, she smelled of salty tears.

"Thank you for coming, Bernie." She took his hand in both of hers. "Thank you."

"I'm sorry," Bernie said.

"You have nothing to be sorry for."

"Your loss."

"Thank you. You're a good man. That's what Billy always—" Gillian's eyes filled up and she went silent. She led us over to the table. "You already know Axel?"

Bernie nodded. Axel dropped the toothpick into an ashtray— beside a cigar butt that was still smoldering—and they shook hands.

"Good to see you," Axel said. "I'm sitting in at Gillian's request. If that's a problem, just say and I'll make myself scarce."

"Sitting in on what?" Bernie said.

Axel turned to Gillian. Sometimes a movement like that wafts interesting smells your way, or at least mine, no offense. This turned out to be one of those times, the smell that got wafted from Axel being Trixie's. Very, very faint, but I know Trixie's smell inside out and outside in and could never miss it or mistake it for anyone else's. It's so like my own, except for the female part. I sniffed around a bit, hoping to pick up her trail. There was no trail. I shifted over and stood next to Bernie.

"Maybe I'm just being stupid, Bernie—or masochistic, which is what Axel thinks—"

"On, no, not at all," Axel said.

"—but I need to know what happened."

"I'll do my best," Bernie said.

"Happy to leave," said Axel.

Bernie glanced around, seemed to take in the boys, drifting by the pool, CeeCee all shadowy under the umbrella, and the long, long view.

"No," Bernie said. "You can stay as far as we're concerned."

Axel smiled. "We is you and the dog?"

"Chet," Bernie said.

"There's nothing like PR," said Axel.

"PR?" Bernie said.

But maybe Axel didn't hear him, because he motioned toward a chair and said, "Sit down, sit down."

At that moment a roly-poly woman dressed in what I recognized was a restaurant cook's uniform, the best human uniform out there, appeared, carrying an enormous fruit bowl. I'd have preferred an enormous bowl of spare ribs but that's something I have yet to see. I haven't given up hope. To tell you the truth I don't even know how to do that.

"Thank you, Mama," Axel said. "Bernie, meet my mom. She keeps everything shipshape around here."

Why did I glance over at CeeCee right then? No idea, but I happened to catch her with her sunglasses off. She was eyeing Mama in a way you couldn't call friendly.

"Mama, say hi to Bernie."

"Hi," she said, not looking at him.

"Nice to meet you," Bernie said.

"Ja," said Mama. She went back inside the house.

"Your mom's German?" Bernie said.

"My father was posted there," said Axel. "Air force. He crashed on take-off when I was a kid."

"Sorry to hear that," Bernie said.

"Life goes on," Axel said. He rubbed his big hands together. "Now Bernie, help us with some of this food! And how about a drink? Just name it."

"I'm good, thanks," Bernie said. He turned to Gillian. "Where do you want me to start?"

Gillian sat down, kind of slowly, in the seat next to his. Axel sat on the other side of the table, facing them. He reached for what I believe is called a decanter and some glasses from the sideboard, somehow holding all that in one hand. I had a strong desire to see Bernie do the same thing—and right now!—but no idea how to make that happen.

Axel looked over to the pool and raised his voice. "Axie! Rustle up some dog treats."

Axie sat up on his float. "Huh?"

"Something wrong with your hearing? Dog treats. Now."

Axie muttered something under his breath.

"What was that?" said Axel.

"Nothin'."

I'd caught what Axie said—as I'm sure you already guessed—but no one else did because eyebrows would have been raised and none were. Axie slid off the float, swam across the pool, climbed out, crossed the deck and entered the house through a sliding door he left unclosed. Lots of info flows by in a job like mine so you have to sort through until you're left with what's important. Once—this was after perhaps an extra bourbon or two—Bernie said, "We're like bears in the rapids, waiting for the right fish." Bears? Us? That's a picture I'd like to forget, but can't. Never mind all that. Right now, I sorted through the info flow out here on this deck, and what was left? Dog treats. I stood up.

"I really don't know where to start," Gillian said. "What was Billy doing up on that mountain in the first place?"

"It was like you said. He was trying to help a former inmate in trouble."

"This Holger person?"

"Holger Niberg," Bernie said. "Did Billy ever mention him?"

Gillian shook her head. "He tried not to bring work home. Not even in his head. The funny thing—" Her voice broke. I could feel her getting a grip inside. She started over. "The funny thing was Billy wanted to hear all about my work at the salon, like what's the hardest kind of hair to cut and did I ever make a mistake and how to fix it." A tear rolled down her cheek. "We had so much fun, just with little things." Axel reached across the table and patted her hand.

I glanced over at the sliding door. Any moment now Axie would be hurrying through with the treats. How long could it take?

Meanwhile, Axel was pouring from the decanter. Tequila, if you're interested: there's no missing the cactus smell. He passed around the glasses. No one except him seemed to be thirsty.

"So, Bernie," Axel said. "This Niberg fellow?"

"Have you heard of him?" Bernie said.

"Negative," said Axel. "Billy never discussed work with me."

"But I thought you'd lent money to ProCon."

"Not lent," Axel said. "Donated. So, yes, we discussed work in that sense." He smiled a big smile. "Caught me in a lie, Bernie!" He clinked his glass against Bernie's and drank.

"How much did you donate?" Bernie said.

Axel was still smiling. "Do we know each other well enough for that sort of sharing?"

Bernie, not smiling, gave him a direct, Bernie-type look, although that little scene seemed oddly distant. Why was that? My goodness. I was no longer standing by the table? But was now rather close to the sliding door? You might say directly in front of it? Life was full of surprises, and who would have it any other way? CeeCee, sitting close by under her umbrella, didn't seem to notice me, had her eyes on Bernie and Axel, although I couldn't be sure of that, on account of her sunglasses being back on. Maybe her eyes were closed. Felix's certainly were. With their eyes closed humans are pretty much helpless. That's just a fact. No offense.

"I'm not interested in your finances," Bernie was saying. "But ProCon's finances are a different story. So anything you know about them—including the amount of your donation—may help with the case."

"There's a problem with ProCon's finances?" Axel said.

"That's what I'm trying to find out."

"Why?"

"Because," said Gillian. She picked up her glass and took much more than a sip, then turned to Bernie. "You don't believe poor old Mr. Parsons was scammed. No, that's wrong. You do believe it but you think he was scammed by his own son."

"My God!" Axel said, putting his hand to his chest. "Could that be true?"

"It's too soon to say for sure," Bernie said.

"But you're not denying it," said Gillian.

I missed whatever came next because by that time I was inside the house, following the trail of swimming pool drops. Swimming pool water has a powerful smell—surely you know this?—so nothing could have been easier. What a house, by the way! The rooms so huge, the floors all marble, more chandeliers than two. The swimming pool drops led me down a broad curving staircase, through a room with a whole bumper car set-up, just like at the State Fair but bigger, a room I hurried through, my one experience with bumper cars—and state fairs, for that matter—maybe best forgotten, then down more stairs and across more rooms, until all at once, and feeling like I was deep in the earth or even a cave, I stepped through a mostly closed doorway and into a sort of office.

A dark, windowless office, so a bit like a cave after all. But no cave I've ever been in—which is lots, especially if you count abandoned mines, exploring them being a fun hobby of ours, mine and Bernie's—had many enormous TV monitors, where all the light came from, or stacks of computer stuff with flashing lights and cables twisting and bunching all over the place in a snaky way. In short, a very unpleasant place, and I would have booked immediately except that Axie was there.

Was he hustling up treats? Had he already hustled them up and was now searching around for something to carry them in? No and no. Instead, he was sitting in front of a laptop, still in his bathing suit, his fingers—the nails rather dirty, but perhaps, like me, he enjoyed digging—poised over the keyboard, ready to tap tap tap. A drip of swimming pool water quivered on the end of his rat tail. I smelled not the slightest scent of treats in this room.

So what were we doing here? I was all set to bark the sort of bark that would remind Axie what he was supposed to be doing when Bernie spoke: ". . . the voice of his own son," he said.

Twenty-five

I glanced around. No Bernie in this office cave or whatever it was. Something in me already knew that, on account of human voices sounding different when they're coming through a phone, or the TV, or some other gadget. They've got a thing for gadgets. We, in the nation within, do not. Just pointing that out.

"But he's a sick old man," Gillian said. "So maybe he actually didn't recognize the voice of his own son, and it wasn't Billy."

Aha! These voices were coming through a small white round plastic thing—soccer ball sized, interestingly enough—with tiny holes in it, which sat on Axie's desk. Those round plastic things with holes had a name, not coming to me at the—speaker! That was it! Wow! Was I suddenly on fire or what? Another speaker just like it but silent rested on a shelf above. Axie opened another laptop, so now he had two, side by side. He did a quick tap tap on both keyboards. For one wild moment I thought the keyboards were using his fingers to tap themselves. How crazy was that?

"Bernie?" said Axel. "Isn't that a good point?"

"Maybe," Bernie said.

"And, if you don't mind me butting into your business," Axel said, "what motive would Billy have—have had, poor guy—in the first place?"

"That's one of the things I wanted to talk to him about," Bernie said.

Then someone—possibly Axel—sighed. It was certainly Axel who then said, "How unfortunate."

Meanwhile Axie was tap-tapping on the second keyboard. A

tiny red light on the shelf speaker began to blink, and lots of action going on both screens, totally beyond me.

"And this Holger guy?" Gillian said. "How does he fit in?"

"I don't know enough to say," said Bernie.

Then came a little silence. I heard a sipping sound, followed by a soft thump, perhaps a glass getting set down. "But if I'm following this right," Axel said, "Holger—what's the last name again?"

"Niberg," Bernie said.

"This Holger Niberg is only tangential," Axel said.

"How do you mean?" said Bernie.

"He's—or he was—your route to finding Billy."

"That's right," Bernie said.

"And now he's your route to finding who killed Billy?" Gillian said.

"But don't we know that?" said Axel. "It was this arson character."

"Werner Irons," Bernie said.

"So there we have it," said Axel. "Finito?"

"We're not done," Bernie said.

"No?"

"We're still looking for Holger Niberg," Bernie said.

"Ah, you're a perfectionist," said Axel. "And who's your client, if I may ask?"

A good question. I, too, was interested in the answer, although Axel and I were probably not alike in most other respects. But before I had a chance to get our answer, Axel's and mine, Axie tapped on the second keyboard and the desk speaker went silent.

Would he now, at last, get around to doing what he was supposed to do, namely rustling up treats? He opened a desk drawer. That got my hopes up even though I knew there were no treats in this room. Funny how the mind works. Axie fished a pack of gum from the drawer and started chewing. Then came more tapping. He chewed and tapped, chewed and tapped, both faster and faster. The swimming pool drop wobbled and fell off his rat tail and onto the floor. I went over and licked it up. There I was right behind him and he didn't even notice. Axie leaned closer to the screens, like they were sucking him in.

At last he stopped tapping, although he kept chewing, and gazed up at the shelf speaker with its blinking red light.

"Come on," he said. "Come on."

But whatever he was waiting for didn't happen. He said some words that Esmé had told Charlie not to say, and then tap-tapped at the second keyboard. After not too much of that, a man popped up on the screen of the second laptop. He had a crew cut, a thin face, and wore a short-sleeved white shirt and black tie. Had I seen him before somewhere? Wow! It came to me. I had seen him, not for real, whatever that is exactly, but on the screen of Esmé's dad's phone.

"Hey, Axie," said the crew-cut dude, his name almost coming to me. "Remember if you run into trouble first check the D386 file, particularly the section after line four thousand fifty four. That's where the wonkiness hides out." Axie tapped a key, and the face of the crew-cut dude froze on the screen. Then he tapped another key—or maybe the same one, all this being not so easy to follow, in fact impossible—and the crew-cut dude came to life and said the same wonkiness thing all over again. Axie tap-tapped and the crew-cut dude disappeared. Then came some time with Axie leaning closer to the screens, where lines of I didn't know what were going up and down, and the tapping and chewing ramped way, way up, and all at once the red light on the shelf speaker turned green.

Axie gazed up at the speaker. At first came the faintest liquidy sound, so close to silence, like the tiniest of trickles. There and gone and there again. Was it actually . . . a kind of silence? Whoa! What a strange thought! And why am I even bothering with this? You'd never be able to hear it. I don't mean that in a bad way.

Then came this, or something a lot like it: "Hey, what's up doc? Twinkle twinkle little deuce coupe how I wander where I wander that's the wonder of you, you-oo, you, you-oo. But don't forget me not that fourscore and more score our forefathers went poop poop pa doop." Axie touched a key and the voice went silent. He threw back his head and laughed and laughed. Was something funny? If so I didn't get it. All at once I wasn't getting a lot of things. But the very most important one was that voice coming out of the speaker. It was Bernie! Bernie's voice for sure, except for the liquidy thing. But did Bernie ever talk like that? Never! And who's heard Bernie talk more than me? No-body!

So that was where we were in this office cave—me, well, off my game, I admit it, and Axie laughing his head off, when I heard footsteps in the doorway behind us. I turned. It was Axel, not in a good mood and somehow looking bigger than normal, which was big enough to begin with.

"What the hell's going on?" he said.

Axie, completely unaware that we had company—in that typical human way—spun around. His gaze went quickly to his father, passing right over me, but then darted back. Of course he hadn't been aware of me either, so now he looked surprised on top of surprised.

"Just, uh," Axie half rose from his chair. "Foolin' around."

"Foolin' around?" Maybe a bad answer on Axie's part, because Axel came striding forward, one hand rising up in the position for backhanding. I'd seen plenty of backhanding in my career— comes with the territory—but never between fathers and sons. Wasn't it impossible? "With what program?"

"One of Holger's." Axie shrank back.

"Didn't I tell you to stay away from all that?"

"But it's fun."

Axel's hand twitched, but before it could do what he wanted it to do, Axel noticed me. Kind of odd that they'd both missed me at first. People didn't usually miss me, mostly catching onto my presence first thing. Axel slowly lowered his hand.

"Didja feed the dog already?"

"Huh?" Axie said.

"Treats. Didn't I tell you to get him a treat?"

"Um?"

"What the hell is wrong with you? Get upstairs."

Axie started walking toward the door. That meant passing close to his father. Axie flinched as he went by, but by then Axel wasn't even looking at him. He went over to the desk, glared at the laptops, smacked them both closed. I followed Axie out the door.

He was walking fast now, headed back the way we'd come, toward the stairs. I went that way, too, at first. But then I heard Axel behind me, leaving the office cave. He was walking down the hall the other way. Sometimes I get a bit curious. How does Bernie put it? "The big guy likes to be in the mix." Exactly. But that's just Bernie's brilliance, one more time. In short, I followed Axel. At a distance, true, although not a huge distance. No need for that, human hearing being what it was.

There were ceiling lights in this corridor, but the light seemed dimmer the farther along we went, Axel moving not how people do when they're out for a stroll, but when there's something to do. We came to a down staircase, quite dark. Axel didn't slow down or turn on any lights. He knew the way.

I waited at the top. That's one of our techniques at the Little Detective Agency. Stairs can be tricky, and are a big subject, which perhaps we'll get to later. The point is there was no way I could lose Axel now, his scent strong to begin with, and trapped in this indoor space.

He reached the bottom and disappeared. I went down, my paws so light on the stairs, doing their job without being told.

Down here we had only one way to go, along a very narrow corridor lit by red bulbs. Axel hadn't nearly come to the end before he stopped at a small door, about the size of a broom closet door. Broom closets always give me a bad feeling on account of the Gail Blandino case, which we solved but too late, as I may have mentioned already.

Axel stood before the door. I could feel him thinking. Then he stepped on some sort of little round pad on the floor. The door slid open. I heard a sound from inside. like someone rolling over, the way humans roll over in bed, for example, although whatever was getting rolled on sounded harder than a bed. But I wasn't sure. I needed—but before I could even figure out what I needed Axel went inside and the door slid closed.

I went up to the door. I heard nothing. Axel's scent lingered in the corridor but I smelled nothing from the other side. The door was metal, metals having unmistakable smells of their own. The gold smell is my favorite, and the taste is also pretty good. This door was not gold, but one of those dull silvery metals you see all the place.

I just stood there, at first waiting for an idea, and then not. I'd been standing still, head kind of down, for what seemed like a long time when I heard sounds far along the corridor. I headed that way, the corridor taking a turn or two and getting darker and darker when suddenly there was a flash of daylight at the end, and I caught a roly-poly figure going outside. Outside was better than inside to begin with, and especially now. I trotted down the corridor and stepped into the sunshine.

Behind me rose the house, so huge from this angle, like a cliff of its own. Before me lay the floor of a small, rocky canyon, with a few houses on the hills at the other side. Mama stood at the other end of a brick walkway, flinging a bowl of what are called slops into the canyon. Slops are an interest of mine but I could hear voices high above, and one of those was Bernie's. What a

voice! Here's something about me: I never want to be away from
Bernie for very long. How long is very long? Any time at all, really. I glanced at Mama. She had her back to me and seemed to
be lighting a cigarette. I turned and trotted the other way along
the brick walkway.

The walkway came to an end at the side wall of the house, but
I spotted a here-and-then-not-here kind of path, on the steepish
side, that led up and up. I took that path, bounding much of the
time, just because I felt like it. Pretty soon I reached street level,
meaning I was back at the front of the house. I trotted past the
front door, with that gold bar above it, came to other side of the
house, then followed it around to the deck with the swimming
pool. The deck was surrounded with a see-through wall, high
enough to keep dudes who'd maybe had one or two too many
from toppling over, although that type of dude was capable of
toppling over just about anything. But none of that had anything
to do with me. I—well, you couldn't call it leaping or jumping or
even hopping. I just sort of strode over that wall, and then pat-
patted across the deck to Bernie, sitting where I'd left him, with
Gillian across from him and Axel back at the head of the table.
Felix was still floating around the pool but now his eyes were
open and he was watching Axel.

Bernie gave me a big smile. "Hey! Where have you been?
Catching a little shuteye?"

Why would I have wanted to do that? I wasn't the slightest bit
sleepy. As for where I'd been, that was becoming a bit of the blur.
And before I could even get going on trying to clear things up in
my mind, Axie appeared with a pack of Cheez-Its.

"What's that?" Axel said.

"Dog treats," said Axie. "You said to get him dog treats."

"Are those dog treats?" said Axel.

Axie shrugged.

"I didn't hear an answer."

Axie looked down. "I dunno."

"Axel, for God's sake!" CeeCee called over from under her umbrella.

Slowly Axel turned to look at her. Their gazes met, although I might have been wrong about that, what with how dark her sunglasses were. CeeCee lowered her head and lowered her voice. "He did his best. We don't even have a dog."

Then came a silence, not the comfortable kind. Meanwhile I now seemed to be standing quite close to Axie. He was a good kid.

Bernie spoke up. "Thanks, Axie. I think Chet could manage a Cheez-It or two."

Axel turned to Bernie. "Whatever you say." He smiled. "You're the master."

Bernie smiled back. "I don't think of it that way."

"Equals?" Axel said. "You consider you and the dog equals?"

"That's right," Bernie said.

Axel sat back, sunshine glinting in his close-trimmed silvery beard. "Then should I ask Chet here whether you have a client in this case?"

Bernie laughed. "That would be like you asking me to sniff for the dead bodies."

Bernie sniffing for dead bodies? Had I just heard that? Bernie's sense of humor to the max, for sure, although Axel didn't seem to get it. Wrinkles deepened on his broad forehead and he glanced over at me, in fact gave me a long look, like there was something very interesting about me. That should have felt good, but it didn't.

"But," Bernie said, "we already have a client. Thanks anyway for the offer."

"I haven't even made an offer yet," Axel said. "What's your rate?"

"Eight hundred a day plus expenses," Bernie said.

"How does two thousand a day sound?"

"Great, but we already have a client."

"You said that. But I'm wondering who this other party might be with an interest in Holger—what was his last name again?"

"Niberg," Bernie said. "Holger Niberg."

Holger Niberg! The crew-cut dude! I was back in the picture and . . . and taking names! Wow! I was coming close to scaring myself.

"And the identities of our clients are confidential," Bernie was saying.

"You said that, too," Axle said. "How about this? On top of the two thousand I'll reimburse your client whatever's been paid so far. Maybe even throw them a little bonus so there'll be no bad feelings. That's one thing I've learned in business. All sides should feel good when the dust settles."

"I'm not clear on what your business is," Bernie said.

Axel turned to Gillian. "You haven't mentioned it?"

"Didn't I, Bernie?" she said. "I thought I did."

"You said Axel was an investor."

"With a capital I," Axel said. He picked up his glass, clinked it against Bernie's, noticed that Bernie's glass was still pretty full. "Hello? Not much of a drinker? Or just not tequila?"

"Tequila's fine." Bernie picked up his glass and drank. "What sort of investing do you do?"

"I invest in people," Axel said. "All these sectors—mining, retail, real estate, entertainment—are unpredictable. But people—that's a different story."

"You find people predictable?" Bernie said.

"But of course!" said Axel. "For example, I now predict that you will end up taking me as a client. Not here and now, not today, maybe not tomorrow, but soon."

Bernie smiled. He has a few smiles meaning different things, not nearly as many smiles as nods. I didn't remember this particular smile, had no idea what it meant. "Thanks for the drink," he said, and then turned to Gillian. "Anything else you wanted to discuss?"

Gillian shook her head. "But thanks for coming. Maybe it shouldn't even matter if I end up knowing all the details."

"It matters," Bernie said.

The next thing I knew we were in the Beast and underway, Bernie quiet and me keeping myself busy. He glanced over. "What you got there?"

My, my. A bag of Cheez-Its? Some things just happen on their own. I'm lucky enough to be there pretty much every time.

Twenty-six

Lou "The Vig" Grotto was at his desk eating the biggest sub I'd ever seen. His office smelled strongly of sub, like a whole wonderful wave of ham, baloney, pastrami, salami, and one or two meats I didn't even know the names of had just come rolling through.

His cheerful round face got rounder and more cheerful when he saw us. Well, when he saw Bernie. That would be closer to the truth. Viggie and Bernie went way back—back to when I wasn't even around, an odd idea I'd picked up from several conversations and never understood in the slightest. How can there be a time when you weren't around? It made no sense.

But forget all that. What I was getting to was Bernie's army days, where Viggie served in Bernie's company, whatever that was, exactly, with Bernie as the boss and Viggie as the cook. In their spare time—I'd picked this up one night when Bernie had told Weatherly all about it, the two of them in bed but not sleeping, and me out in the hall, also not sleeping—the army guys and gals played card games for money. Viggie told them not to worry about playing when it was just the company folks, but if they ever saw him at a table with outsiders then stay away. Weatherly laughed when she heard that. She has a lovely laugh, by the way, not one of those tee-hees but actually kind of booming. But back to Viggie, who got kind of rich on his tour of duty and now ran Lucky's Golden Desert Diamond Casino, having taken over from Lucky Chan, whom I'd met only once and briefly before he went down in what I believe is called a hail of bullets.

"Hey, Captain!" Viggie rose from his chair and hurried over to us, wiping his mouth on the end of his necktie, a nice-looking necktie with a slot machine pattern. Then he and Bernie were hugging and pounding each other on the back, a pounding that left a mustard smear on Bernie's shirt. "Don't tell me you saw the notice on LinkedIn?"

"What notice?" Bernie said.

"I'm looking for a head of security. Pays competitive but the perks can double that, value-wise."

"No thanks," Bernie said.

Viggie appeared not to hear. He turned to me. "And we can probably find a way to slide Chet here onto the payroll. All's we need would be a last name and some sort of social. But my God! Can he still be growing?"

"It doesn't make sense," Bernie said.

"Hey, pal," Viggie said, going pat pat on my head.

Wow! The smell of this hand! I wanted to lick it so bad. But he withdrew it before I had a chance.

"Whatever you're getting fed I want some," Viggie went on.

The Cheezits were gone. I felt a little badly about that. I'd have been happy to share. Up to a point.

"We're looking for a poker player named Holger Niberg," Bernie said.

"Doesn't ring a bell," Viggie said. "Professional?"

"More like a high-stakes amateur."

Viggie sat back down at his desk, waved Bernie into a chair, took a notebook from a drawer, plucked a nice round salami slice from the sub, and tossed it my way. And all of that in one motion! Viggie's hands weren't things of beauty like Bernie's, in fact were on the short and stubby side, but he was very good with them.

He leafed through the notebook. "What I got is the names of every serious or even semi-serious player who's come through the joint in the past five years." He stabbed a page with his finger.

"Here we got Nesterenko and then Nilan, nothin' in between."
He looked up. "Where Niberg would be. You follow?"

Bernie nodded. His eyes were sparkling, like he was having a
great time. And he hadn't even had a single salami slice. Bernie
knows how to have fun with the little things. In this case the thing
was so little I'd missed it completely.

Viggie closed the notebook. "So what else do you know about
him?"

"He's a tech guy, worked for the that space outfit run by Meelo
Morster."

"Him I heard of, but he don't grace my establishment," Viggie
said. "But I love when tech guys show up."

"Yeah?"

"They're good with numbers, right? That makes them confident. Confident players think—naw, they know—that it's all about
numbers, which is true, and since they're whiz kids at numbers
it'll all come out right in the end." Viggie took a big bite off the
sub, talked around a mouthful. "But the numbers are on our side.
That's ironclad. It's the whole . . . what's the word I'm looking for?"

"Point," Bernie said.

"Bingo. You should have my job."

"Ha," said Bernie.

"The whole point," Viggie went on. "Think we'd be in business
if some tech kids could waltz in and whip our ass?" He chewed
thoughtfully. "No, sir, Captain, hell freezes over." He burped and
thought some more, then waved a finger, tipped with mayo, at
Bernie. "But there's one or two private high stakes games down
here in Gila City. Want I should write them down?"

"That would be great."

"Tell 'em I sent you." Viggie opened the notebook, tore out a
sheet, wrote with a stubby pencil. "And that security job's open
whenever you want."

Bernie smiled. "What if it gets filled?"

"It would still be open whenever you want."

Bernie reached out and tapped the edge of Viggie's desk, a soft one two. Did it mean something? I didn't know, but a look appeared on Viggie's round and now somewhat greasy face that was almost loving.

"Just say the word, Captain," he said.

Bernie sat in front of his laptop. I curled up at his feet, or perhaps right on them. Did Bernie mind? What a question!

"That place of Axel's gotta be worth millions," he said. "But he doesn't show up on the internet at all. Is that good? Bad? Neither?"

Bernie had lost me completely. That generally happens when humans are involved with their gadgets. Except for cars, their best invention by far. Trucks are also nice. Now Bernie closed the laptop, a fine idea, and went to the fridge. I followed. When someone goes to the fridge I follow. That's basic.

He took out some eggs, got busy, ended up making an egg salad sandwich. I've never seen Bernie eat an egg salad sandwich but he's an ace at making them which he does for Charlie from time to time and Charlie eats every bite, unless a bit of egg salad happens to ooze out from between the bread slices and fall to the floor. Life—mine, anyway—is full of tiny fun.

Bernie popped the sandwich in a baggie and we went over to the Parsons' house. He knocked on the door and I got ready to snatch Iggy when he came flying outside. I heard Mr. Parsons coming, slow and heavy, but there were no Iggy-type sounds. The door opened.

"Ah, Bernie," Mr. Parsons said. He wore nothing but pajama bottoms. His chest, arms, shoulders were just bones covered in bone-colored skin. "You brought Chet over to play? I'm afraid Iggy's feeling a bit poorly."

"What's wrong with him? We can take him to the vet if you like."

"The vet came. She really is wonderful. Apparently there's nothing wrong with him, not physically. Edna's back in the hospital, and then there was the . . . the service for Billy. Do you think dogs can get depressed?"

"For sure." Bernie raised the baggie. "How about a sandwich?"

"Does Chet get depressed?"

All eyes were suddenly on me? How come? I was doing basically nothing, simply minding my own.

"I don't know," said Bernie, after some thought. "But if he does he bounces back real fast."

"How does he do that?"

"No clue," Bernie said. He jiggled the baggie.

"So nice of you," Mr. Parsons said, "but I haven't got much of an appetite."

"Maybe you'll change your mind after a bite or two. I added dill to the mayo—specialty of the house."

"You made it yourself?"

Bernie nodded.

Mr. Parsons reached out like he was going to touch Bernie's shoulder, but his hand didn't quite get there. Was he distracted by the sudden sight of his own bare arm? He blinked a few times and waved us inside.

We went into the kitchen where Iggy lay on his little bed, gazing at nothing. I gave him a poke, not hard, just saying hi. He didn't look at me, but the tip of his odd corkscrew tail twitched slightly. I took that for a good sign. Meanwhile Mr. Parsons stepped into the laundry room, which was right off the kitchen, and when he came out he was wearing a white dress shirt with his pajama bottoms, although was having trouble with the buttons. Bernie fastened them for him. He didn't say anything, just did it, like it was a routine they had.

Mr. Parsons sat at the table and started in on the egg salad sandwich, first one slow bite and then more and faster. Bernie leaned against the counter.

"We're still looking for Holger Niberg," he said.

"Have you mentioned him?" That was the moment a little clump of egg salad got free and dropped on the floor with a quiet but very satisfying plop. It disappeared before you'd know it. "Please remind me."

Bernie started in on a long story about Billy, Holger Niberg, Werner Irons, ProCon and lots of other stuff that seemed a bit familiar. But Bernie had it all down pat! Sheer brilliance was the reason why, amigos. He was so brilliant that I stopped listening to the words and just sort of bathed in the wonderful sound of his voice.

"I'm a little lost," Mr. Parsons said after a while. "But I believe I have a photo of the Holger fellow."

"Oh?" said Bernie.

Mr. Parsons rose and began rummaging through drawers. Bernie went over to Iggy's bed, crouched, and—and started giving him a belly rub? Excuse me? Iggy's tail did some more twitching, a lot more. Humans have this expression about being of two minds about something or other. At the moment I was of one mind only, but I kept that to myself, being a very good boy and a visitor, after all.

"Ch-et?"

Or maybe I kept it almost to myself, a pretty decent performance under the circumstances. Perhaps, if this belly rubbing had gone on longer I might not have done as well, but Mr. Parsons interrupted.

"Here we go."

He held up a photo of two smiling men standing side by side in front of a building. Wow! I knew so much about it. I'm a pro, after all, but still. The building was the ProCon office in Gila City. The shorter of the two men was Billy Parsons, looking relaxed, happy, even on a roll. The taller—a thin dude with a crew cut and wearing short-sleeve white shirt—was Holger Niberg. Not only had I seen his face before but I'd even heard him talk. Something about wonkiness, a complete mystery.

"See what Billy wrote?" Mr. Parsons said. "'Me and Holger, the smartest guy I know.' He sent this to us the day he became director."

Bernie moved closer, took a real good look. "Did Billy ever say anything about him?"

"Not that I remember. Sorry, Bernie."

"That's all right."

"I'd like to help."

"Thank you, Daniel," Bernie said. "Maybe you've got some thoughts on Billy's domestic situation."

"You mean . . . ?" Mr. Parsons raised his hands in a way that made the hands themselves look confused. Are hands like very small humans? I didn't want to go one more step in that direction.

"Anything about it that comes to mind," Bernie said.

"Like the fact of his being a stepdad?"

"Sure," Bernie said.

Mr. Parsons nodded, thought, nodded again. "Billy doesn't—he didn't think of himself as a step dad. Not yet. That's what he told Edna. Not yet. It came out of the conversation we had—well, she had it, but I always back her up whether . . ." He gave Bernie a sideways look that was almost shifty-eyed. Shifty-eyed from Mr. Parsons? How could that make sense?

"Go on," Bernie said.

"Well, you know marriage," said Mr. Parsons.

"Not the long lasting successful kind," Bernie said. "Give me some pointers."

"No one's ever asked me that."

"To give marriage tips?"

"Tips on anything. I'm not complaining. I'm a type B person. Although Edna said—the one time it came up—that I may be a type B person except I'm type A at the core. But I'm wandering. Here's a marriage tip. Even if you're inclined to disagree about some little thing, keep your trap shut. Only disagree if it's big and you're damn sure. Like if she says take the next left and you know it goes right off a cliff."

Mr. Parsons was right about that. Take that recent little cliff-side outing with me, Bernie, and Werner Irons. I wasn't eager for a repeat anytime soon, and of course a repeat with Werner was off the table. Off the table? Had I come close to a funny thought? I tried to find it but it backed away from me. I went over to Iggy, still lying on his bed, and gave him another poke. His eyes were blank, looking right through me, but the tip of his tail quivered slightly. Something wasn't right with Iggy, poor guy.

"The stepdad issue is an example," Mr. Parsons went on. "We both want—wanted. God in heaven. I keep making the same mistake. Edna and I both wanted a grandchild and were happy to see Gillian's boy in that light. That was when Billy made the not-yet remark. Edna . . . didn't take that in silence. It's just not her way. She started interrogating—well, not that, more like discussing what you were asking about, Billy's domestic set-up. Edna just up and said, 'What are you waiting for?' That's when Billy got to talking about the domestic situation. It seems the father—I'm talking about Felix's dad—have you met Felix?"

"Yes."

"Us, too, just for an hour or so last summer when they dropped in, Billy and Felix. What did you think of the boy?"

"He's quiet," Bernie said.

Mr. Parsons nodded. "Was he playing on his tablet thing the whole time?"

"That's the norm."

"Can't be good in the long run—like living in an endless tunnel. But there I go, wandering again. Where was I? The father? Right. Gillian's ex. He's remarried now, too, apparently, a former model, I believe, and has another son not much younger than Felix. They're buddies, apparently, and the father—a rich private equity fellow or some such—also lives in Gila City and is a presence in Felix's life. So that was Billy's point. There really wasn't room for a traditional stepdad. He couldn't see a way to make that happen. Edna put down her teacup and said, 'You've got it backwards, Billy. To make it happen you start by thinking of yourself as the stepdad, inhabiting the role.'" Mr. Parsons smiled. "How many people do you know who can slip inhabiting into a conversation?"

"Just the one," Bernie said. "What did Billy say to that?"

"'Oh, Mom.'" Mr. Parsons sat still for a few moments. Then he said, "They left soon after. We gave Felix a goodbye hug whether he liked it or not." He glanced over at Iggy, whose eyes were now closed. "I think I'll take a nap long about now, Bernie. Just a shortie. Can you believe I've already had a nap today? How can anyone justify that when there's so little time left?"

"Don't be so hard on yourself." Bernie rose. "Call if you need us for any reason."

"You're a good man, Bernie." Mr. Parsons yawned a huge yawn. At the front of his mouth were lots of teeth, but things emptied out at the back. "Was there something else I meant to tell you?"

"Like what?" Bernie said.

Mr. Parsons shook his head and then yawned again. Iggy, eyes still closed, had himself a real good stretch, his paws doing that slight vibration thing that was very Iggy. So this little visit ended well. That was my takeaway.

* * *

Back home an envelope was taped to the door. Bernie opened it, unfolded the sheet of paper inside, and read to himself, his eyes going back and forth real fast. Inside him things were changing, also fast. We get monsoons in these parts, although it wasn't monsoon season now. You can see them coming from far away, boiling in the sky. Some kind of storm like that was rising in Bernie now. He finished reading, tore the sheet of paper into tiny bits and tossed them away.

"They took our license."

Bernie said that quietly but inside him the storm was starting to rage. His mighty hands balled themselves into fists. He turned to the house and . . . and gave it a look like he hated it! Hated our own house on Mesquite Road, the nicest house in the whole Valley. This was terrible, and then it got even more terrible when Bernie drew back one of those fists like he was going to smash our own house, knock it down, turn it to smithereens. I poked him, kind of how I'd poked Iggy but harder. A lot harder, no denying that. Bernie whirled around toward me, his eyes furious and not seeing, and then seeing and not furious. The storm began to die down.

We went inside. Bernie poured himself a shot of bourbon and gulped it down. He raised the bottle to pour another, but paused, glanced at me, and put the bottle away.

I drank water. Bernie took the .38 Special and went into the office. I heard the safe open and close. He returned with the .45, our stopper, formerly belonging to some real bad guy and now ours, although he'd tried pretty hard to hang onto it. He had no need for it now, of course, up at Northern State Correctional. Bernie loaded up the .45.

Twenty-seven

"Poker might not be my game," Bernie said.

Nighttime on the road to Gila City. I already knew poker might not be his game, had gotten the idea at that Valley PD poker night where we found out about mortgages beyond two. Baseball was Bernie's game. He'd pitched at West Point and been on his way to the big time—even if he says he wasn't—until he blew out his arm. But he can still throw a ball a country mile, much farther than your mile, city folks. No offense.

"Fifty-two cards," he said, interrupting a long, pleasant silence. Not a complete silence, since we had the constant low rumble of the Beast, letting the traffic, of which there wasn't much, know what was what. Also, there'd been no interrupting. How can Bernie interrupt? He's what's going on!

"Four suits," he continued. Four was one of those mysteries but four suits seemed like a lot. Bernie himself had just the one, the very dark gray, perhaps black long ago, that he'd worn to the old Spanish mission.

"Spades were always my favorite, just from the appearance." Approaching headlights lit up his face, and we had ourselves one of those moments when he and Charlie looked a lot alike, although there was no toughness in Charlie's face and plenty in Bernie's. "But now I'd go with hearts." The headlights flashed by and Bernie was back in the shadows. "The whole set-up is feudal, I guess. Is the jack a prince or a fool? And what about the ace? More powerful than the king and yet sometimes counting as a mere one? Above the king—wouldn't that be a kind of god? But what god is also the lowest of the low?"

Over to you on all that. Meanwhile Bernie went silent and stayed silent all the way into Gila City. We rolled down the main drag, past the restaurants, shops, art galleries, all nicely lit— but I had the odd thought we weren't part of that, at least not tonight—then turned down a side street and parked in front of what had to be a pool hall. You get to know pool halls in my line of work. We're part of that.

"Poker's not my game, gotta remember that," Bernie said as we walked up to the door, those old-fashioned swinging doors you sometimes see in these parts, a type of door I favored, although I can open a surprising range of doors by myself, something Bernie and I have worked at a lot, resulting in many many treats. But back to knowing pool halls, and now comes something I shouldn't even have been thinking: Pool wasn't his game either. Please forget that immediately.

We walked through the swinging doors—what a refreshing breeze they made—and entered a pool hall like so many, with tables under hanging lights, dudes with cigarettes dangling from their mouths peering at colored balls from different angles, chalking the ends of their sticks, leaning way over the tables with their butts sticking out. The best parts were the smell of the chalk and the sound of the balls clacking off each other. Balls, I should add, with an unpleasant mouth feel, probably the most unpleasant of all the balls out there, baseballs being the best by far. Who could disagree with that?

We headed to the bar at the back. There was one customer at the end, gazing at his drink like . . . like he was waiting for it to do something! What a crazy thought! Like start dancing across the bar, for example. Hey! Even crazier. We walked over to the barkeep, polishing glasses at the other end.

"What'll it be?" she said.

Bernie took out the sheet from Viggie's notebook, unfolded it, smoothed it out. "We're looking for . . ." He squinted at the page. ". . . Earl Westie."

"And you are?"

"Bernie Little, and this is Chet."

"Uh-huh. Earl know you?"

"No. Lou Grotto sent us."

"Lou Grotto?"

"Yes. You know him?"

"Wait here." The barkeep turned toward a door that stood between the shelves of bottles.

"Hey," said the dude at the end of the bar. "Can I get another?"

"You ain't done with the one you got." The barkeep opened the door, went through, closed it firmly behind her.

The dude who wanted another drink glared at Bernie, like Bernie'd been the one to blow him off.

"That dog on a leash?" he said.

"Are you?" said Bernie.

The dude turned away. My Bernie.

After not very long, the barkeep returned. "Follow me," she said.

We walked around the bar, followed her through the door between all those bottles, up wooden stairs that were real worn and old, a treat for the paws. At the top we took a few steps down a narrow corridor, also with an old wooden floor, and came to a door with one of those pebbly glass windows in it, a sight I'd actually only ever seen in old black and white movies Bernie and I sometimes watched, like the one that's all about some sort of black bird, so of course things go south, wherever that is exactly.

The barkeep knocked.

"Yup," said a man on the other side.

The barkeep opened the door. We went in. She closed the door and walked back down the narrow corridor, her sneakers going pad pad.

"Hi," Bernie said to the guy standing at a small bar and pouring himself a drink. "I'm Bernie Little and this is Chet."

The guy turned to us. He was older than Bernie, tall and lean like the ranchers and the cowboys we've got around here, and like them wore jeans and a denim shirt, plus a white cowboy hat and, most important, cowboy boots with a black and red pattern. That leather! So rich and supple! Had I ever smelled such superb leather? No. I searched my mind for some sort of plan, not necessarily even a good one, and came up with nothing.

"Earl Westie," said this . . . this current possessor of the boots. "How do you know Viggie?"

"We served together overseas."

"Were you a cook?"

"No."

"Wasn't Viggie a cook?"

"He was much more than a cook."

"Was he ever in action?"

"Action?" Bernie said.

"A firefight," said Earl.

"Several."

"Was he good?"

"Very."

"He never talks about it," Earl said. "At least not to me."

"No," Bernie said.

Earl nodded. Then he glanced my way. "Fine looking companion you got there."

"Thanks."

Companion would be what again? Before I could get going on that Earl said, "I've known Viggie a long time. He never recommended anyone to me. Why you?"

"You'll have to ask him," Bernie said.

"True." Earl picked up his phone, went tap tap. "Viggie? Earl. Got this fellow Bernie Little, looks like maybe a cop of some sort, says you recom—"

I could hear Viggie's voice rising on the other end. You might have been able to hear that, too, although maybe not. But you certainly couldn't have heard what Viggie was actually saying. I myself caught every word, most of them the kind Bernie tells Charlie not to say.

Earl got off the phone, setting the thing on the desk with a little push, like it was hot. "What can I do for you, Bernie?" he said.

"Does the name Holger Niberg mean anything to you?"

"Sure. I take it you're not a cop?"

"Correct."

"Some kind of private operator?"

Bernie said nothing.

"Never mind," said Earl. "Don't matter. Yeah, I knew Niberg. Haven't seen him in years. Is he still locked up?"

"He's out," Bernie said.

"Maybe he smartened up," Earl said. "He hasn't been in here."

"Smartened up how?"

"We run a poker room, a selective poker room. Ante's five grand each. Our cut's five percent of the ante, one point five of every pot, drinks on the house. My family's owned this place since 1879 and the game goes almost that far back. Doc Holliday and Johnny Ringo both sat at our table."

"Not on the same night," Bernie said.

"Ah," said Earl, sitting back. "You knew they were enemies? I'm guessing your people also go back a ways in these parts."

Bernie nodded. "Enemies are what we're looking for. Specifically Holger's enemies."

"From where I'm sitting that would be himself," Earl said. "You play poker?"

"Some," Bernie said.

Earl gave him a narrow-eyed look, and he was the narrow-eyed type to begin with. "I'm bettin' you do," he said.

Bernie looked . . . well, he looked pleased to hear that. It's a look you don't often see on his face. That was odd. Also odd was the fact that he'd very recently been saying poker was not his game. I was a bit confused.

"So you already know," Earl went on, "the game's in three parts."

Uh-oh.

"First, you get managing the cards, knowing the odds—the odds for in your own hand, everybody else, what's still in the deck. Math dudes like Niberg are real good on that one. Second, there's the betting. That depends on the odds—up to a point. The math dudes are real good there, too, till you get to that point. Third, comes sizing up the opposition. I'm talkin' psychologic now. You follow?"

"I do." Bernie was listening as hard as I'd ever felt him listen to anyone.

"Then that's it. When it comes to the psychologic, math dudes are math dudes, finito. Niberg dug himself some deep holes back there—" He nodded toward one of the side walls. "—and tried to double down. Or more like recapitalize. Which he did by stealing if the jury got it right."

"Who did he owe money to?" Bernie said.

Earl shrugged. "All the actually good players, most likely. But they're not the kind that advertise they can't collect. They just freeze you out."

"Any idea where we can look for him?" Bernie said.

"He took you, too?"

"Kind of," Bernie said.

"Before they put him away or after?"

"After."

"Son of a bitch," said Earl. He drummed his fingers on the desk. "You could try asking the boys, at least some of them."

"What boys?"

"The poker boys. There's a game every night 'cept Mondays." Earl checked his watch. "They take a break in five minutes or so." He pointed. "Down the hall on your right. Tell 'em you're askin' for me."

"Thanks," Bernie said.

They shook hands. Earl gave me a scratch between the ears on the way out. Quick and on the heavy-handed side, but nice.

We walked down the hall, me and Bernie side by side, meaning I was slightly ahead, and stopped in front of another one of those pebbly glassed doors. Bernie opened it and we looked in.

Cigar smoke, booze, playing cards, cash, and stacks of those plastic chips—their mouth feel, like the pool balls, disappointing—and a bunch of men seated at a round table. One of the men was about to turn over a card that lay face down and all the others were watching real close and unaware of us. One of those men, watching real close and unaware of us, was Axel. Bernie touched my collar. We backed out of the room. Bernie closed the door without making a sound. After that we found a side staircase out of the pool hall and down to the street and hit the road.

Twenty-eight

Hitting the road, yes, but at first we didn't go far, only to the end of the block where we hung a U-ee and parked on the other side of the street, Westie's pool hall in view. Were we waiting for someone to go in? To come out? Either was fine with me, sitting on a place being one of our best techniques at the Little Detective Agency. The case was going well, if in fact it was a case. I tried to line up all the facts, but they turned out to be shadows that melted away. Still, if it was a case someone had to be paying. Otherwise our finances would be . . . would be kind of like how they were. A bad thought, but right away came a good one, which was how I liked to roll. Wasn't Axel paying? I certainly remembered something about that, remembered very clearly, although not clearly enough to advance beyond the something about that stage. But good enough! Axel was paying and we were waiting for him to come strolling out and fork over a fistful of green.

Then, just when I'd gotten the whole thing down pat, Bernie opened the glove box and took a peek inside. There was the .45, kind of like the .38 Special's big brother. Bernie flipped the glove box closed. Were we planning to shoot Axel after he came through with the cash? That didn't sound like us but I had no other ideas.

The phone beeped.

"Bernie? Dan Parsons here."

"Hi, Daniel. Everything all right?"

"Well, I don't know. Are you at home?"

"No."

"Some lights seem to be on."

"That's the timer. It turns them on at night."

"Ah, that explains that. I could never get ours to work. Lights kept going on and off at the oddest times." Mr Parsons went silent.

"Um, is that why you're calling?" Bernie said. "To set the timer? I'd be happy to when we get back."

"No," said Mr. Parsons. "No, no, no. But thank you. I get it now—you're not at home. So that's the explanation."

"Explanation for what, Daniel? Is something wrong?"

"I wouldn't say wrong. More like unusual. It was Iggy who noticed first, barking by the window. The one in the front hall, with a view of your place. He stands there on his back legs and watches. Edna calls him our little sentry." He went silent again.

"And what did he see, Dan?"

"Tonight, you mean?"

"Yes."

"Well, he might not have seen at first. You know dogs. He might have heard or smelled. It's a whole different approach to life. Maybe gets you out of your own head a little more. Preferable, if you see what I mean. But here I am pontificating. What I'm trying to get to—the purpose of the call, you might say—is that Iggy started barking. You know that bark of his, especially when it goes on and on? You're a prince not to complain. That's how Edna puts it. She says that Chet doesn't bark much and when he does it's to let you know something, whereas Iggy barks on account of being all roiled up inside."

"But in this case?" Bernie said.

"Excuse me?"

"Iggy's barking—was it to let you know something?"

"Exactly! You're so easy to talk to. He was going on and on the way he does, and shouting Iggy, pipe down, did no good so finally I hauled myself up and went to his window. And—this is why I'm calling—there was a stray dog outside your house, standing right in front of the door."

"Alone?"

"I think so."

"One of the neighborhood dogs?"

"No. At least not one of the neighborhood dogs I know. The funny thing is at first I thought it was Chet, locked out or some such."

Bernie sat up straight. "Why did you think it was Chet?"

"Spittin' image, Bernie, that's why. Same powerful build, same coat—black as night with that one pearly ear. I rapped on the window and he—well, maybe she—turned, and I saw that this dog was a bit smaller than Chet. She—I'm really thinking she's a she—gave me a look that seemed highly intelligent, maybe even more so than . . . well, let's leave it at that. But the whole thing is, I don't know, off in a way. Thought you should know."

Bernie started the car. "Is she still there?"

"I'll have a look see." Some time passed, time with clumping sounds, meaning Mr. Parsons was back on his walker. "Yup," he said. "On the doorstep."

"We're on our way," Bernie said. "Ninety minutes. See if you can get her to come inside your place."

"With treats?"

"She likes those chicken jerkies, the same ones you have for Iggy," Bernie said. "And her name's Trixie." He turned the wheel and stepped on the gas, hard enough to make the Beast roar. Trixie was in the picture? Treats were being handed out? To her and not to me? Faster, Bernie!

We flew through the night, the open desert between Gila City and the Valley alive with all sort of creatures, although I heard and saw none. But I smelled them, smelled them hunting and being hunted. We were hunters, me and Bernie. Others worried about us, although one strange thing about this night was how worried

Bernie was. His worry grew and grew. I could smell it, something like human sweat but just the bottom layer, if that makes any sense. He called Weatherly a whole bunch of times on the ride but she didn't pick up.

We squealed to a stop in front of our place, the car rocking back and forth, and we hopped out, Bernie, too, like the Beast was rocking us right out of itself.

"Get ready," Bernie said as he knocked on the Parsonses' door, meaning get ready to snatch Iggy out of the air when he bolted the way he did whenever a chance came his way. I was already ready.

The door opened—actually opened wide, kind of careless on Mr. Parsons' part—and there was Mr. Parsons, still wearing the dress shirt and pajama bottoms combo. No Iggy. Yes, he was on the premises, all right. I could see him in the background, sitting in front of the stairs and panting, but making no attempt to flee the coop. How strange! Also strange was the fact that we had another member of the nation within in the front hall, standing between Iggy and the door.

"Is that Trixie?" Mr. Parsons said.

"Yes," said Bernie, as we entered, Bernie closing the door behind us. "Thanks for letting us know."

"No problem. Would you believe she has Iggy under total control? Like she's got him on a leash. It's amazing. How do you know her?"

Hello? Trixie had Iggy on a leash? I've heard many strange things—it's that kind of career—but this was the strangest.

"She's Weatherly's," Bernie was saying. "Have you met her?"

"Not to my knowledge. Or rather recollection!" Mr. Parsons chuckled for reasons unknown to me. "I've certainly met Weatherly. Didn't Edna tell me you're getting married?"

Bernie nodded. I'm sure I've mentioned he has many nods,

meaning all sorts of things. This particular one was the most special. It could mean anything.

"If I can say something without being too personal, Bernie, she's a real genuine beauty. A knockout, as we said back in the day. Somewhat reminiscent of Ava Gardner, if that means anything to you."

"I've heard of her, but I can't picture her face."

"Now you can," said Mr. Parsons.

Bernie opened his mouth, perhaps a little on the early side, because he seemed to be a bit lost on what to say. Not lost, of course, no way Bernie is ever lost, so it must have been that he had too many brilliant choices. Before he settled on the best, Trixie walked over to him in that way she had. So uppity! It couldn't be more annoying. And then what did she do? She pressed against his leg, pressed hard. That was my job. I turned toward her but before I could . . . fix things, let's put it that way, Bernie crouched down, took Trixie's head gently in his hands.

"What is it, girl?"

Trixie made a tiny whimpering sound. That was unusual, so unusual I forgot all about whatever I'd been planning. At that moment Iggy, too, made a whimpering sound. Trixie wheeled around toward him and barked. Just one solitary bark, but savage, as scary—well, no, but close—as one of my very best. Iggy rolled right over and stuck his paws in the air and lay still, tongue hanging out the side of his mouth.

Bernie rose. "Can you do us a favor, Daniel?"

"Anything."

"Watch Trixie for a while."

"Of course. What could be easier? She couldn't be better company."

Trixie looked at me. I looked at her. We had what you might

call a brief looks contest. I won, as I'm sure you guessed already. Except I lost. Forget that last part.

The little lemon-colored house, namely Weatherly's, was empty, which I knew before Bernie knocked.

"Tallula?" Bernie called. "Tallula?" He glanced at me. "Maybe she's gone to bed." He raised his voice. "Tallula!" No answer, although a light went on in a house down the block.

Bernie took out his phone. "Have I even got her number?" He did this and that, finally tap-tapping and holding the phone to his ear. I heard nothing on the other end. "She's probably back north on the Nation. Service can be iffy up there." He was sliding the phone back in his pocket when it beeped.

"Tallula?" he said.

"Tallula? My, my, you do lead an interesting life, Bernie."

"Hi, Etta," he said.

"What do I have to do to get some of that Tallula excitement in your voice?" Etta said. Voice was the subject? Etta's was fine, in my opinion, like when the door opens to a nice smoke filled bar on whiskey tasting night. "What's she got that I ain't got?"

"Actually there are similarities," Bernie said. "She's Weatherly's mom."

"Of my vintage, then," said Etta. "I picture her as somewhat better preserved. I didn't preserve myself as prudently as I might have."

"Well, um—"

"Don't even try," Etta said. "Water under the bridge—and not the purpose of the call. I did some digging on Werner Irons and came up with a morsel or two."

Whoa! We needed to see more of Etta, and not only on account of that voice. She could also dig! And dig successfully! Morsels! Perhaps a personal visit would be better than a phone call for whatever we were doing right now? I sat on Bernie's foot. He didn't seem to notice. I tried to think of a way to sit harder but came up empty.

"Werner had a long series of wives and girlfriends, some simultaneous, mix and match et cetera, but nothing lasting, none in the till death do you part category. Although he happened to have a girlfriend in tow at the end, so I suppose they were parted by death, but I'm not feeling romantic about it. Some other impediment would have intruded sooner or later, my money on sooner."

"Her name?" Bernie said.

"Don't rush me," Etta said. "I was about to tell you the kind of thing I never tell a soul."

"Oh?" said Bernie.

"Yeah, oh," Etta said. "Remember that excitement in the voice I was referring to?"

"It was only moments ago."

She laughed. "Uncanny. He had that exact same delivery."

"Who are you talking about?"

"Your father, of course. And that excitement was what he stirred up in me. It stayed there, mostly dormant, long after he was gone."

Bernie said nothing.

"Maybe you're the wrong audience for that," Etta said. "More water under the bridge. Water's what I should have been drinking tonight but it was whiskey instead. Still with me?"

"I am," Bernie said.

"She's a retired stripper, lives in those Cactus Grove casitas overlooking the upscale trailer parks, can't remember what they're called."

"Good Life Gardens," Bernie said.

"Perfect," said Etta. "Her stage name was Delilah. Her real name's Janet Carbo. Casita 17C."

Twenty-nine

Once I heard Esmé telling Charlie that casita meant a little house. Charlie was chewing off the tip of a fingernail at the time so what he said in return was a bit unclear but it was something like "What's the word for no house?" Which I didn't get at all and neither did Esmé, to judge from the look on her face, like she'd just bit into a lemon, a mistake I once made myself and then again and possibly once more after that.

That was water under the bridge, as Etta would say, although what did it actually mean? For example, there's no water under the Rio Calor bridge, the Rio Calor being empty. But now I was even farther off track. What I was trying to get to was the fact that casita 17C in the Cactus Grove casitas on the little rise over trailer parks as far as the eye could see was the smallest casita I'd ever come upon. All these casitas were crowded together and connected by cement paths lined with plants that weren't doing too well and the occasional ground lantern, the light strangely orange and flickering in just about every one.

We walked toward the door of 17C but it opened before we got there. A woman stepped out, maybe Bernie's age or a little older. There was nothing else little about her. Lots of big blond hair shining in the light of the door lamp, big this, big that, but not a fat woman. Just big is what I'm getting at. She was carrying a couple of suitcases, a couple of shoulder bags, a purse, and also had a cigarette sticking the side of her mouth.

"Going somewhere, Janet?" Bernie said.

Janet—and she had to be Janet, Bernie never making a mistake on this sort of thing, or on anything, really—stopped in her tracks, took in Bernie, me, then Bernie again. "Who the hell are you?"

"Bernie Little. And this is Chet."

Janet dropped the suitcases and the shoulder bags, but not the purse. The purse she swung around, digging her hand inside, whipping out a gun, in fact a .38 Special just like ours, except for ours not being pink. That was interesting although not amazing. The amazing part was how quickly she did all that. Once Bernie and I went to a quick draw contest at the state fair, where I had what you might call an encounter with a prize pig name of Sir Francis Bacon, our departure coming soon after. But those quick-drawing dudes were something to watch, except no matter how closely I watched I didn't really see. Janet was like that. The time from gun in the purse to gun pointed at us was nothing at all. Luckily for us, in less than nothing at all I was in midair.

"Ow," Janet yelled, clutching her wrist and doubling over, the pink gun tumbling down and clattering across the cement path. That doubling over was a bit much, and the amount of blood involved not worth a mention. I trotted over to the gun, collected it, and gave it to Bernie.

"Let's get in out of the cold," Bernie said, which was odd, the night being on the balmy side for this time of year. But no one objected. We entered casita 17C, me first, then Janet, and Bernie last, the pink gun dangling from his hand. Our techniques at the Little Detective Agency are pretty damn smooth, whether . . . whether our finances were in good shape or not! Wow! I came close to understanding something, something that gave me a good feeling so I didn't bother to try understanding any better. I had other things to do, whatever they might turn out to be, and I had to be ready.

✿   ✿   ✿

"I should call the cops," Janet said, holding her wrist under the faucet at the kitchen sink, the cigarette still in the corner of her mouth.

Bernie was in the living room, checking out the pictures on the walls, but the living room was only a few steps from the kitchen and there were no walls in between, so our security set-up was good. Security is always on my mind. I'm a pro, don't forget.

"I can give you a few names," Bernie said in a distracted sort of way. His attention seemed to be on something else, possibly those wall pictures, all of them about fires: forest fires, house fires, office tower fires, car fires, airplane fires, even one of a burning match, but a very close up burning match so it looked huge.

Janet dabbed at her wrist and peered at the paper towel. Not a spot of red. She balled it up and tossed it across the room and right into a wastebasket. Was she a perp or a gangbanger? I was starting to like her anyway.

Meanwhile Bernie was taking a close look at the burning match picture, his back to us.

"Are you going to kill me?" she said. Which was kind of upsetting, what with me starting to like her and all. Why would we do something like that? Just because she'd drawn down on us? If we'd killed everyone who'd done that then . . . then the traffic wouldn't be so bad in these parts. Whoa! Where had that come from? The truth was I didn't even get it.

"Why would we do that?" Bernie said, without turning. Just as I'd thought. We're alike in some ways, me and Bernie. But more important, the fact that he hadn't turned meant he was missing how Janet was glaring at him, like she wanted to do something real bad. I reminded myself that we already knew that from what had just gone down outside, and eased my way a little closer to her.

"Are you stupid or somethin'?" She stubbed the cigarette out in the sink, stubbed it out real hard. "You murdered Werner. Now you come for me."

Bernie turned. "Who told you we did that?"

Janet shrugged. "Some guy from the DA's office. I didn't catch the name. And I happen to know you lost your license. So you have no right. Scram."

The expression on Bernie's face changed. Janet caught that. Perhaps she realized we never scram. She backed away, bumping into the sink.

Bernie glanced over at all her baggage, piled by the door. "Where were you going?"

"Huh?"

"Just now."

"None of your damn business."

"Fair enough," Bernie said. That surprised her, her eyebrows, not the kind with any hair in them, rose. "How about why?"

"Why?" she said. "Why? I've had enough of this godforsaken place. That's why."

"You're talking about this house?"

"Call this a house? It's a dump. I'm talking about the Valley."

"How long have you been here?"

"Too damn long. I'm drying out in this dustbin of yours. Already dried out so it's probably too late. That's my world class timing for you."

"Your leaving has nothing to do with Werner?"

Her glare relit itself, like one of those fires that wasn't out after all. Whoa! Fire. We had lots of that going on in Janet's pictures and now in her eyes as well. If there'd been time to think about that I might have. "You've got some nerve," Janet said. "Talking so . . . so casually about a man you killed."

"It was self-defense," Bernie said.

"Not the way I heard it."

"From the DA's office?"

She nodded. "They said you set him up. I don't know or care. Werner was involved in so many goddam schemes something like this had to happen. Can you believe I actually loved him? For a few days anyway. Werner himself had no love in him. Well, not quite true."

"He was in love with fire?" Bernie said.

Janet went still. "You're scary." She glanced at me. "Your dog is scary, too."

Scary? Me and Bernie? I didn't get that and then I thought of the night of the broom closet case and how we'd brought justice and I sort of did. Also Bernie's face happened to be somewhat scary at the moment. "His name's Chet," he said.

"Okay, okay," Janet said. "Back off. You thinking of hitting me? I know that look."

What was this? Bernie hitting Janet? Wasn't she a woman? It was off the table. But he did back off, moving into the living room, and taking another look at the fire pictures.

"Did Werner collect these?" he said.

"Werner? That wasn't him. I did the whole thing—buying, framing, hanging."

"It's an interest of yours, too?"

"Pyromania?" Janet said. "What do you take me for?" She gestured with her chin toward the pictures. "I gave them to Werner the day he moved in here." Her eyes got an inward look. "He had love in him that night." She turned to Bernie. "Or something close to it. Close enough."

"Are his things still here?" Bernie said.

"I got rid of them."

"Where?"

"Tuesday was trash day."

Then came a silence. They both eyed that close-up of the burning match.

"We were done," Janet said. "But he wasn't as bad as you think.

Nobody got hurt and insurance covered the losses, meaning it was one of those victimless crimes."

"Bullshit," Bernie said.

My ears went up. Had Bernie ever said that before about anything? I'd had experience with bulls, none of it good, and bullshit itself is a huge subject we may never have time to get into.

"He killed Billy Parsons up on Buzzard's Peak the other night," Bernie went on, "so what are you talking about?"

"That wasn't supposed to happen," Janet said. "Werner told me that astronomy lab or whatever it was—"

"Observatory."

"Observatory, whatever. It was supposed to be deserted."

"What made him think that?"

Janet shrugged. "The client must've told him."

"Who was the client?" Bernie said.

"We never talked about things like that. We had this pipelines thing. Werner read some book about business. It was all about flow charts. We stayed in our own pipelines." Janet thought for a few moments. "Was he an astronomer, Billy what's his name?"

"Billy Parsons," Bernie said. "He worked with ex-cons."

"I don't get it," Janet said. "Werner was an ex-con. Was Billy working with him?"

"I doubt it," Bernie said. "But I actually hadn't thought of that."

Uh-oh. There was bullshit and now this other first. Bernie not thinking something and someone else getting there ahead of him? I got the feeling this case had taken a sudden bad turn and did my best to ignore it.

"Any chance Billy was a poker player?" Janet said.

"I don't think so," said Bernie. "Why?"

"Because," Janet said, "the client was a poker player."

"How do you know that?" Bernie said, his voice getting real quiet. I knew that one. It sent a tingle down to the end of my tail.

"Werner told me. The job was all about payback on some deadbeat."

Bernie was silent for a moment. He stood very still. So did I. So did Janet. Were we all waiting for something important to happen. If so, what?

"And the client's name?"

"I told you—I don't know. Tear the place apart if want. That's what she did."

"Who are you talking about?"

"Bitch who came pounding on the door this afternoon—actually what made my mind up about blowing this goddam town. She didn't give her name. Or ID. No nothin'. I'd say a cop, the rogue kind. But maybe a criminal? There was something wild about her. She had her gun out the whole time."

Bernie went so still, as though he'd turned into a statue. But you don't hear heartbeats from a statue, and I was hearing Bernie's heart beating like I'd never heard it before.

"She searched the place?" His voice was quiet but shaking slightly at the same time. It came close to scaring me.

"That's what I said."

"Did she find anything?"

Janet opened her mouth, then closed it.

"This would be a real bad time to make a mistake," Bernie said. He didn't move at all but suddenly seemed to be looming over her.

Janet gazed up at him. "A little cash might be nice."

Bernie reached into his pocket, thrust over a wad of crumpled bills. Not a big wad, but still.

Janet stuffed it in her purse. "A burner," she said.

"A burner?"

"You know, a burner phone, one of those cheap—"

Bernie's voice rose. "I know what a burner is."

Janet raised her hands like this was a bust. "Werner used

burners all the time, part of his what do you call it? MO? This one musta fallen out of a jacket or something when I was clearing out his stuff. She found it on the closet floor and took it. I didn't try to stop her, even gave her the password. Fire, with three exclamation marks, Werner's password for everything. She scared the shit out of me."

And we didn't? I was a little . . . miffed, would that be it? Maybe we'd meet this scary someone somewhere down the road and show her what's what.

Thirty

What's with the moon? Every so often, you see it in the daytime, but the moon prefers the night. Not every night, it's true. Some nights it's simply gone. But when it's hanging around up there it likes to play tricks, tricks that are all about changing shape. My preference is the big round fat moon. Sometimes I just sit out on our patio behind the house and gaze at it. If Iggy's up he does the same thing, only from behind a window at his place. The sight of that big fat moon, so close, tends to make him howl. I get that, although Iggy has the kind of howl that grows old real quick. Almost before he starts in you can hear shouts rising from houses in the neighborhood. And even from a house or two across the canyon. Iggy's my best pal for a reason. Why I started in on this was because on this particular night the moon was taking on that horned shape, reminding me of devils—true, quite small—knocking on the door on Halloween, my least favorite of all the holidays. Other than the horned moon this drive was a lot like that last wild ride on the broom closet case, which happened under a moonless sky. We brought the night then, and we were bringing it now. I could tell by Bernie's jaw, green in the dashboard light, a little muscle jumping in it from time to time, like it couldn't wait.

We drove into Gila City, climbed into the hills where the houses got nicer and bigger, and rolled slowly toward the wall with a tall gate in the middle. Last time it opened all by itself. Now it stayed closed. Bernie pulled over and parked in a little space between two mesquite trees with low branches that hid the Beast nicely. I was all set to hop out when Bernie turned to me with his finger across his lips. I knew that one. He took the .45 from the glove box, grabbed a coiled rope from under his seat and we walked in silence to the metal gate with black bars spear tipped in gold.

"What do you think?" he said, his voice soft and calm like a night breeze. How pleasant that was, especially since we had no breeze tonight! That was Bernie, stepping up as usual, taking charge of the weather. What a guy! That was what was on my mind as I soared over those gold spear tips with plenty of room to spare, and if not plenty at least some. Don't be surprised. Leaping is my best thing. How then had I flunked the leaping test at K-9 school? My memories of that were blurry but one thing for sure: a cat was involved. There were no cats tonight, amigo.

Meanwhile Bernie had tied a loop at one end of the rope, turning it into a lasso. From what I'd heard, possibly from his old baseball coach at Chisholm High on a case involving something or other, Bernie had worked on a ranch before baseball took over his summers. Now he spun that loop around with a kind of thrilling whoosh whoosh and floated it up up and then set-tling perfectly down and around one of those gold spear tips. He drew the loop tight and climbed up the gate like a rock climber, maybe not the fastest rock climber but pretty fast for a man with a wounded leg from the war—Bernie never wears shorts, by the way—and then twisted around at the top without the slightest trouble I'm going to mention and lowered himself to the ground. I bounded—well, not bounded on account of how quiet we were being, more like I simply crept over to him and nuzzled that poor leg. He grinned down at me, his teeth the color of the moon but not so devilish.

Night is full of shadows. We made our way through them as we approached the Spanish-style mansion with the gold bar over the door, the mansion that didn't seem very big at first. What had Bernie said? Don't be fooled—it turns its back to the road? Something like that. You can't be fooled when Bernie's got your six. He's mine, by the way, just a reminder. As for six, it may be a number of some sort, but far beyond two, and not my responsibility.

All the windows were dark. We didn't go near the door, but began walking around the house. There was no need for any back and forth. We're a team, me and Bernie, which is probably clear by now. Since I'd walked around it once already I led the way, although I actually never need a reason. Also I seemed to be trotting. We were in the shadow of the house now, not easy to see much of anything, but in the nation within we're fine with not seeing much of anything. I rounded the house, pit-patting alongside, and stopped at the see-through wall with the ground level deck on the other side, where we'd had that little get together with Axel, Gillian, CeeCee, and the boys. Bernie came up behind me, perhaps stumbling just the slightest bit. Not seeing much of anything doesn't work quite as well for humans, no offense.

He gazed down at me. "You seem to know your way around here." He whispered that. I loved that whisper of his, don't hear it nearly enough. It's very soft but there's a deep rumble of power behind it that I feel instead of hearing. But enough of that. I leaped over the see-through wall, not as tall as the gate out front, easy peasy. I turned to Bernie.

Uh-oh. Did we have a problem? Maybe, since there were no spear tips to lasso plus we no longer appeared to have the lasso. Bernie stood on one side of the see-through wall and I stood on the other. I looked at him. He looked at me. Then he sort of bounced up and down on his toes? What was he thinking? Whatever it was he stopped bouncing and reached as high as he could, just barely getting his finger tips on the top of the glass wall. Not a thick wall—I should have mentioned that already. More like the thickness of, say, a nice juicy steak. I smelled no food at all at the moment. Maybe not an important fact, but all the same I suddenly found myself on the peckish side.

Meanwhile Bernie bounced once more and then again, but on this second bounce pulled himself up and over the see-through wall, sticking the landing right beside me, and making the whole thing look easy. And if not easy, then at least he did it, so let's not split hairs, one of those strange and somewhat frightening human sayings. He flashed me a quick grin, his teeth shining in the light of that horned moon. How nice! He was pleased with himself. This little expedition was already a success, although I got the feeling we weren't calling it a night.

We moved across the deck. Were we planning on entering the house? That was my guess. I headed for the slider where I'd gone in before, following Axie in his search for treats, but now it was closed. Bernie grasped the handle, gave it a little push. Locked. No biggie. Bernie could handle just about any lock that's out there. Once I'd seen him open a padlock as big as his hand with only a toothpick, a toothpick he'd taken right out of the mouth of a passing wino who turned out to be not a wino but the actual perp. But not important. The important thing was that Bernie was now feeling in his pocket for the exact right opener. A ball of lint, perhaps? How amazing that would be! But before he came up with anything, I heard footsteps in the house. Bernie did not. I gave him a slight push. We moved out of the moonlight and into the shadows.

The slider opened. Mama stepped out. She wore a robe and slippers and her hair, white as the moonlight, was wild. She lit a cigarette and walked off toward the pool, leaving the slider open. We slipped inside, moving as one, me first.

It was dark inside the house. That didn't matter to me. I could sort of hear and smell all those huge rooms, and of course my paws already knew the feel of the marble floors, hard and soft at the same time. My paws ended up taking over, leading us down the broad curving staircase, along a broad hall, through more rooms, down more stairs, and finally we reached the office cave, deep inside this enormous space. The door was slightly open. Blue light leaked through. From inside came the sound of Weatherly's voice: ". . . so don't worry about me. I just need some time. Maybe down in Mexico or a bitch in—" She suddenly went silent. I looked up at Bernie. His eyes were lost in darkness. Then Weatherly spoke again. ". . . need some time. Maybe down in Mexico or a beach in Costa . . ."

She talked on—maybe in a very slightly liquidy way, not sounding quite like herself—but meanwhile Bernie shoved the door open wider with his toe and we moved inside, Bernie closing the door softly behind us. No sign of Weatherly. A man in a white short-sleeve shirt, his back to us and wearing headphones, sat before all those enormous TV monitors, stacks of computer stuff, twisted cables, little round white speakers, with different colored lights flashing here and there, almost like this was all one enormous creature, a bit of a scary thought. Other than that, I wasn't scared at all. We moved across the floor, Weatherly talking about alone time and thinking things over, the man with headphones hunched over a keyboard. We stood right behind him. He smelled of sweat, the anxious kind and the scared kind. Bernie tapped him on the shoulder.

That sent a jolt through the dude, quite pleasant to see. He whirled around, whipping off the headphones, and took in the sight of us. Meanwhile I took in the sight of him, crew-cut, thin-faced, although not wearing a tie at the moment. I'd only seen Holger Niberg in pictures and kind of liked how he looked. Now, seeing him in person, I did not.

Holger started to rise. Bernie put a hand on the top of his head and pushed him back down.

"Where is she?" Bernie said. He didn't raise his voice but something in it made the fur on my neck rise.

"I—I don't know who you mean," Holger said. "I don't know who you are."

"You do and you do," Bernie said. "Try again."

Holger's eyes shifted one way and then another. He was having so many thoughts, so fast! "Yes, I know who you are. I apologize. I didn't mean—"

"Where is she?"

"I don't know. I swear. He keeps things compartmentalized and—"

Bernie grabbed a handful of that white short-sleeve shirt, right below the chin, and jerked Holger up off the chair, in fact, off the floor, his feet in the air. Their faces were close together. The expression on Bernie's was murderous. The expression on Holger's was that of a man about to be murdered. I've seen both in my career. I know.

Holger raised his hands in the giving up position. Bernie lowered him to the floor and let go. "He's got her somewhere—that's all I know." Holger tilted his head to the stacks of computer stuff. "I'm supposed to create this message for you, so you won't come looking."

"You sample her voice and then make it say anything you want?" Bernie said.

"Basically," Holger said, his eyes lighting up a bit, like at last something interesting was happening. "The program I've designed is a self-learning algorithmic pyramid that exponentially—"

Bernie's hand made a whooshing slash though the air. I could hear the whoosh. Holger went silent.

"Did you pull the same deep fake with Billy?"

"Oh, no," Holger said, suddenly hoarse like he might have been about to cry. "Billy was a wonderful man. I'd never have done anything to hurt him. Even though I was in so deep I—"

Bernie's hand made just the suggestion of an air slash, but

now that was all it took. "Are you saying Billy's call to his dad was real?"

"Real in the sense of . . . ?"

Bernie reached out to grab Holger's shirt front again, but Holger started talking fast before he could. "They hated each other—"

"Billy and Axel?"

"Yeah. But because of the domestic situation it was all sublimated. Axel loves his kids. In his own way, but he does. When I got out I still owed him a million two. I thought maybe he would have let it go—I did three years—but he didn't and now he was into the possibilities of A.I. to supercharge all his schemes—the back door blockchain edits, Tapp, some innovation in the NFT space—"

"Tapp or Zapp?" Bernie said.

"Tapp. Zapp's a pretty simple app. Tapp will be much more sophisticated, a way to tap into the banking system like tapping maple syrup from the tree. The point is he wanted me to work off the debt. I refused and Billy was right behind me. Putting himself second to me. You understand?" And now the tears were flowing, streaming down his face. "The call to the dad was a warning, to get Billy to back off."

"By stealing all his father's money?"

Holger dabbed at his eyes. "I had nothing to do with that program. Axie wrote it. By no means perfectly but . . ." He looked down. "Good enough."

"Axie?"

"He's a natural," Holger said.

"A natural criminal?" said Bernie.

"A natural programmer. Axie didn't even know the purpose. Axel made it seem like a game. Like Billy and Axel were just goofing on each other."

"But you taught Axie."

"Just one or two A.I. online lessons before my release date. Axel got in touch. I thought those lessons were all he wanted from me. When I got out and it was clear there was more, I . . . I took off. Billy helped. The plan was to get me to Estonia. I know the place. I'd be safe."

Bernie waved all that away. "What's Greta Analytics?"

"Never heard of it." Holger glanced past us at the door. "But Axel's mother's name is Greta." He bit his lip. "She lives here."

Bernie nodded, like that made sense. Not to me, but right there is why we're a team, me and Bernie. "If Billy knew what had really gone down," he said, "why didn't he tell us? Or the cops?"

"Maybe he would have. But first he thought he could get Axel to return his dad's money. Involving law enforcement is against the ProCon philosophy."

Bernie gave him a long look. "Instead, he got himself killed."

"That was an accident."

"What are you talking about?" Bernie said. "We were on the mountain that night."

"It was meant to be a warning, bring me back into the fold. Axel knew how much I loved that little observatory, but he thought we weren't there, Billy and I."

"You believe that?"

Holger looked down.

"Where were you?"

"Camping in the desert, both of us. The plan was to drive to L.A. the next day, where I'd take the overnight flight to Tallinn."

"Why did Billy leave? Why did he go up to Buzzard's Peak?"

"I didn't know that was where he was going. He just said he'd be back soon."

"Did Axel call him? Luring him there on some pretext? Like maybe to negotiate restoring the forty-seven K?"

There was a dark flash—if that makes any sense—in Holger's eyes. "I don't know," he said.

"You do," Bernie told him. "You just don't want to."

Holger said nothing. He sat down in the chair—sat down hard, like his legs wouldn't hold him up—and didn't come close to looking Bernie in the eye.

"What about the call to me?" Bernie said. "Supposedly from Meelo. Who made that deep fake?"

Holger took a deep breath. "Axel's big on stalking drones. They've got an acoustic component, can scoop up conversations from a thousand feet in the right conditions. Such as those prevailing the other day in Empty Wells."

"That's not what I asked," Bernie said. "Who made the Meelo deep fake? Axie again?"

Holger shrugged. "Practically any decent programmer could, once it's up and running. But it was Axel."

"And now you're back in the fold," Bernie said.

"Do I have a choice?" Holger started crying again. "I had no idea Billy was up there. That's the truth."

"Tell yourself whatever you want," Bernie said. "Where's Weatherly?"

Holger shot another glance at the door, this one real quick. "I told you—I don't know."

Bernie drew the .45. "Any reason I shouldn't shoot you right now?"

Holger shrank back. He was still doing that when the door banged wide open

All at once we had a very complicated situation, very complicated and very bad. Axel stood in the doorway, but he was mostly hidden behind Weatherly, with one arm around her neck. In his free hand he held a gun. Duct tape covered her mouth and her wrists were duct-taped together. I saw all kinds of things in her eyes but fear wasn't one of them. And there was more. Behind Weatherly and Axel I could make out Mama, her face twisted and a shotgun in her hands.

Axel smiled. "Excellent question, Bernie," he said. "I can't think of one single reason." Then, real quick, he raised the gun, pointed and squeezed. *CRACK!* The crack of a gunshot, followed by a cry from Holger. He tried to bring his hands to his chest but couldn't quite do it. Instead he toppled off the stool and lay motionless on his back. The front of his short-sleeved white shirt turned red.

Axel slowly turned the gun, now pointing it at Weatherly, the muzzle touching her ear. "Drop it, Bernie."

Drop it? Why would Bernie do that? Yes, Axel was hiding behind Weatherly but was he completely invisible? No. I could see part of his face, a part of his face that was much bigger than a spinning dime, and Bernie can shoot spinning dimes out of the air. Axel didn't know that and now it was going to cost him. Shoot him, Bernie! Shoot him! And now in Weatherly's eyes I saw the same message: Shoot him!

But Bernie did not shoot him. Instead, his fingers moving very slowly, he let go of the .45. It fell to the floor, somehow making no sound at all, at least that I could hear. Imagine that, what with me who hears everything!

"Thank you, Bernie," Axel said. In no hurry, he now swung the gun forward, aimed right at Bernie.

At that moment an amazing look rose in Weatherly's eyes, a furious look that said she'd had enough. Then, so quick and so strong, she twisted around—or at least half-twisted around—and drove her shoulder into Axel's chest. Maybe not hard enough to do much, or even make him let her go, what with no ramp-up space between them, but by then I, too, had had enough. I didn't think, not for a second, a lucky break since I'm at my very best when thinking is off the table. I sprang. That was all. I simply sprang at Axel, easily reachable in a single spring, at least one of mine.

He turned the gun on me and squeezed the trigger. At the same

time, Weatherly made a muffled cry—muffled but enraged—
and shouldered him again.

CRACK!

I felt that round part the fur on my shoulder and zip on by.
Then I was on him, Weatherly wriggling free. I knocked Axel
to the ground. We rolled, first with me on top, then him—a big
strong bad guy, no doubt about that—then . . . But no. Not then
me on top again. Instead he stuck that gun right into my muzzle
good and hard and—

BLAM!

That was the .45. The top half of Axel's head—well, I won't
describe that part. Axel slumped off me. I scrambled to my feet.
Bernie was on his knees, the .45 still trained on Axel. Weatherly
had fallen to the floor and was slowly rising. At that point Mama
stepped into the room, raising the shotgun, her face showing you
what rage was all about. She wrapped her finger around the trigger, which was exactly when Weatherly kicked out and knocked
the shotgun from her hands. It spun away, hit the door jamb butt
end first and then went off, all by itself.

BOOM!

The blast blew Mama clear out of the room. She lay motionless in the hall. I won't describe her either.

Then it was just me, Bernie, and Weatherly. We started moving closer to each other, like closing a circle. They both patted me
all over, checking for who knows what. Hey! I was fine!

Through one of the little round speakers came Weatherly's
voice, or close to it: "Don't worry about me."

Thirty-one

Their feet were touching under the table, Bernie's and Weatherly's. I could see that from where I was enjoying my steak tips, the table being on the deck at the Dry Gulch Steak House and Saloon. Strip for Bernie, ribeye for Weatherly, red wine for them, water for me. We had a couple of visitors at that dinner. First came Fritzie Bortz, an old motorcycle cop buddy who'd gotten into too many wrecks and was now sheriff of the county next to ours, this rise, quite surprising to lots of folks, following his recent marriage to Rayette, who'd grown up in West Texas with her best pal Randa Lee, who was now the governor's wife and running things on account of the governor being non compos, whatever that means.

"Hi, lovebirds," he said. "Got something for you, Bernie." He laid an envelope on the table.

"What's this?" Bernie said.

"Your license. Reinstated. Good to go. Signed by me personally."

"Why you?"

"I'm the new DA. You hadn't heard? Rayette and Randa Lee took a dislike to the previous gal. I'm stepping in for the time being. Still sheriff. Wearing two hats. Two hats Bortz—might be my campaign slogan."

"What campaign?" Bernie said.

"For governor, when the time comes," Fritzie said. "Meanwhile the two hats thing will look good on my . . . what's the word for it? Starts with C and got a V in it?"

"CV," Weatherly said.

"Bingo, little lady," Fritzie said. "Don't let this one get away, Bernie."

Bernie and Weatherly exchanged a quick, private look, very nice to see, in my opinion.

Not long after that we got a call from Trummy.

"Guess what? The fraud squad chief's retiring next year and I'm on the short list."

"Congrats."

"On the strength of this case," Trummy said. "I don't feel right about it."

"Why not?" Bernie said.

"You did the work."

"You managed it," Bernie said. "That's what a chief does."

The second visitor was Meelo, wearing a suit and now shoes as well.

"Word is you had no client on this recent affair," he said.

Bernie nodded.

"Then allow me to be the client after the fact. Here's a check for one hundred K."

"Why you?" Bernie said, not taking the check.

"Why me?" said Meelo. "Because if my information is correct, you put an end to someone who was deep faking me. Surely you can see how dangerous that could be, not just for me personally but for my plans and therefore the whole future of . . . well, everything. No sense in false modesty at a time like this."

"Please divide it in thirds," Bernie said. "One for the Parsons, one for Gillian, one for CeeCee."

Meelo blinked. "And how much for you?"

Bernie smiled. "You're the math guy."

"Meaning zero? I'm a little lost. And if that's really how you want it, why not distribute it yourself?"

"It's better like this," Bernie said.

❋   ❋   ❋

"I didn't know the voice of my own son," Mr. Parsons said.

"Please," said Edna. "Stop." Her hands and wrists were all purple from getting stuck so much, but otherwise she was looking not so bad.

"But—"

"No buts. It's a deep fake. That's the whole point. Isn't that right, Bernie?"

Bernie nodded. This was the morning after the Dry Gulch dinner. Weatherly had slept over and now we were having breakfast at the Parsons, Trixie included. One thing about having Trixie around, I didn't have to worry about Iggy at all. Trixie handled that without even trying. For example, he was curled up in a corner, his gaze never leaving her, and she was napping on a footstool, not even close by.

"Now just try these pecan buns," Edna said. "I bought them myself."

And they smelled very nice, but before anyone could get going on them the doorbell rang.

"I almost forgot," Mr. Parsons said. "We invited Gillian over."

"Good," said Bernie.

"With the boys."

Bernie sat back.

"With Billy gone," Mrs. Parsons said, "we've changed our will."

Weatherly is not a crier, as I may have mentioned. But now her eyes teared up. "The boys are the beneficiaries?" she said.

Mrs. Parsons nodded. Meanwhile, Mr. Parsons opened the door. Gillian, Felix, and Axie came in, the boys stopping in their tracks at once. Bernie rose and went over to them. He pulled up a chair, sat down at their level.

"Anything you want to say to me?" he said. "Anything at all? There's no wrong answer."

Felix and Axie glanced at each other. Then they looked everywhere except in Bernie's direction. But finally right at him.

"You   " Felix began, and then turned all red and came to a halt.

"Killed our . . . our dad," said Axie.

Felix nodded.

"I did," Bernie said.

"He was mean sometimes," Felix said. He tried saying more but his voice broke.

"You killed him cause he was mean sometimes?" Axie said, his voice rising to a shout. "You . . . you . . . !" He balled his hands into fists.

Bernie spoke very quietly. "I killed him because it was him or us—Chet, Weatherly, me."

The boys both went very pale. Axie seemed to calm down almost right away, but Felix began to cry. Axie punched him on the shoulder, but very softly, perhaps what humans call a love tap. Felix stopped crying.

"These pecan buns are best when hot," Edna called. "Come and get 'em."

It turned out that somehow Iggy had been the first to get the message that the pecan buns were best when hot. Now he had the whole bag and appeared to be headed in the direction of the stairs. That led to a certain amount of chasing, much of it involving rapid changes of direction and also changes of possession. Was it fair to say that in confined spaces such as this, Trixie was better suited to rapid changes of direction? No it was not. It was very unfair. During these proceedings, which seemed to last for some time, I was pretty sure I heard the boys laughing once or twice, at what I had no idea.

ACKNOWLEDGMENTS

I'm blessed to have such a wonderful team at Forge. Many many thanks to Kristin Sevick, Troix Jackson, Libby Collins, Jennifer McClelland, Anthony Parisi, and Linda Quinton. Chet and Bernie couldn't do it without you!

Turn the page for a sneak peek at
Mrs. Plansky's newest thrilling adventure

Available Summer 2025 from Forge Books

One

"What's your favorite sports cliché?" said Kev Dinardo.

"In general?" Mrs. Plansky said. "Or possibly useful at the moment?"

Kev turned to her and smiled, a sweat drop quivering on the end of his chin. They hadn't known each other long, just a few months, mostly getting together on the tennis court, but it was enough for her to have learned he had two smiles: a big one when he was happy about something, which was often, and a small, quickly vanishing one that flashed when he was struck by an unexpected insight. This particular smile was the second.

Mrs. Plansky searched her mind. Her background was not one of those sports-free backgrounds, so she knew many sports clichés, but now she came up empty. That was frustrating. This whole situation, taking place on Court #1 at the New Sunshine Golf and Tennis Club, was frustrating. Her face felt flushed, and not just from the exertion and the heat. Mrs. Plansky loved playing tennis. She liked to win. She did not hate to lose. Her son Jack out in Arizona, a gifted player with professional experience on the satellite tour and now a teaching pro, hated to lose. He liked to win. Did he still love or had he ever loved playing tennis? She shied away from that question. What if he'd devoted his whole professional life to something he didn't love? What kind of toll would that take? But this wasn't the slightest bit relevant, not at the moment. What was relevant? The fact that although she didn't hate to lose, she hated to lose like this.

"Here are some," Kev said. They were on a changeover between games, sitting on a courtside bench. The sweat drop wobbled off his chin—a strong, squarish chin that might have been a bit much on some male faces but not his—and fell, somehow landing on her bare knee, cooling a tiny circle of her skin. "It ain't over till it's over. One play at a time. Go down swinging."

Mrs. Plansky was unmoved by any of them, especially the last. Over on the other courtside bench their opponents had set aside their energy drinks and were rising. Changeovers lasted forty-five seconds, but at club level events no one was strict about it, although the umpire in her chair did seem to be glancing down at them. Also the opponents, representing the Old Sunshine Country Club in this North Beaches Sixties and Over Mixed Doubles Championship match, were now on their feet and bouncing a bit, eager to get this—what would you call it? Demolition? Close enough. This demolition over and done. The two clubs were ancient rivals, ancient for this part of the world, going all the way back to the 1995 founding of New Sunshine. Old Sunshine dated from 1989 and had old Florida pretensions. Its members had to wear white on the court. Half white was the rule at New Sunshine: Kev, for example, now in white shorts and a crimson tee, and Mrs. Plansky in a sleeveless peach-colored tennis dress with white trim perhaps making up ten percent of the whole, or not even. She could be something of an outlaw at times.

"Just choose one," Kev said. "I hate to point it out, Loretta, but we're running out of time."

Mrs. Plansky rose and picked up her racket. The opponents were striding onto the court, the woman, Jenna St. something or other taking her place at the net and the man, Russell Curtis or possibly Curtis Russell, heading to the baseline to serve. Neither of them looked older than forty-nine. They'd had work done, of course, but still. Mrs. Plansky, too, had had work done, just the once a few years ago, on an afternoon outing with her daughter Nina, down for a few days from her home in Hilton Head. A nice mother-daughter Botox bonding experience that had resulted in temporary simulacrums of rejuvenation here and there on her face. She was trying to recall some funny remark of Nina's on the subject of needles when Kev said, "Loretta?"

"Right," said Mrs. Plansky. She sipped from her water bottle and took in the here and now. They had an audience, maybe fifty or sixty members of both clubs, sitting in lawn chairs and on the clubhouse patio, some fanning themselves. It was the first hot and humid day of the year. Mrs. Plansky was unsure of Kev's age but probably no more than five or six years less than hers, and she herself was seventy-one. She had an artificial hip, in no way detrimental, and in fact the best joint in her body, a sturdy body that had served her well in many ways, even capable of some foot speed at one time. She'd been a tomboy as a kid, played peewee hockey with the boys back home in Rhode Island. But actually irrelevant to the present situation, the headline for which would be: trailing 6–1, 5–love in a best-of-three set match. She didn't have to look to know that some of the spectators were glancing at their watches, planning drinks, dinner, perhaps a quick sail or swim. That was the overview. Mrs. Plansky, going back to her days in business, believed in overviews. Norm had been more about winging it; a bit strange since he'd been the one with the engineering degree.

She put her hand on Kev's shoulder, a thick shoulder, much more muscular than Norm's, Norm being husband, business partner, tennis partner, and love of her life, with whom she'd played countless matches and had looked forward to many more when they retired down to Ponte d'Oro, but one of those quick and merciless cancers had felled him soon after. How she'd loved playing with him! But Kev was the better player. The thought gave her a pang of disloyalty. Was this the time for all that? Certainly not! Overviews yes, but you could overdo the over part and end up with a blurry picture. Focus, Loretta!

"Kev," she said. "You're wrong about running out of time."

"Oh?" he said, an expectant expression crossing his face. For a second or two she could see how he'd looked at a kid.

"There is no clock in tennis. Let's stretch it out, way, way out."

Kev laughed. "Like Einstein's relativity!"

"I don't know about that," said Mrs. Plansky.

And they were both laughing when they took their places on the court to return serve. Puzzled frowns appeared on the faces of their opponents. Who laughs when they're getting their asses kicked?

Late afternoons in April could bring enormous thunderheads looming in off the sea, and somehow those four players—Russell Curtis, Jenna St. something or other, Kev, and Mrs. Plansky— were still on Court #1 to see those thunderheads closing in. By that time Mrs. Plansky knew that Russell was the first name, since Jenna had taken to hissing to him after some of the points, as in "Russell! Hit to the open court!" And "Russell! He's getting you with that wide serve every goddam time!" Also, "Her backhand volley, Russell? Hello? How many times do you need to see it?"

Mrs. Plansky and Kev chipped and sliced, lobbed and dinked, came to the net, stayed back, served Australian, used signals, pretended to use signals, went down the middle over and over until Russell and Jenna were squeezing in so close that they whacked each other's rackets trying to make the shot, which Mrs. Plansky and Kev took as an invitation to start hitting down the line. Time expanded beautifully. Mrs. Plansky stopped feeling flushed, her flush perhaps finding its way to Jenna's face. Mrs. Plansky's kick serve even appeared, after an absence of fifteen years. Not a word was spoken, not between Mrs. Plansky and Kev. There was no need. Had she actually patted him on the

butt as he pulled off yet one more killer backpedaling overhead?
Good grief.

Final score: New Sunshine 1–6, 7–6 (11), 6–4. They'd hugged
at the end, pretty standard in mixed doubles. Kev had lifted
her right off the ground—which was not standard—somehow
making it look easy. She'd been struck by a strange and simple
thought at that moment: *More.*

The first raindrops were falling by the time Mrs. Plansky and Kev
left the clubhouse. He'd come on his bike, so they stowed it in
the back of her SUV—Mrs. Plansky, a mother and grandmother,
drove SUVs by long habit—and she took him home, their two
trophies bumping together in the backseat.

"Wow," Kev said. "Unreal."

Mrs. Plansky nodded. She tried to think of any other time in
her life when the unreal had really happened, and found several right away. For example, there was the camping trip when
the kids, Nina and Jack, were small, Norm working at a small
engineering firm and making little, Mrs. Plansky a paralegal
and making slightly more, when she, fixing sandwiches, said,
"Wouldn't it be nice if the knife could toast the bread while you
sliced?" An unreality that just popped out. Norm, dozing in his
sleeping bag, sat right up. Three years later came the Plansky
Toaster Knife, and the small fortune—quite small given the kinds
of fortunes that are out there these days—that followed. Or how
about Norm on his deathbed—Norm, who couldn't hold the
simplest tune—suddenly singing "My Funny Valentine" in a
smooth, lovely baritone? And he a tenor to boot? Or take that
fairly recent Romanian adventure where after decades of law abid-
ance, she'd purloined—

"Next left," Kev said, gesturing toward a lane lined with silver
buttonwoods and paved with sun-bleached seashells. His hand

touched down on Mrs. Plansky's hand, resting on the console. He gave a little squeeze. Her hand, acting strictly on its own, rolled over and squeezed back. Rolled over? Rolled over like . . like some . . . some eager beaver rolling over in bed! Eager beaver? For God's sake! Get a grip. The flush, maybe just on loan to Jenna, returned to her face. What with endorphins and all that, Mrs. Plansky knew she was in a heightened state, just from the length of the match, never mind the triumphant conclusion, but still. Was something about to happen? If so, what? Despite the fact that she was not dating—although she and Kev had had dinner together at the new sushi place by the marina once or twice, which couldn't be called dating—and had never visited any of those apps—Match.com, OkCupid, Mishmash.net, whatever all those names were—and was perfectly content with things as they were, deep down Mrs. Plansky knew the answer to what could happen. It could be . . . anything! Somewhere in the middle distance thunder boomed.

Kev's hand moved away. He pointed. "Second driveway."

Ah, a baritone. She hadn't realized that until this moment. A full-time baritone. The rain was pelting down now, the windshield wipers on max, the car steaming up inside. Steaming up would be an example of that literary technique where nature imitates the moods of man, the name not coming to her at the moment, although she could picture Mr. Cabral, tenth-grade English teacher, a little guy with nicotine fingers and nicotine mustache, explaining the whole thing. Mrs. Plansky took the second driveway. Thunder boomed again, closer now, and the sky tried out a rapid color selection, settling on purple.

Kev's house rose at the end of the driveway, an elevated house with hurricane-resistant curved lines, streamlined and perhaps bigger than it appeared. Through the gun barrel pilings she could see the ocean, a strip of beach, a white, crimson trimmed boat with a tall tuna tower, tied to a wooden dock. Perhaps yacht would be the right word, more precise than boat. How big? Mrs. Plansky was no expert on yachts—Norm prone to seasickness in anything bigger than a kayak—but she guessed about fifty feet, although the yacht, streamlined like the house, also might be bigger than it appeared.

Mrs. Plansky parked in front of the house. "My, my," she said, "what a lovely—"

Time, which had slowed down so nicely on Court #1 now sped up in a way that made it hard to keep track of things and was not nice at all. First came another boom, this one the loudest yet, practically right on top of them. Then—but more accurately at the same instant—the sleek white yacht with the crimson trim burst into flames, exploded, was replaced by a ball of fire.

Kev jumped out of the car and ran under the house, toward the dock. Mrs. Plansky jumped out, too, and ran after him through the pouring rain, for no reason, just instinctive heart-pounding thoughtlessness on her part, her mind completely empty of thought. Well, not quite true. There was one thought: What about the lightning that always preceded thunder, thunder actually being the sound of lightning, as Norm had explained to the kids on another one of those camping trips? Mrs. Plansky had seen no lightning.

TWO

Too late. There was nothing to be done, the fire already in its roaring mid-life stage. Mrs. Plansky realized all that but at the same time she found a hose coiled on the dock, turned on the faucet, and was now sending a limp stream of water into the conflagration, somehow all the more pitiful since it was still raining pretty hard to no effect on the fire. From where she stood she could see the name of the boat, gold-painted on the stern: *Lizette*. The name melted away, slowly at first and then fast. The lines tying the boat burned up and *Lizette* tilted toward the sea and began drifting off. Roaring amped down. Sizzling amped up. Mrs. Plansky glanced at Kev. He stood by a mooring bollard, arms folded across his chest, face impassive, the fire reflected in his eyes. Mrs. Plansky turned off the faucet, recoiled the hose, and moved beside him, putting her arm around his back. They were both soaked through and through.

At first he didn't seem to notice her, might as well have been a statue with a pulse. She thought about saying, *It could have been worse*, but that was stupid. What would be helpful or comforting or at least relevant that wasn't stupid? She still hadn't come up with anything when the rain stopped all at once. Kev suddenly came to life, turned, took her in his arms, and kissed her, a kiss that grew deep, passionate, intimate, and took Mrs. Plansky completely by surprise, but which she returned in kind. Surprise number two, although in kind might not have been accurate, since she'd been out of practice with Norm gone—as long as you didn't count the events of one unplanned night during her

Romanian adventure, a sort of sub-adventure. But now the memory of that got mixed in with present-time action, a super-charging combo of mind and body, so who knows what would have come next there on Kev's dock, with *Lizette,* her fire flickering out, now mostly underwater, only the sport tower and the ends of the outrigger rods still showing? Mrs. Plansky's heightened state had heightened some more, so much that she felt like a different person and not a seventy-one-year-old widow with an artificial hip and perhaps—well, no perhaps about it—a few extra pounds on board a body that had always been strongly built, which was how she preferred to look at that whole question. So the truth was that anything could have come next out on Kev's dock despite—or because of!—the end of *Lizette,* but right then sirens sounded, close by and urgent. They let go and backed away from each other. Thunder boomed one more time, distant now and in the west, the storm drifting inland.

A fire truck rolled up the driveway, lights flashing, siren off, seashells crunching under the big wheels. Three firefighters hopped out and hurried toward the dock, two men and a woman. They had numbers on their helmets—27, 99, 133. They took in the remains of the fire and didn't bother unspooling their fire hose. 99 snapped a few photos on his phone and 133 made a call on his. 27, the woman, turned to Kev and Mrs. Plansky, gave them each a quick, close look.

"Anyone on board?"

"No, thank God," Kev said.

"This your place?"

"Yes. Well, mine. My name's Dinardo."

27 motioned toward what remained of *Lizette.* "What happened, Mr. Dinardo?"

"We were just driving in and the rain was coming down hard but I got a pretty good look. It was a lightning strike. Toward the stern, I think, but I'm not sure. It was just a big bright flash."

27 glanced at Mrs. Plansky. "Anything to add to that?"

Mrs. Plansky didn't quite know what to add. She would have preferred subtraction, specifically regarding the lightning strike. There had to have been one but that wasn't the same as seeing it. She ended up saying, "I don't think I've ever heard a louder boom." And thus sounding stupid.

27 didn't seem at all surprised by that. She turned back to Kev.

"What kind of vessel?"

"Bertram 50S."

"Diesel?" she said.

"Yes."

"Tank capacity?"

"Twelve hundred and some."

"How full?"

"Only about a quarter, maybe less."

27 turned to the other two firefighters, standing on the edge of the dock. "Any slick on the water?"

"Nope," said 99, a short, broadly built guy with a grizzled beard.

"Musta all combusted," said 133, a tall, skinny kid who looked like he might still have been in high school.

"Uh-huh," said 27, her tone discouraging further comment on his part. The kid looked down at his shoes—not shoes, of course, but heavy rubber boots with yellow toe caps. "And get hold of the harbormaster."

"Already done," said 99.

27 turned to Kev. "How's your insurance?"

"Good," said Kev.

"Don't want to jump the gun but the harbormaster will be wanting to short haul what's left down there."

"Should be covered," Kev said.

27 nodded. "Act of God."

"Yeah," said Kev. He shot Mrs. Plansky a quick glance. "How about we get started on the paperwork?" 27 said. "Sure." Kev gave Mrs. Plansky a little smile and followed 27 to the fire truck.

The sky began to darken, night moving in fast the way it did down here, down here being how Mrs. Plansky still thought of Florida. A bright light appeared to the south, grew brighter very fast, and soon the harbormaster's patrol boat was gliding into the dock. 133 helped the harbormaster tie up. 99, the short, thickly built guy with the grizzled beard, approached her.

"Mrs. Plansky?" he said.

"Uh, yes?"

"Thought I recognized you."

That was the moment Mrs. Plansky realized she was still wearing her sleeveless peach-colored tennis dress with white trim, not at all a water-repellent garment and still soaked from the rain and therefore on the clingy side. Very clingy, in fact. She could feel just how clingy it was, especially here and there, but dared not look.

"Ah," she said, "I'm sorry but I don't—"

"No, we never met but I've seen you a few times."

"Oh?"

"From out in your parking lot. Picking up Lucrecia when her car was in the shop. I'm her worser half, Joe Santiago."

"Of course, of course." Although she would have preferred to somehow arrange her arms in a body shield position, she shook hands with Joe Santiago. "I don't know what we'd do without Lucrecia."

"Same," said Joe.

Lucrecia was the home health aide who came to Mrs. Plansky's place for four hours every weekday to . . . well, to basically entertain Mrs. Plansky's dad—who despite being 98 had no apparent health problems, although he himself in toto was just about unfailingly problematic—and Mrs. Plansky regretted her last remark immediately. Did it sound patronizing? What could she say to smooth things over? Nothing came to her. Then something sizzled out on the water, actually more of a hiss. They both turned to look but there was nothing to see except dying embers. *Lizette* was gone.

"We were just playing tennis," she said.

Joe sounded very surprised. "You and Lucrecia?"

"No, no, although I'm sure it—" Mrs. Plansky slammed on the brakes before she began a description of the fun she and Lucrecia would have on the tennis court, both she and Joe knowing full well that Lucrecia had no interest in tennis or any other sport. She gestured toward the fire engine, where Kev was saying something and 27 was writing it down on a notepad. "With Kev. Mr. Dinardo. He lives here."

Joe glanced around. "Where's the court?"

"Not here, but earlier, over at—"

Before she could make herself even more ridiculous, the man at the wheel of the patrol boat called over. "Joe? Got a sec?"

"Nice seein' ya," said Joe, walking away.

Mrs. Plansky wanted to call after him: *I'm not even rich! Just comfortable!* In her mind she heard what that would sound like before she could speak.

She stood alone on the dock, watched the harbormaster's crew shine flashlights on the water. Somewhere farther off a piece of wreckage burst into flame. She watched it die down to nothing. Did people still use the word *comfortable* to mean whatever the hell she meant by it? Probably not. Your language gets outdated as you age. You end up becoming like a foreigner. My goodness! What thoughts were these? She heard Norm's voice in her head. *Hook.* Just the one word, his customary signal that it was time for them to leave wherever they were, the hook being the kind that whisked vaudeville performers offstage.

Mrs. Plansky walked off the dock, slowing down when she reached the fire engine. Kev interrupted whatever 27 was telling him and turned to her. "Sorry for all this, Loretta."

"I just hope everything's okay," she said.

"Should take a few days to sort out. I'll be in touch."

"When you have time," said Mrs. Plansky. In her mind—and so brazen!—she thought but absolutely did not say, *To be continued.* Instead she waved what she imagined was a noncommittal goodbye, then got into her car and drove away. The fire engine lights kept flashing in all her mirrors until she made the turn onto the coast road. She dialed up the heat, hoping it would dry out her tennis dress but it only made things clammy. First thing when she got home would be a shower.

As she passed the Green Turtle Club, a Bahamian-style bar with conch fritters Mrs. Plansky craved now and then, she hit a little pothole and the trophies bumped together in the backseat. What remained of her heightened state lowered itself back down to ground zero. Mrs. Plansky's eyesight was kind of marvelous since the cataract surgery, a tiny, personal miracle. But she hadn't seen the lightning strike. She probably didn't see a lot of things.

Sometimes Mrs. Plansky pictured abstractions in her mind. She'd been doing it since childhood, had never really thought about it, or wondered if others did the same. For example, she now pictured a door, just a plain simple wooden door, like you'd find in millions of homes. She closed it on the lightning question.

ABOUT THE AUTHOR

Lannan O'Brien

SPENCER QUINN is the pen name of Peter Abrahams, the Edgar Award–winning author of forty-seven novels, including the *New York Times* and *USA Today* best-selling Chet and Bernie mystery series, *Mrs. Plansky's Revenge*, *The Right Side*, and *Oblivion*, as well as the *New York Times* bestselling Bowser and Birdie series for younger readers. He lives on Cape Cod with his wife, Diana—and Dottie, a loyal and energetic member of the four-pawed nation within.